ALMOST LIKE PRAYING

JOEL SAMBERG

Black Rose Writing | Texas

The author grants the final approval for this literary material.

First printing

This is a work of fiction. Names, characters, businesses, places, events, and incidents are either the products of the author's imagination or used in a fictitious manner. Any resemblance to actual persons, living or dead, or actual events is purely coincidental.

ISBN: 978-1-68433-936-5
PUBLISHED BY BLACK ROSE WRITING
www.blackrosewriting.com

Printed in the United States of America
Suggested Retail Price (SRP) $20.95

Almost Like Praying is printed in Book Antiqua

*As a planet-friendly publisher, Black Rose Writing does its best to eliminate unnecessary waste to reduce paper usage and energy costs, while never compromising the reading experience. As a result, the final word count vs. page count may not meet common expectations.

For Eileen Kindl, who Bonnie and I
never cease to admire as a gift whose
mere presence brings hope and joy.

ALMOST LIKE PRAYING

"Instead of cursing the darkness, light a candle."
— **Benjamin Franklin**

PROLOGUE: DANIEL'S LETTER TO DOUG

To open the rickety screen door, Doug Kelleher had to kick it with his right foot because he had a large yellow manila envelope in one hand and a Budweiser in the other. It was a good thing, really, that the fastener that used to keep the screen door latched shut had fallen off months ago.

Outside, as he stood on the cement slab that served as the cabin's front porch, Doug yawned and then groaned; not only was he dead tired, but the thought of crouching down to sit on the slab made him remember just how achy he was from last month's accident at the Cardinal Motor Speedway. Doug was a member of the speedway's in-house pit crew, which serviced novice drivers who did not yet have pit crews of their own. A pneumatic jack had malfunctioned, and the front end of the three-thousand-pound Chevy Camaro on which he had been working fell nine inches to the ground; Doug rolled away in the nick of time to avoid getting crushed to death, but fractured his left arm and severely bruised his left shin. After a visit to Lee County Hospital, where he was x-rayed, bandaged, and drugged, he was sent home in an ambulance and instructed to rest up for a few weeks.

His cabin, while also in southwest New Mexico, was an hour-and-a-quarter from the speedway and an hour from the hospital. To Doug, who grew up in a Long Island suburb, everything in New Mexico seemed too far from everything else. He had discovered that shortly after he settled in the state almost three years ago. Ever since then, he had jested to his friends and coworkers that his mailbox was "like a hundred goddamn miles" from his front door. While certainly an exaggeration, the joke revealed his constant state of fatigue.

Earlier that morning, the first thing Doug did after he woke up was to put on his torn jeans (one of three pairs of pants that he owned), his Eagles tee-shirt (one of four), and his favorite moccasins (which over the last two years had lost all its embroidery). Then he opened the refrigerator to make sure there was at least one can of beer for breakfast. (There were three.) Satisfied, he limped a quarter mile down the road to the row of mailboxes that served the entire block of cabins. It was a journey he hadn't made in a week, though to a stranger it might have seemed that the mailbox was emptied every day, for there was a very light load inside. There was a new copy of *Playboy*, four small leaflets, and one large manila envelope. That was all. Doug grabbed the load and limped the quarter mile back home. He was exhausted when he entered the cabin. The lingering aches from the accident were no help.

Inside, he took a can of Budweiser out of the refrigerator and sat next to the metal tray stand that tripled as a kitchen table, desk, and junk drawer. He put the *Playboy* on the floor under the tray stand. Then he quickly flipped through the four advertising fliers, all of which he crumbled one by one into little balls and tossed carelessly and mostly successfully toward the plastic garbage pail by the sink. The one that he missed he left on the floor; he had ceased being concerned with neatness the week before, when his latest live-in girlfriend moved out. Doug was alone now, once again, and knew it mattered little if a few crumbled balls of junk mail were part of the permanent kitchen decor. After all, the place was just a rental, a cheap bungalow that was one step away from homelessness, as he joked with friends from time to time. It may be sloppy but never out-and-out dirty, he often thought to himself with an odd sense of pride. It even smelled sufficiently agreeable because Doug had gotten into the habit of lighting scented candles every night to keep the other odors at bay.

Doug saved the manila envelope for last. The return address label showed it was from Daniel Hillman, in New York, New York. Daniel had been a childhood friend of his on Long Island, in a town called

Westbrook Hills. There was something weighty inside. He said "Let's go, buddy" to his beer can, and took the yellow envelope outside.

Standing on the cement slab, Doug ripped open the top. Inside were three sets of documents on white paper, each set bound with a black metal clip. The top page of each of the three documents had a typewritten title in bold letters. The first said "The Farrells and the Kellehers," the second, "Officer Doug Kelleher," and the third, "Maria and Dolores." There was also a typed two-page letter from Daniel. Before he sat, Doug read the letter:

> *Dear Doug,*
>
> *Believe it or not (and I hate to break the news to you, but you have no choice but to believe it), I have spent the last two-and-a-half years painstakingly researching and writing about your family.*
>
> *I won't be so vain as to assume that you know all about my work and career, but suffice it to say that I live in Manhattan and write for a living. For reasons to be discussed in a moment, I felt compelled to explore and then reveal a few fundamental episodes of 1) your maternal heritage in Sherborn, MA, 2) several more episodes of your family life on Pearl Drive in Westbrook Hills, and 3) a single year in that same Westbrook Hills house, several years after you left New York.*
>
> *A few things prompted this literary endeavor, Doug, which required quite a bit of sleuthing, phone calling (siblings, aunts, uncles, you name it), traveling (Sherborn, Westbrook Hills, the Bronx), international phone calls and document requests (Ireland, Puerto Rico), knocking on doors, making some educated assumptions, and so on. Well, those are the heartbeats of my trade anyway, so I wasn't really doing anything I wasn't already used to doing. The only person I tried but failed to reach was you. No one knew where you were, and you covered your tracks exceedingly well, buddy boy. Quite impressive, actually. But my*

reporter's nose finally sniffed out your trail (I guess I was blessed with a good nose for that, if nothing else), though it was too late to use for my literary project.

Here's what prompted it. First, your mother stopped by my parents' house one day in the fall of '85 to talk to my mom. The conversation they had, which my mom told me all about on the phone, sparked in me a certain interest about your family. In fact, I must admit that I always held a certain fascination in the back of my mind about your parents, your sisters, and your brother, and even your extended family in Massachusetts. Every once in a while when we were kids, you used to tell me about your occasional visits to Sherborn, and to me it seemed like a million miles from Long Island, and sometimes it even seemed like a different century. Listening to some of your stories was like reading a book about American history from an Irish-Catholic perspective.

Then, a few weeks after my mom told me about the conversation she had with your mother, I stopped by my old house to help my parents get ready to move to Florida. While I was there, I went into my old bedroom, looked out the window, and happened to see your mother and little Maria sitting on your front stoop. Your mother had her arm around Maria's shoulders. They looked very pensive. Pensive but happy. Those two incidents — the conversation between our mothers, and seeing your mom and Maria on the stoop — merged in my mind to spark the idea which became the project that turned into the three manuscripts you are soon to read — if, of course, you decide to read them. I sincerely hope that you do. I think you'll discover some things that will give you the kind of pleasant a-ha! moments that I myself experienced while working on them. You'll find out some noteworthy things about your grandparents (R-rated, at the very least). You'll find out some interesting things about your parents (though I guess it wouldn't take a genius to know that your mother loved Massachusetts and that your father could not have cared less). You'll find out some intriguing details about your sisters, and something very important about your brother. And I'd bet good money that you'll find the story of that little girl on the stoop quite... well... how should I put it? I really don't know. I guess I'll just wait and see.

Here's the thing, Doug. In some ways, what you have in front of you are three completely separate stories. But in other ways, they are inexorably linked. Which, I'm afraid, has made it difficult for me to decide precisely what to do with one, with two, or with all three of them. A single, all-inclusive book? Two books? Three? A movie? A long-form, serialized magazine feature? A screenplay? I just don't know.

You're probably very confused right now, Doug, and I'm really sorry about that. I wish I had more time to explain it in a clearer and more comprehensive manner, but I'm actually on my way out the door right now to catch a flight to Dallas for a magazine assignment. I'm running late.

My point in sharing all this with you is actually very simple: depending on what I end up doing with this project (if anything at all), I may — and I emphasize the word _may_ — be required to ask you to sign a release form, just for my protection and the protection of whatever publishing or production company is willing to go along with me on this literary journey. To further complicate matters (again, I'm sorry for that), I may decide to change all the names, alter some of the details, and place some of the action in surrogate locations. (Right now, I use all the real Kelleher and Farrell names and places.) If I change all that, I won't need a signed release form because I'll be able to call the whole thing fiction. In such a case, this package will serve you no purpose at all, except as a *bit of free leisure-time distraction (if you choose to be distracted).*

I'll get back to you on the matter of the release form as soon as I can.

Doug, I'm sure you've had some adventures over the last few years that would allow you to one day sit on a mountaintop and shout out to the world: 'Hey! Most of you assholes out there lead goddamn boring lives — but I don't!!!" There's something to say for that, buddy boy, regardless of all else. Maybe you and I will partner on writing about it one day, just like we used to partner a long time ago in our backyards playing Batman and Robin and the Green Hornet and Kato.

In the meantime, stay well, and make sure your next adventures are safe enough so that you live long enough to share them! Write back if you have a chance. I'll be happy to answer any questions you may have about this package of 'stuff.' The return address is on the envelope. I'll be back from Dallas in about two weeks from the date this envelope goes to the post office.

Regards,
Daniel
02/18/1989

It was a long letter, and Doug stood while he read the entire thing. When he finally attempted to sit on the cement slab outside, his aches and pains announced themselves once again in no uncertain terms. And along with the aches and pains of his body came a certain discomfort to his mind. Doug wasn't certain that he really wanted to read the manuscripts. He didn't know if he had the emotional strength to look at even one of them, let alone all three. He thought it might be too painful.

But by this time, he was already on the cement slab. So he leaned back against the rickety screen door, popped open the Bud, and began to read.

PART ONE:
THE FARRELLS AND THE KELLEHERS

SHERBORN, MASSACHUSETTS

"At least Ken's last name is Kelleher, not Valenti, and his skin is fair, not dark. I'm telling you — Ken Kelleher has to be mostly Irish. He just has to be!"

Skerries was a seaside fishing village in the county of Fingal, on Ireland's rocky east coast. Dolores O'Farrell was born there to Alexander and Mary Ann O'Farrell in the spring of 1921. She was the youngest of three O'Farrell daughters; the others were Katherine and Patricia, older by eleven and twenty-two months, respectively. Dolores was baptized at St. Patrick's Parish at two weeks of age. The ceremony was followed by a small congregational gathering in the Parish courtyard that was arranged, decorated, and catered by Mary Ann O'Farrell, who was as devout as she was eager to acknowledge family pride.

Alexander O'Farrell was a university instructor in Dublin, well admired by the students in his English and Irish literature classes for his sometimes-whimsical ways of teaching. For example, he wrote short stories in which he disguised his students as noble suitors and country maidens, and would then ask the boys and girls in class to read the stories aloud and try to guess who was who.

Though life in Skerries was safe and assured, Alexander knew it would be even safer and more assured in America. So he applied for, was offered, and accepted a job at Boston College as a professor of English literature and, in 1923, crossed the Atlantic with Mary Ann and the three girls to settle in Massachusetts. They left their old lives, their aged parents, and the O in their last name behind. Mary Ann gave birth to Timothy twelve months after they arrived in the town of Sherborn, and then to Randall another twelve months later.

The Farrells lived in a small yet stylish white Colonial that sat on an acre of land surrounded by a beautiful lawn and gardens. For years, Sherborn was strictly farm country, but after the Farrells arrived, it transformed into a comfortable Boston suburb. Brian Donnelly, a Boston-bred author of a book called *The History of Sherborn*, credited the Farrells and five other local families with having encouraged the transformation. Donnelly, an effusive writer, also explored his poetic side by adding flavorful heritage-based imagery to his descriptions: "Alexander and Mary Ann Farrell enjoy the additional distinction of authentic Irish brogues," Donnelly wrote in his book, "having come directly from the County Fingal to the illustrious Massachusetts Colony, where Benjamin Franklin was born, where the Sons of Liberty spawned a Revolution on the Harbor, and where the clam chowder is second to none."

Although Alexander Farrell earned significantly less than a princely salary, his skill in financial prudence stretched dollars in such a way as to make it appear his family wanted of nothing. And Mary Ann's ability to give the simple Colonial a dignified appearance made the house seem rather stately. Dozens of other Sherborn homeowners tried to mimic what the Farrells had started.

· · · · ·

Dolores, the youngest Farrell daughter, loved art and music from early childhood. Because of Dolores's interests, the small Sherborn house seemed even smaller because of the number of instruments and easels that Alexander purchased for her every so often.

The house became smaller still when relatives arrived from Ireland who, though they had purchased their own homes, often visited Alexander and Mary Ann and their five children. In 1929, Alexander's sister Gillian, and Gillian's husband Grant O'Reilly, settled in Holliston, next door to Sherborn. They, too, left the O in their surname on the Emerald Isle. In 1930, Mary Ann's brother Connor McDolan, and Connor's wife Diane, crossed the Atlantic and moved to Cambridge. They became the Dolans.

Before long, Grant Reilly was a successful financial advisor in Boston, and Connor Dolan opened an art and music studio, which doubled as a gallery, also in Boston, called Connor's Corner.

Young Dolores spent many blissful afternoons as her uncle's assistant at Connor's Corner. Among other amenities, the venue featured on its second floor two painting lofts, on the third, a dance studio surrounded by mirrored walls, and on the fourth, a half dozen small rooms with upright pianos and music stands. Dolores visited Uncle Connor's studio whenever time allowed. Sometimes she would disappear for minutes at a time to explore its artistic nooks and crannies.

Novice and celebrated painters and musicians stopped by often to render, compose, or practice. One day in 1931, in one of the small piano rooms, a young crooner named Bing Crosby, not yet nationally known, rehearsed a song called "I Found a Million Dollar Baby (in a Five and Ten Cent Store)," which shortly thereafter became popular on the radio. Ten-year-old Dolores watched Crosby from the open doorway, even though her uncle had warned her not to bother paying customers. Crosby noticed and asked Dolores if she could please bring him a glass of water. Dolores complied. Uncle Connor accompanied her back upstairs. Dolores said to the singer, whose name she had apparently misheard, "You can stop by Connor's Corner any time you want, Mr. Bingsby." Crosby laughed. Uncle Connor apologized for his niece's impudence, but the singer said that no apology was necessary.

The eminent watercolorist Edward Hopper came by for a week of work while his own studio, damaged by a flood, was being rebuilt. Hopper was friendly, but had an eternal scowl which prompted Dolores to avoid him. She cleaned up the studio one late afternoon after Hopper had left for the day and noticed an incomplete painting of a full-bodied nude woman whirling about on a stage. The woman's large, firm, and protruding breasts practically leapt off the canvas and bounced on air. Uncle Connor found Dolores staring at the unfinished painting and tried to explain what he believed to be Hopper's motivation. He then begged Dolores not to mention the episode to her parents. "You know how they are," he said to her. "You can never tell…"

Dolores wondered what Uncle Connor had implied by those comments about her parents. Were they Victorian prigs? Alexander and Mary Ann Farrell? How could that be? Dolores recalled all the times in the past, particularly when they thought no one was nearby, that her mother and father were very affectionate with one another. No—they were not priggish at all. She refused to entertain the notion. After all, Alexander played practical jokes now and then, some of which involved the ruse of making someone believe that he wasn't wearing pants when, in fact, he really was. Also, Dolores's parents often took long rides alone and never said where they going. Whenever asked, Alexander would say, "That's for us to know and for you to never find out." Victorian prigs? Not a chance.

· · · · ·

Dolores sometimes spoke of becoming an artist, dancer, or musician when she grew up. She commented once to her father that when she sang or danced in her bedroom, she no longer felt like just one of the five Farrell children, but someone entirely unique. Singing and dancing, she said, felt almost like an invitation to have a special life of her very own. Alexander commended her on her fine turn of phrase and asked if he could use it one day. Dolores asked what for, but he simply responded by telling her she was still too young to worry about what to do with her life as an adult.

Mary Ann, having heard similar sentiments from Dolores, did all she could to instill in her youngest daughter the notion that it was a far more sensible, secure, and satisfying endeavor to concentrate on the *business* of art—to discover it, encourage it, promote it, and bring it to people who might otherwise have no access to it. "Artists," she told Dolores, "even great ones, are bohemians at heart and eccentric in nature. They rarely exhibit impeccable manners, because their art is far more important to them than anything else."

"But *you* like to sing and play the piano," Dolores countered, "and I once saw you doing ballet at Uncle Connor's studio when you didn't know I was watching."

"That was just for fun, dear. Nothing more. You see, Dolores, the Farrells, and on my side the Dolans, carry themselves with distinction, and therefore are favored in the eyes of the Lord. And in return, we are treated with the respect and admiration we deserve."

This was an important ideal for Mary Ann Farrell to impart to all her children, for until about 1890, both the O'Farrells and McDolans were among Ireland's most impoverished families. O'Farrell and McDolan men were laborers then, many of them drunkards, several always in jail. Their wives were timeworn housekeepers, each of whom gave birth to eight or nine children, two or three of whom inevitably died at childbirth or in infancy. People in other Irish villages who had more and fared better mocked and derided their families. "We worked hard turning all that around and leaving it behind," Mary Ann explained to her children many a Sunday as they walked to mass at Saint John's Catholic Church. "And now, here in Massachusetts, we can justifiably call ourselves American royalty. Why do you think Father McDermott looks so happy whenever we arrive?"

Indeed, whenever the Farrells took their seats in the first row of pews at St. John's, Father McDermott always smiled, for he regarded them among the church's most generous and admirable parishioners. The girls, Katherine, Patricia, and Dolores, were pretty and grew more appealing as they became young women. They attracted many young men who might otherwise want to skip Sunday services. Father McDermott considered that a harmless little ploy of God's will to fill up the venerable sandstone church. That was important as Sherborn grew and welcomed several new churches, most of them catering to other denominations. "God bless those delightful girls," Father McDermott often said while he watched the Farrell sisters walk along the brick path at the front of the church.

The two brothers, Timothy and Randall, were bright, strapping boys who often helped at St. John's when furniture needed to be moved or fences mended. There were many times when one or both of the boys saw something on a Sunday that required repair and, after school on Monday, attended to the repair without being asked. "Such handy young men, God bless them both," Father McDermott would smile as he watched them run ahead of their sisters.

The Farrell children always dressed well, and Father McDermott was far from the only one who noticed. Neighbors, local shopkeepers, and even some teachers from Trinity Elementary School commented on it from time to time. Dolores also believed—and this she told her brood in words they could easily understand and appreciate—that the Farrell children were afforded special treatment wherever they went not just because the girls were attractive and the boys handsome, and that they were all well dressed, but because they had exemplary manners. "And with good manners," she said, "pretty becomes lovely, and handsome becomes dashing."

Katherine, Patricia, and Dolores were slim and even-featured, with easy smiles, hazel eyes, and almost noble profiles. Each had very wavy light-brown hair that some women in town suspected was a style copied from magazines, but which actually grew that way naturally, long before those magazines ran advertisements for products that could make it happen. Timothy and Randall, both muscular and solidly built, had dimpled chins, dark and expressive eyes, and hardy complexions that resulted from years of summer sailing and winter skiing. All spoke with accents decidedly more Boston than Irish. That didn't bother Mary Ann one bit, for in her mind, this part of America was her old country relocated, and whatever happened naturally in terms of one's look, speech, and demeanor was divinely ordained. Besides, the Farrell children had so many friends and were busy with so many activities outside of the home that *not* having attained Emerald inflections was a foregone conclusion.

•   •   •   •   •   •

While the Farrell boys embarked on sporting events and led many of the town's athletic programs, the girls tended to more charitable pursuits. They helped with church socials for disadvantaged families and, with their mother's help, turned unused plots in Sherborn into glorious gardens with walking paths and old, weathered, wooden benches that were refurbished into sanded, painted, and comfortable new ones. Whenever they embarked on such projects, Mary Ann called it "another gay flora day in Sherborn."

At Christmas and Easter there was always much singing in the Farrell home, and from early morning to nearly midnight the house smelled of holiday treats baking in the kitchen. All the Farrell children helped Alexander and Mary Ann with the decorations, inside and out. Young Dolores, in particular, always looked forward to the holidays. One time, a week before Christmas, she asked her mother why every day of the year could not be thought of as a holiday. Mary Ann considered the comment and said, "Because it's nice to have something to look forward to, dear." She then stepped outside to the front porch to see how Alexander and the boys were coming along with the old wooden reindeer, which they were positioning on the lawn. Mary Ann had restored and repainted them by herself. While outside, she glanced up and down the block and announced how pleased she was to see that every other house featured festive Christmas decorations. It was another validation for her, one of many over the years, that Sherborn was the proper setting for the Farrell family.

•　　•　　•　　•　　•

By most outward appearances, Mr. and Mrs. Alexander Farrell abided by traditional gender rules. Mary Ann, however, deliberately, and with self-assurance, pushed that boundary ever so slightly, for she wished not to be pigeonholed into a traditional woman's role. She took care of her five children, but also repaired furniture, hung paintings, measured spaces, and did many other chores often associated with the man of the house. She built toys for the children, including the sturdy wooden rocking horses and small shoebox locomotives that the five Farrell children and their friends enjoyed in the playroom. She had also constructed the playroom on her own, which she nicknamed the Farrell Fun and Frolic Farm. Mary Ann's sisters and brothers — Dolores's aunts and uncles — sometimes discussed among themselves their collective belief that Mary Ann assumed this character out of necessity, not purely desire. Alexander, as decent a husband and father as he was, and as good a provider as he proved to be, did little in the house. He did not like to build things or fix things. Instead, much to Mary Ann's chagrin, when Alexander was home from the college, he preferred to relax in a small, book-lined alcove by his bedroom, where sometimes he wrote on pads that he kept hidden in a desk drawer. More often, he liked to recline in the living room easy chair, in loose trousers and an undershirt, to read books and plays— Shakespeare, O'Neill, Hawthorne, Fitzgerald—and the *Boston Globe*. Alexander also enjoyed sports and games with the children, including treasure hunts of his own design. He enjoyed taking Mary Ann to faculty events, where he made it clear by his introductions just how proud he was of his beautiful and accomplished wife. Mary Ann, however, enjoyed few if any of these outings, for many of the academics in attendance were too peculiar for her taste; they were professors of creative writing and drama and art who arrived in sarongs or corduroy jackets or other odd attire, and often used sassy language.

Young Dolores admired Mary Ann's strength and independence, yet sensed that her mother may have been discontent. Mostly, she supposed, it was because of her father's behavior, which prohibited Mary Ann from living the full image of Sherborn royalty that permanently lived in her head. For a long while, Dolores did not know what to make of her suspicion. Then, one day after school, her Aunt Diane, Uncle Connor's wife, stopped by for a visit with Mary Ann. The two women chatted in the kitchen. Dolores was in the living room mixing up the pages in that day's *Boston Globe* so that her father, when he came home from the college, would have an impossible time reading the long articles. (This was in response to a harmless gag Alexander had played on her the day before, when he mixed up five of her school-book covers.) From the living room, Dolores overheard her mother and Aunt Diane talk about their husbands. Mary Ann said that she sometimes wished Alexander had become a banker or an attorney. "Not a college professor, but someone who dresses nicely even in the house, fixes things the minute they need to be fixed, enjoys the fact that his wife is not only an exemplary mother and housekeeper, but is her own person, as well. And I wish he would take me to fancy restaurants in Boston so that he could say these things in public, instead of dragging me to those pitiful college jamborees where the most important thing to do is say something wittier than the last thing someone said."

Young Dolores never doubted that her parents loved each other very much, so she easily dismissed the hushed conversation between her mother and her Aunt Diane. Besides, she was certain that her mother and her aunt had been sipping wine while they chatted that afternoon, and Dolores had read enough novels to know that emotions swell and lips loosen after just two or three glasses.

．　．　．　．　．

In 1937, when Dolores was sixteen, she volunteered her mother, without her knowledge, to help design and build the sets for Saint Theresa High School's production of an old musical called *Follow Thru*. She was proud of her mother's skills and wanted to show them off. But Mary Ann seemed indifferent when Dolores told her about it.

"I play the part that Eleanor Powell played on Broadway," Dolores said eagerly, hopeful that the news would boost her mother's enthusiasm. It did not; the comment merely turned Mary Ann's doubtful look into one of genuine concern.

"Don't entertain any ideas of becoming an actress, young lady," she said sternly.

"It's just for fun, mother," Dolores replied quickly. "Please don't worry."

Mary Ann agreed to help build the set, but regretted it almost immediately. She knew she would have to work alongside many other parents and loathed them seeing her in the outfits she would need to wear in order to accomplish the task. At home, when she built and repaired things, she wore a pair of Timothy's faded slacks and one of Randall's Boston Red Sox sweatshirts. She was alone then, however, or with just her family. To wear knockabout clothing like that would be inappropriate at Saint Theresa's. Yet, what choice did she have?

Around this time, there was a distressing incident in the Farrell home that took up much of the family's attention for several months. Five Boston businessmen sued Alexander Farrell for "inhabiting private land" (as the official complaint stated) to which he had no legal right. Apparently, the twelve empty lots in Sherborn that Mary Ann and her daughters turned into 'public gardens' were actually owned by developers who intended to build houses on them. The businessmen, who were eager for a fight, did not accept a simple apology from Alexander, but wanted to bring the matter to court. Alexander had to hire an attorney to help end the matter quickly and avoid a trial.

Dominick Hollister, Esquire, was the attorney hired by Alexander Farrell. Hollister was first in his class at Harvard Law, but only five months into his law practice. His scant time as a member of the Massachusetts bar was precisely why he took on the case for a guaranteed fee, win or lose, of just twenty-five dollars; he needed to build a reputation in the competitive legal environment in Boston, and he needed to do it quickly. Even if the case never went to court, which was the goal, Hollister knew that his eloquent public comments and official published statements on the matter would help establish himself as an attorney of prominence. Alexander had approached him with that very logic after he researched the Class of 1936 at the Harvard Law Library.

"He's extremely skilled and eager to work for a song," Alexander said to Mary Ann when he told her that Mr. Hollister would stop by the house for a discussion.

Hollister was very handsome, and though they would have been shocked to hear it pointed out, Mary Ann, Katherine, Patricia, and Dolores all had fanciful looks on their faces whenever he visited the house in the days following that initial chat with Alexander. On those days, perhaps without even realizing she was doing it, Mary Ann dressed extra stylishly and took more time with her makeup and perfume. So did the girls.

One day after school, Dolores went to Boston to work at Connor's Corner and found herself three blocks out of her way, in front of a tiny storefront with brand new lettering painted on the window that said Dominick Hollister, Attorney at Law. She lingered there for a few moments. When Hollister, who was alone, noticed Dolores outside, he invited her in. He apologized for the condition of the small office and said it was all he could afford at the moment. "Meager, but serviceable," he called it. "After two or three cases, I'll move up to something a little nicer. If I win. Maybe in Boston, maybe someplace else. Depends on fate. And whichever way the wind blows."

Hollister told Dolores that the print shop run by James Franklin, who was Benjamin Franklin's older brother and master of young Ben's printing apprenticeship, was originally located just around the corner. Benjamin Franklin, he explained, was smarter than James and knew the day would come when he outgrew both the small print shop and what Benjamin considered the small, stubborn minds inhabiting the colony. He was barely seventeen years old when he illegally broke his apprentice's contract and stowed away to Philadelphia. It was in Philadelphia where Franklin began to make his mark on history. "I'm already twenty-six," Dominick Hollister said. "I don't work for my brother—I'm an only child—but who knows? Maybe my Ben Franklin moment will happen after your father's trial."

For the next hour, Dominick and Dolores chatted about many things. Dolores said that lawyers were very much respected in her family, and that when her father said he was doing some research at the Harvard Law Library, everyone was excited about the prospect of his changing professions from college professor to attorney at law. But he was simply researching the Harvard Law class of 1936.

Dolores tried to act older than her sixteen years during her conversation with Dominick Hollister by mimicking some of her mother's gestures and expressions. When the young attorney asked her about *Follow Thru*, she slipped back into her mid-teen self. That embarrassed her greatly.

At one point Hollister said, "Can I tell you a secret?" He walked around his desk to stand next to the chair in which Dolores was sitting. He bent down to her and whispered, "Everyone thinks I'm confident about this case. But I'm really scared right down to my socks."

Dolores felt his breath in her ear, smelled his cologne, and sensed a tingle down her spine when Hollister put his hand on her shoulder. She excused herself, went home, and hid in her room for hours.

The mean-spirited businessmen who had initiated the lawsuit against Alexander eventually dropped it (and left five of the gardens intact for the next eleven years), and Dominick Hollister ceased being a presence at the Farrell home. His law practice struggled, though he eventually joined a large firm in Hartford as a junior associate.

Follow Thru, the play in which Dolores appeared at school, was well-received. "Did you hear that applause, all for me?" Dolores asked her mother after the first performance.

"You were wonderful, and I enjoyed it immensely, Dolores — but boasting is not pretty. It reeks of desperation. And desperation breeds contempt. You don't ever need to be desperate."

"I'm almost seventeen, and I've never had a boyfriend," Dolores said in an uncharacteristic act of boldness that surprised even her. "Maybe I *should* boast sometimes." Mary Ann looked at her daughter with a combination of astonishment and compassion. "You'll have plenty of boyfriends, Dolores," she said without a trace of anger. Then she leaned over and said quietly, "If Dominick Hollister were five years younger, or if you were five years older, you would have a boyfriend this very day. And I would be very jealous. Don't ask me how I know, Dolores. I just know." It was the most exciting and intimate moment between mother and daughter in years. Dolores had never been prouder to be the daughter of Mary Ann Farrell than she was that afternoon.

•   •   •   •   •   •   •

Once Dominick Hollister ceased coming to the Farrell house, and once *Follow Thru* was but one of many memories of her sophomore year, Dolores began to think about herself as a future housewife and mother. She thought daily of ways to become just like Mary Ann, albeit with a few minor modifications in personality and style so that she could be her own person. The plan was to marry an Irish-Catholic man — an attorney, she decided — and live with him in Cambridge, in the shadow of Harvard University, where her five children would be students one day. They would live in a gorgeous though modest-sized Victorian home she would expand herself, slowly, as one child after another was born. She would start a nonprofit agency (when the youngest turned three) whose goal would be to bring disadvantaged New England youth to Boston's many fine museums, galleries, and concert halls. Even though her surname would no longer be Farrell, she would continue the Farrell legacy in every way possible.

Often Dolores would sit on the front stoop of the Sherborn house and visualize her future children playing at the side on a beautiful spring morning, while she, in the same fantasy, mulled over a speech she would give that night after being honored by Boston's mayor for the good work she had accomplished in the city. Indulging in these pleasing flights of fancy seemed to her to be not merely daydreams, but divine inspirations.

When she turned eighteen, Dolores began studies in arts management at Boston College. She worked on the publicity committee for the drama society, whose faculty director urged her to try out for shows, though she never did. She was president of the garden club, volunteered with many school-affiliated charities, and helped organize several socials intended to enable students from different disciplines to meet other students with whom they may not have otherwise engaged. It was at one such social, toward the end of her junior year, that Dolores Farrell met a graduate student in first-year law named Kenneth Kelleher. Even before they were introduced, she knew by his looks that he was a handsome Irish-Catholic; like her father, Ken had a head full of golden-brown hair and a cluster of half-moon strands near the hairline that always fell onto his forehead. Brushing them back with one hand gave Deloris a good excuse to touch him without seeming too brazen in public. She enjoyed doing that. Ken ran around to so many classes, clubs, and events that the half-moons returned day after day, often hour after hour. As most students did in those days, Ken wore a suit while on campus, and he always looked sophisticated. Dolores came to believe that his disobedient hair was not just acceptable, but equally distinguished. As she told her friends and eventually mentioned ever to her mother and father, someone involved in so many activities, and was just steps away from becoming a famous Boston attorney, can afford a few wayward strands of hair. Mary Ann smiled. Alexander once again complimented her on a well-turned phrase.

Ken had served in the army for two years after high school and enrolled at Northeastern University as an undergraduate at twenty years of age. He began law studies at Boston College four years later, and was twenty-five when he met Dolores Farrell. At Dolores's prompting, they attended many lectures together. Ken insisted he enjoyed these lectures, as well as the movies and plays in Boston that Dolores took him to see, although he rarely had much to say about them afterward. Dolores repeatedly showed him the five Sherborn gardens that still existed that she and her mother and sisters had created. Ken seemed to enjoy himself as the two of them sat on garden benches, holding hands. Sometimes, when they were alone, they kissed. They double-dated several times with a college classmate of Ken's named Ted, and Ted's fiancé Joanna. Ken and Ted avoided discussions of law school and the legal profession and instead chatted about the Indianapolis 500 and the Grand Prix races in Europe. Dolores and Joanna laughed and said that their "boys" merely had trouble accepting the fact that they were now men. Ken and Ted also enjoyed games of pool in the basement of Ted's apartment building, while Dolores and Joanna researched magazines and newspapers to see what cultural events they could oblige their boys to take them to see.

One day, Dolores suggested to Ken that they motor up to the Massachusetts countryside, in the Berkshire Mountains, to see the beautiful foliage. Ken liked the idea. On the ride up, he was very much relaxed, yet also animated behind the wheel of his beloved Plymouth P7 Roadking. He had purchased the car five years earlier, after his army discharge, with money he had saved throughout his teenage years. Dolores thoroughly enjoyed the three-hour drive and observed her beau's eager confidence as he drove. She asked him about the car, but not much else about his family, or his past, or even his plans for the future; she believed that in an honest relationship, all the most important information would eventually spring forth. Besides, she was confident that whatever information finally sprung forth would be exactly what she wanted to hear.

· · · · ·

"My father was twenty-four when he married my mother."

This is what Dolores said to Ken one day in an uncharacteristic reversal of strategy. She had hoped for him to come up with the idea on his own and propose to her in the Berkshire Mountains, under the stars, after that exhaustive and exhilarating car ride. That would have mixed tradition with distinction. But when the six-month anniversary of their first date came and went, Dolores knew she had to take matters into her own hands.

"Six boys in my American history class got married over the winter break," she said as she strolled with Ken through Boston Common. Ken said he was not ready for marriage, that he wanted to be established first, with a few professional roots firmly planted. While it was not the response she hoped for, Dolores assumed he had said it simply because it sounded like the sort of thing a young man about to be married was supposed to say. So, for the moment, she let it pass.

Alone in his apartment, Ken thought about it some more. He was torn, for he did not like playing what he called 'the game of pursuit' with young women — the one-sided quest to have to always predict what a paramour was thinking, what she would like to do, where she would like to go, what she would like him to say. He had played that game with three other young women before Dolores came along and always tired of it quickly. But Dolores had decisive ideas and more readily conveyed them, so maybe with her he needn't play that exasperating game anymore. On the other hand, he wondered if her decisiveness was a sign that she might just be a bit too much to handle.

On the last day of his first year of law school, which was also the next-to-last day of Dolores's senior year of college, Ken Kelleher gave Dolores Farrell an engagement ring and proposed. She accepted.

Plans were made. The wedding was to be held in the fall at the Heritage House in Sherborn. Ken's family in New York agreed to drive up north. With the help of her mother and sisters, Dolores purchased a dress, selected the menu and decorations, and privately delighted in the fact that the youngest Farrell daughter would be the first to marry.

●　　●　　●　　●　　●

Dolores, never a fan of surprises, had an unwelcome disclosure a month before the wedding. Ken told her he had decided to discontinue his law studies.

He said that the thought of being an attorney no longer appealed to him. The law students he knew were too severe, too single-minded, too shifty. He did not like them, and if *they* wanted to be lawyers, then he did not. The legal profession was not for him, he said. Dolores tried to change his mind. She considered it a foolish decision. Hollow and rash. Ken said it went deeper than that — that his heart was never really in it to begin with. Dolores contemplated calling off the engagement, but knew that her mother would consider that equally foolish. Mary Ann would certainly tell her that O'Farrell and McDolan women, even in the most dire of circumstances, never gave up. Surely Ken would find another profession for which his skills and appearance would be well-suited. This is what Dolores and Mary Ann concluded when the two of them discussed Ken's startling decision. Banking, perhaps. Or financial management, like Grant Reilly. Dolores even talked her Uncle Grant into having a chat with Ken, but when she asked Ken to accompany her on a visit to the offices of Buono, Feingold & Reilly in Boston, he refused to go. He said he had important plans of his own that day.

Two-and-a-half weeks before the wedding at the Heritage House, Ken accepted a position as a sales representative with Aster-Paxton Pharmaceuticals for the northeast territory. After she questioned him for more than an hour about the job, Dolores gave a secret sigh of relief; Ken, she learned, would still have to wear a suit to work, carry a briefcase, and impress people both with knowledge and personality. Dolores had also discovered by asking her friends that some salesmen often earn more money than attorneys. Ken spent the next sixteen days in a row training for the job.

The wedding, on the second day of October 1943, was a fine affair. All the Massachusetts Farrells, Dolans, and Reillys were there. A handful of Dolores's close friends attended, as did some of Alexander's colleagues, a few of Mary Ann's co-committee members from Sherborn women's clubs, and Dominick Hollister. Father

McDermott performed the ceremony. Dolores dreaded the possibility that Mr. Hollister would ask her to dance. He did not.

There were few Kellehers at the wedding, for Ken did not have a large family. Peter and Lucille Kelleher, his parents, were accompanied by their widowed older son, Joe, and Lucille's childless brother and his wife. There were, in fact, just six attendees from the Kelleher side, including Ken. Dolores met Peter and Lucille for the first time on the morning of the wedding. The elder Kellehers seemed somewhat befuddled by the affair, and Dolores and Mary Ann assumed it was because they lived exceedingly simple and humble lives, which they admitted to themselves was as decent a choice as any other lifestyle. Conversations were brief between the Farrells and the Kellehers. Mary Ann whispered to Alexander that she wished not to overwhelm Ken's parents; there would be time enough to get to know them once Ken and Dolores were husband and wife.

When Ken and Dolores returned from their Atlantic City honeymoon, they moved in with Alexander and Mary Ann in Sherborn while Ken started his new job with Aster-Paxton Pharmaceuticals. They agreed to wait until early 1944 to look for a home of their own. For the time being, there was more than enough room at the Farrell house; Dolores's younger brothers, Timothy and Randall, were away at college, Timothy at Cornell, Randall at Penn State, and her older sisters, Katherine and Patricia, had moved into apartments of their own in Beacon Hill. Both sisters craved the kind of independence many of their friends now enjoyed. Katherine, a nurse's aide, would marry within the year. Patricia, a librarian, would remain single until her thirties.

Ken did well as a pharmaceutical salesman in the first few months of his tenure with the company. Although he spent countless hours in his Plymouth and invested more money in its upkeep than he had expected (only salesmen who had been with the company more than a year had access to company cars), he enjoyed his success on the road. Affable, funny, and bright, he won over new clients with ease. As a result, his income was exemplary for the time. So for Dolores, the deviation from her original design seemed to have no objectionable consequence.

But then, another deviation came along, and for Dolores, this one *was* objectionable. One evening after work, in the middle of January, Ken told Dolores that he had decided they would move to a Long Island suburb, not far from where he had grown up and where his parents still lived. Peter and Lucille Kelleher had a small apartment in a neighborhood called Rego Park, in the New York City borough of Queens. Dolores had assumed that the elder Kellehers lived in Manhattan. When she asked Ken why he had never mentioned Queens, Ken reminded her she had never asked.

"Rego Park?" she repeated. "That doesn't sound very Irish."

"It's not," Ken replied. "But even if it was, I'm only half Irish anyway, so what's the difference? My mother's Italian."

Peter Kelleher had met Lucille Valenti at the Coney Island Amusement Park in 1909, when they were teenagers. They were both native New Yorkers. Peter's parents had emigrated from Waterford, Ireland, and Lucille's from Messina, Sicily. After she was filled in on these and other ancestral details, Dolores tried to avoid the appearance of any negative impressions. In her mind, though, she could not deny the fact that many of the Italians she knew in Sherborn seemed a bit too loud and easily swayed toward less-than-genteel comments and gestures. Irish families didn't behave that way, she felt, nor did the Jewish ones or the handful of Koreans she had encountered from time to time. Dolores thought about it for days and finally ignored this latest transgression of her grand plan: at least Ken's last name was Kelleher, not Valenti, and his skin was fair, not dark. "I'm telling you—Ken Kelleher *has* to be mostly Irish," she told Julie O'Malley, her childhood friend from the neighborhood. "He just *has* to be."

The week before he mentioned his plan to Dolores, Ken had visited a new housing development in Nassau County when he was on Long Island for a sales call. He described for Dolores a house on a street called Pearl Drive in a town named Westbrook Hills. So spirited was he in his description of the house and the neighborhood that it rendered Dolores almost speechless. Ken was impassioned about the rationality of residing in a place where their children would have so many others to play with. He was resolute in his belief that living close to Manhattan would provide endless excitement for the family. And so, after she listened to her husband's discourse about the house on Pearl Drive, Dolores said that with his kind of oratory skill, Ken could have been a fabulously successful defense attorney. He chuckled, then went outside to wax his car.

WESTBROOK HILLS, LONG ISLAND

"I have five children. One is missing a leg. One is married to a fat Jewish man. One loves to show the world her tatas. Don't I deserve to have a little fun?"

"No, no, no, I do *not* hate it. I really don't," Dolores insisted while she talked to her mother. "It has so much potential. Really it does."

The Farrells drove to Long Island to visit the newlyweds three months after Dolores and Ken moved into the high ranch in Westbrook Hills. As Ken and Alexander chatted in the living room, Dolores and Mary Ann sat in the kitchen. Dolores listed for her mother several things she wanted to change in the house. The foyer, she said, was ill-planned; not only was it too dark, but the access to the dining room was too close to the front door, making the house appear tiny to anyone just entering. The brickwork on the chimney, inside and out, was sloppy. All the bedroom and closet doors were a fraction of an inch too small. The cement patio should have been a few inches higher to eliminate the need for those unsightly and treacherous cement steps at the back of the house. "It's certainly not as well constructed as our house in Sherborn," Dolores said when she concluded her list of objections.

"I'm sorry you hate the house," Mary Ann sighed gently.

Dolores instantly regretted having shared her personal list of grievances, for it put a cloud over the first half of the visit from her parents. She tried to convince her mother that she was not as miserable as Mary Ann seemed to believe. Or at least not as miserable as she appeared.

"I'm glad, dear," Mary Ann said. "Well, Ken surely seems to adore the house, doesn't he?"

That was not at all debatable. Everyone knew how much Ken revered the newly-constructed home, with its sizeable backyard—the largest on Pearl Drive, he was proud to point out—and the spacious garage with its modern electric door up front and its convenient dark green access door at the back. He was proud to have been able to buy the house at just twenty-six years of age. He told Alexander and Mary Ann of his plans to turn the basement into a poolroom one day, and to paint black-and-white squares on the electric garage door. That was a design that Ken associated with professional car racing, although the Farrells seemed unaware of the connection.

As Dolores and Ken escorted Mary Ann and Alexander to their car by the curb, Dolores commented, almost under her breath, how she wished the house differed a bit from the others on Pearl Drive. Mary Ann gazed at her sympathetically. Then the Farrells returned to Sherborn.

It was Dolores's goal in those first few months to transform the house into one she felt was more appropriate for the family she planned to raise there. She started small and spent as little money as possible so as not to arouse Ken's suspicions. Inside, she repainted most of the walls with brighter colors. She adorned the living room and dining room walls with watercolor paintings by novice New England artists who she believed would be famous one day. On the living room table she kept several oversized, artistically covered books, with titles such as *Gardens of New England* and *The Emerald Isle*. Although smaller than the others, also featured on the table was a copy of *The History of Sherborn*, by Brian Donnelly, which her mother had graciously relinquished. Dolores put ornamental pewter music stands in every room, which mimicked the atmosphere of the many antique shops in the Beacon Hill section of Boston that she had frequented as a college student. On some of the music stands she positioned artificial vines and roses, and on others she placed sheet music for such songs as "Moonlight in Vermont" and "Weekend on Cape Cod."

"I left New England nine weeks ago," Ken grumbled one day when he returned from an exhaustive sales call in upstate New York, "and now I'm back! You've done a lot to this house, but I don't know if I like you becoming a bloomin' magical leprechaun, Dolores

28

O'Farrell!" he said with an exaggerated Irish brogue. That was the day of their first major argument as husband and wife.

As Ken earned and saved more money, Dolores felt freer to make bigger changes in the house, and when they had been there a year-and-a-half, she hired a contractor to install a shingled awning over the front steps, which was supported by two wooden columns. She painted the columns by herself, using a ladder to reach the upper portions. They were now sparkling white from top to bottom. The following year, she had a circular window added just below the awning and above the front door, which let more natural light into the foyer. Dolores extended the front garden another five feet from the facade of the house and lined it with a meandering border of decorative paving stones. After four years, the Kelleher house looked like none other on Pearl Drive.

From the beginning, what gratified Dolores most was the fact that the house was roomy enough for a large family. Upstairs, there were four bedrooms and two bathrooms. Downstairs, besides the dining room, kitchen, and living room, there was a small study, a family room, and a third bathroom. Ken might use the study as an office one day, she surmised, and perhaps she would eventually turn the family room into an office of her own, to do work for whatever charitable organization she knew she would run in a few years.

In time, Dolores came to accept the house as one with which she was content. What bothered her, though, was that other than her own large family from Sherborn, and Ken's small one from Queens, few visitors stopped by to enjoy her domestic handiwork. Over the years, she attempted to befriend the housewives she met at Saint Matthew's Church, where her children were baptized, and at Holy Name Elementary School, where they were students. She was not as successful as she had hoped. She found most of the women too shrill for her taste, even the Irish-Catholic ones. "Must be a Long Island thing," Dolores shared with her sisters, Kathleen and Patricia. Some of the other housewives, she explained, used phrases like 'He's full of piss and vinegar,' which she found crass, or 'Well, just have me stuffed and mounted,' which she found vulgar. Three or four of the women dressed in sweaters that accentuated their bosoms, and once the late nineteen fifties and early nineteen sixties arrived, their sweaters revealed far too much cleavage. One woman smoked cigarette after cigarette, and another, Dolores overheard, had had an affair with her gynecologist. The one who smoked cigarettes had apparently graduated to marijuana once her children got older. Many a Sunday, Dolores went to confession with Father Thomas Woodward at Saint Matthew's to cleanse herself of having seen such unseemly attire and having heard such profane gossip.

True, there were a handful of women more like Dolores, but they, too, remained distant. Once, at Holy Name Elementary, Dolores overheard two mothers chatting in another hallway. One said, "That Dolores Kelleher is a little standoffish, don't you think?" The other responded, "Must be a Boston thing."

Dolores had one good friend, her neighbor Donna Kelsey, who grew up in Queens and moved to Westbrook Hills when her husband Darren accepted a job as an engineer for the Grumman Aircraft Corporation, in nearby Bethpage. Donna and Darren were a few years older than Dolores and Ken. Dolores had little in common with Donna, but neither did she find her vulgar. Every few days, the two would sit and chat over coffee and slices of pie. Donna always brought the pie. She loved to bake and eagerly shared recipes and cooking secrets with Dolores. Donna enjoyed Dolores's stories of Sherborn and Boston and how she had transformed the Pearl Drive house practically on her own. Donna complimented her often. As if to return the favor, Dolores said she was impressed with the minor alterations Donna made to her own house, although she was really not all that impressed.

Ken had an amicable relationship with Darren Kelsey, although Darren spent most of his time at Grumman testing aircraft engines for the military. Their conversations were infrequent, though when they did bump into each other outside they could end up chatting for fifteen or twenty minutes, mostly about homeownership, utility companies, and how they both dreaded shoveling snow only to have snowplows push it back onto their driveways. More than once did Darren joke that he hoped Ken and Dolores would have a couple of muscular sons one day to help both of them out after winter storms. He said that he and Donna did not plan on having children.

Dolores and Ken would eventually have five children of their own, three girls and two boys. Alexis was born in 1945, Bridgett in 1947, and Caroline in 1949. Bridgett and Caroline shared an upstairs bedroom. One night when Caroline was four, with all the girls asleep, Ken and Dolores stayed up late, drank a few glasses of wine, and agreed to try for another child. They both dreamed of a son. Ken said he would love to have a little boy to play ball with and teach how to drive home-built go-carts. Dolores said that she, too, would love to have a son who would one day go to work in a three-piece suit and carry a leather briefcase.

"A leather briefcase? Not when he's five, I hope," Ken smirked. "I mean, you don't want the briefcase to have a picture of Howdy Doody on it, do you?" That prompted yet another marital spat between Ken and Dolores.

Still, the wine won out. Douglas Kelleher, conceived in 1953, was born the following year. Ken believed that stopping at four children was a wise choice, but Dolores was not as committed to the idea. Michael arrived in 1957. The plan was for Douglas and Michael to share another upstairs bedroom once Michael no longer needed a crib. But that plan derailed after Michael suffered a terrible injury.

• • • • •

Michael was Dolores's easiest birth. He had the most agreeable infancy. Even as a toddler, he looked more like a Farrell than any of the other children. Dolores loved all her children, but always had a secret smile for Michael. One day in 1959, when he was two-years-old, Michael was playing on the front lawn while Dolores, inside the garage, attended to one of her many projects. Michael toddled over to the open garage door to show her the dandelions he had picked from the lawn. The garage door suddenly came loose and crashed down with a thunderous boom, crushing little Michael's right leg almost to the point of complete detachment, and severely damaging the left. Dolores rushed him to the hospital in her own car. Unable to be saved, his right leg was amputated just below the waist, which rendered him wheelchair-bound from that point on. The doctors said that a prosthetic right leg was not possible because of the severe nerve, bone, and tissue damage where the prosthetic would need to be attached. The left leg, because of the muscle mutilation, would be all but useless, they said.

Timothy Farrell, by then an attorney in Newport, Rhode Island, asked Dolores if she planned to sue the original contractor who had installed the electric garage door, and offered whatever help the family needed. Dolores said she would much prefer to devote her efforts toward making Michael's life comfortable and meaningful and not squander vast amounts of time arguing in lawyer's offices and courtrooms. Timmy argued with her about that for several months after the accident and tried to get her to reconsider, but Dolores prevailed.

Two weeks after the accident, Darren Kelsey stopped by with a box full of tools, metal brackets, and bolts and screws from Grumman. He and Ken reattached the garage door to the motor with what Darren called the strength and integrity of a jet engine. Ken was unreserved in his thanks; Dolores, though appreciative, didn't know how to say so without revealing her rage and sorrow.

When Michael turned four, Dolores, with the help of a contractor who lived down the block and had offered his services for free, had a ramp built that led out of the kitchen door and descended gently to the backyard lawn. Michael could finally come in and go out of the house without the need to have his wheelchair lifted. The downstairs study became his bedroom. Being wheelchair bound, and thin, made Michael appear frail and disheveled as he approached adolescence, but he had always been very active within the limitations of his chair. He had a ready smile, an impish grin, and an easy laugh. Still, all Dolores saw was the way he struggled to do the simplest of tasks. For the first three years after the accident, a nurse-specialist stopped by the house once a day to assist. She, Ken, and Douglas helped Michael with his bathroom chores until Michael, at age six, took the initiative to learn those tasks on his own by maneuvering off and onto the wheelchair. It was rigorous and time-consuming, but day after day he did it without complaint, and got better at it as time went on.

Over Michael's objections, Dolores bought him special games and toys geared to the handicapped and, also against his will, took him to several physical and mental health specialists. The mental health specialists insisted Michael needed no help in that regard. Dolores more than once retorted that it seemed impossible that Michael would not require some psychological scrutiny given that he was the only child in the neighborhood so afflicted. "Please take no offense, Mrs. Kelleher," said one specialist, "but it seems to bother you a hell of a lot more than it bothers Michael." Dolores was offended and stormed out of the office.

That afternoon at confession, Dolores told Father Woodward that she had taken the Lord's name in vain while she glanced at the garage door. "It just came out," she said. "I didn't realize it until after I said it." She asked Father Woodward why Michael had to be the one to get in the way of the faulty door; why it couldn't have been her instead? The kindly priest said that only God knows the answer to that question.

"I shouldn't have broken the chain," Dolores added. When Father Woodward asked what chain she was talking about, she explained how all her children had names that started with consecutive letters of the alphabet—Alexis, Bridgett, Caroline, and Douglas—and that she broke the chain with Michael. "I should have named him Edward," she said without a trace of flippancy.

"Maybe you named him Michael," Father Woodward responded, "because in some way *he's* destined to be the one to break the chain. Maybe he'll be unique in ways you cannot even imagine right now."

Father Woodward told Dolores to thank God that Michael was alive and happy, to stop taking on the burden of needing to know God's plans, and to stop assuming the role of God's interrogator. Her penance, he said, was to go home and have a glass of wine.

She complied.

As the children grew, the Kelleher household became one of constant activity, though Dolores also commanded a measure of calm as a protective balance.

"Four active kids, a beautiful home, a husband who provides well. You must feel very fulfilled, Dolores," said her sister Kathleen one day during a visit. Dolores smiled.

As young girls, Alexis, Bridgett, and Caroline were respectful at home and diligent in school. Dolores expected nothing less, and the appearance of nothing less made her proud. Yet, she had concerns. She worried Alexis lacked motivation, that Bridgett wittingly masked her femininity, and that Caroline was developing an unbecoming sense of self-absorption.

Alexis was far too content to watch television, talk on the telephone, and read movie magazines. More than once did Dolores have to hold her own tongue when compelled to mention to Alexis that inactivity was most likely the cause of her build; while never fat, Alexis was stouter than her sisters and many other girls her age. She belonged to not a single club at school or church, despite her mother's pleas. Often Dolores took Alexis shopping with her, and then out for lunch without the other sisters, and through stories and compliments tried to build up her motivation and enthusiasm. Alexis enjoyed the outings, though her motivation and enthusiasm remained forever sluggish.

Bridgett became one of the busiest and most-feted athletes at Sacred Heart Junior High and Our Lady of Mercy High School. Her rough behavior on the field mimicked the reckless way she began to dress when she reached her teen years, and the reckless way she behaved off the field. Ken and Dolores attended most of her games. Ken's shouts of enthusiasm when she made goals, and his yowls of contempt when referees issued terrible calls, made Dolores feel ill at ease. She feared Bridgett's indelicate persona would plague and seriously hinder her in years to come. On three occasions, the principal of Sacred Heart Junior High School asked Ken and Dolores to stop by because Bridgett punched boys who had called her a dyke. Each boy had a black eye.

"What are we going to do about this tomboy thing, Ken?" Dolores asked her husband one evening. "It's nearly unbearable."

"Oh, I don't know," Ken replied. "Next door, Donna and Darren just put in a very expensive alarm. We have Bridgett instead! We're saving a ton of money."

Dolores and Ken had another battle that night.

Caroline, the youngest daughter, seemed to be on a mission to get people to take notice of her. She never sat still. In one way or another, she always performed, such as using a hairbrush to pretend to talk into a microphone, or opening up a schoolbook and placing it under her chin to mimic a tanning ritual at the beach. She was academically gifted and belonged to the Debating Club, the Model Congress Club, the Silly Skits Club, and a half dozen others. As often as she was kicked out of one club for impertinence, she would be reinstated after passionately defending her actions. Ken found it all very amusing. "As long as she's ambitious and respectful and does well in school..." he said to Dolores one night.

"Ambitious? Respectful?" chided his wife. "Last week at a debating club event, she went up to the microphone and called her opponent a horse's ass."

Ken was uncertain if it was the anecdote itself or his wife's retelling of it that made him laugh. He soon wished he hadn't.

One weekend in the summer of 1961, the family drove to Sherborn to celebrate Alexander Farrell's sixty-fifth birthday. Dolores's sister Kathleen had three daughters of her own, and her brother Timothy had three sons; all six nieces and nephews engaged easily in conversations with the adults, while the Kelleher children stayed mostly with each other and out of the way. The nieces and nephews seemed not to mind the graceful attire they had on; Dolores's children complained about the clothes she had insisted they wear and, as if to protest further, were very cavalier in their behavior.

"I need to build something in them," Dolores said to Ken when she was alone with him in her parents' kitchen. "Something that's not there now."

"Build something in them? They're not patios, Dolores, that you can just add shingled awnings onto. They're children. Happy, smart children. Leave them alone."

The argument ended there, but that did not stop Dolores from silently acknowledging how the Kelleher girls hardly fit the Farrell mold, physically or otherwise. As she saw it, Ken's side of the family had introduced into the line some features, postures, maybe even attitudes with which Dolores was uncomfortable.

"They are who they are," Father Woodward said when Dolores discussed it with him at confession one day. She was there for that very reason—to acknowledge how she sometimes harbored low-spirited thoughts about the way her children were developing into young adults. "Not only are they who they are," the priest continued, "but they're wonderful, to boot! So get off your Irish high horse and love those adorable ponies for who they are. For your penance, pray to God that I don't kick you out of this church for good."

Dolores knew not whether to laugh, cry, or just chalk it up to a quirky priest whose job it was to protect his entire flock, no matter how he chose to do it.

•   •   •

Dolores loved her children. She knew she loved them. And it was not seldom when each one of them said something, did something, or even looked a certain way, in a certain light, that gave her an extra measure of pride when she least expected it. Douglas, despite his complexion, which came from his paternal grandmother's side of the family, had Farrell eyes and the Farrell smile, and in many other ways could have grown up in Sherborn. In some ways, he reminded Dolores of her brothers; he did marvelously well in school, was good at baseball and basketball, and was always active, moving with great speed and competence from one hobby to the next. In elementary school, he was the leader of a club charged with making a time capsule to bury behind the playground. In a church youth group he was asked to teach younger children the game of checkers. In junior high, he was appointed as student leader of the hall monitor team, a role he embellished by wearing a cap that resembled the kind worn by police officers and by sticking a small water pistol into his belt (which he was asked to remove on several occasions). But because of his aptitude, curiosity, and determination, Dolores might have considered Douglas a nearly exemplary child. What hampered that conviction was his occasional lapse of good behavior. If Douglas deemed something unworthy of his time, he ignored it. What Dolores disliked even more was his refusal to abide by her rules. How she detested the occasional phone call when Douglas was stuck somewhere after having taken a long bike ride for which she had earlier denied permission. Douglas loved to ride his bicycle, and he loved to ride it fast and sometimes farther than he promised his parents he would. On a number of occasions, he reached his distant location when it was already dark outside

"Phone calls from the principal about Bridgett aren't enough?" Dolores complained to Donna one afternoon. "Now I have to get phone calls about Douglas from a grumpy store owner ten miles away?"

Dolores was furious at Ken for buying Douglas a dirt bike for his twelfth birthday. She considered the bike dangerous and unnecessary. As she watched from the living room window as Ken and Douglas took turns with it on Pearl Drive, Dolores was convinced that her husband bought it as much for himself as for their son.

As a teenager, Douglas discovered he sang and danced well and had a flair for acting. He joined the O.L.M. Stage Society at Our Lady of Mercy High School. Dolores volunteered to help with costumes, publicity, and rehearsal refreshments. She recruited Donna to provide the cupcakes and help hang posters around town. Dolores enjoyed the backstage visits and often fell into daydreams while the students rehearsed. She was pleased that Donna was there so that it wouldn't seem as if she were lingering there on her own for no apparent reason. Donna roused her out of her daydreams without knowing she was there to serve that very purpose.

There was one additional blemish on Douglas's character with which Dolores had to deal. For all his attributes and promise, Douglas had developed what his mother considered a streak of vanity. She tried to justify it; after all, he was gifted at so many things that it must have been hard for him to accept direction or criticism or to be told to do something another way. Over the years, he alienated several friends, teachers, even a relative or two, with his lack of modesty. Dolores was certain it would dissipate in time.

What made that even easier for her to overlook was the fact that Douglas seemed destined to become an attorney. Though he watched television rarely, when he did, he almost always insisted it be a crime show because of how well he could figure out the perpetrators, thieves, or murderers, and because of how passionate he was to justify or condemn the plot's outcome. Many of the shows, Dolores realized, featured lawyers and courtroom scenes, and she was certain that it would spark in Douglas a desire to enter the legal profession one day, a vocation for which she and several of Douglas's teachers knew he was well-suited. She was counting on it. From time to time in the privacy of her thoughts, Dolores delighted in the paradox that, despite some serious social shortcomings, a restless nature, and a penchant for moving from one hobby to another at lightning speed, Douglas seemed primed to end up the most successful Kelleher child.

•   •   •

Michael, three years younger than Douglas, created publicity posters for many of the plays in which his older brother appeared. Michael loved to draw, and as early as age five showed remarkable talent. Dolores made a small desk out of plywood that attached to Michael's wheelchair with plastic clasps. She glued thin strips of wood on the front and sides of the tabletop so that his pens and pencils would not fall off as he wheeled from one room to another. Michael drew faces and animals and nature scenes, some in near-realistic form, others as cartoon sketches. Dolores encouraged Michael's artistic bent, though she found it difficult to restrain her anger when he would draw on surfaces not meant for drawing, such as walls and bed sheets. Ken thought that Michael's tireless artistic whimsy was funny. Dolores was outraged at her husband for thinking so.

So adept did Michael become with artists' tools that he could pull off practical jokes on his father, such as when he changed the page numbers in the *Sunday New York Times* so realistically that Ken could not find the continuation of the article he was reading.

"Not so funny anymore, is it?" Dolores sneered at Ken.

Michael heard this from his bedroom and smiled.

Like his father, Michael enjoyed traveling, and urged Ken to take him on long rides in the car. If his father refused, Michael convinced Bridgett, who was physically strong, to wheel him a mile away to a track where Douglas often rode his dirt bike. Michael would sit by the track drawing on a large tablet pad and root his brother on at the same time. Sometimes he would tell Bridgett to leave him there and that he would wheel himself back home, since the return trip had no rising hills. He had the strength to wheel long distances, for he kept himself fit. His father had put up a basketball hoop above the garage door and played with Michael as often as he could. This became more infrequent as Ken's sales territory expanded and his out-of-state business trips increased. He also played more golf on weekends with clients than ever before. During these times, Michael would play basketball with Douglas, and sometimes Bridgett or Caroline. Michael asked Dolores to play two or three times, but she deferred, much preferring to stay with him inside.

"Afraid I'll make you look like a loser on the court?" joked ten-year-old Michael one day, after his mother turned him down.

Only once did the Kellehers go to Jones Beach as a family. Years of practice enabled Michael's parents and siblings to manage his collapsible wheelchair with relative ease and get him in and out of the car and in and out of the chair. But the sand proved to be insurmountable. Jones Beach, the famed leisure-time destination on the south shore, to which thousands of Long Islanders and families from New York City flocked on sunny days, was on the summertime wish lists of many friends of Alexis, Bridgett, Caroline, and Douglas. So it was with their friends' families with whom the Kelleher children, save for Michael, often went to the beach during the summer. Michael claimed not to mind, for he was fair-skinned and light-haired, and had once gotten a stinging sunburn just from sitting in the backyard.

"Besides," he said more than once, "I like big waves and hot sand about as much I like skin cancer." Each time he said it, his mother chastised him for making an indelicate joke, although she was secretly pleased that there would be no more Jones Beach stress because of Michael's dislike of the waves and the sand.

* * *

As Bridgett and Caroline entered their late teenage years, Dolores realized how boys paid more attention to Caroline than to Bridgett. Bridgett seemed not to care, and Caroline snubbed her admirers in such a mocking way as to charm them even more.

On the handful of occasions when she was at Caroline's school, Dolores wondered if some of the older boys were looking at her instead of her youngest daughter. After all, Dolores had maintained her weight through all the years her children were growing, wore smart clothes that endorsed her figure without accentuating it, and always stood tall with her head held high. She prayed that no one, least of all her daughters, ever noticed the fleeting, embarrassed glances some boys at school threw her way. Internally, she debated what to do to discourage it. But just as she turned a thought or two through her head, her mind went on to other things.

School events were hard for Dolores for yet another reason. She had to listen to mothers talk exuberantly about their various clubs and charities, while her own attempts to get involved were met with disappointment. The year before Caroline was born, Dolores joined a county-wide organization whose mission was to establish branches of each town's public library in spruced-up abandoned storefronts, making books more accessible to everyone. But the organization folded three months later because of mismanagement. When Douglas was two, Dolores joined a group whose goal was to strengthen the bonds between religious schools and public schools. Each member was given a role as a committee chairwoman—except Dolores, for reasons never made clear. She quit. When she was pregnant with Michael, she joined an arts promotion group as one of three assistant directors. Against her advice, the group concentrated exclusively on

Black and Hispanic communities, and no others. Dolores considered that a poor use of its resources and decided not to return. When Michael was in kindergarten, Dolores and Donna established an organization of their own, run out of their kitchens, that advocated the limiting of commercial development on Long Island. They called it Long Island Vistas, but were turned down for funding by private companies and government agencies twenty-one times before the two partners abandoned the effort.

Dolores gave organizational life one last try when Douglas was fourteen. She attended a meeting of the Mid-Nassau Garden Society. However, as she quickly learned, the women in the society discussed gardens far less than they discussed shopping centers or the sex appeal of various county officials. During one such discussion about the Roosevelt Field Shopping Mall, Dolores described the little family-owned shops along Main Street in Sherborn, but saw only a landscape of blank faces in return. She went to only one more meeting.

From time to time, Ken offered to help. Some nights, he sat up with Dolores past midnight to discuss it, even though he had to wake early the next morning to drive out of state. They would sip brandy on the couch, beneath the large "Nantucket Mist" watercolor by Sherborn native Tara O'Shea. They would discuss plans of action and try to figure out how to avoid past mistakes. Once or twice, when the brandy kicked in, the discussions became animated, and young Michael, whose room was nearby, would yell out, "Can you lower the volume, elder folks? You have a handicapped adolescent son in here trying to sleep."

Sometimes Ken asked around at Aster-Paxton Pharmaceuticals to see if anyone had a spouse who was involved in something similar to what Dolores wanted to do. Nothing ever came of it.

Dolores appreciated the effort, for it was rare that Ken took seriously anything other than his work, his golf outings, and his easy chair in the living room. She thought of Ken as a good provider with a gentle soul and a warm smile, but it was his general indifference that troubled her. It troubled her and strangely amused her, too, for Ken often reminded her of her own father, Alexander Farrell, and that could be a comfort. Still, the comparison was not entirely parallel: Ken enjoyed watching car races on television, and occasionally the news, whereas Alexander took far more of an interest in science, art, history, and politics. To Dolores, that made her father a more interesting person. Ken was reliable—he took care of all the bills, car maintenance, and various other family tasks—but Alexander was a better disciplinarian. Ken never wanted to yell at his children and steadfastly refused to strike them. Sometimes Dolores demanded it, such as when Caroline's tongue ran loose with a fifteen-second-long string of one- and two-syllable curse words, or when Bridgett refused to change out of her ripped blue jeans to go to church, or when Douglas shattered the glass atop a curbside lamppost with his BB gun. It was usually Dolores who had to dole out the punishments—mostly a stiff, angry grasp on their arms, or sometimes a silent, icy stare that the children regarded as even more painful than the arm-grasping.

Yes, Dolores loved Ken, but by the time Michael was a teenager, she questioned her ardent love for him. Their time together was comfortable yet unexciting, respectful yet passionless. If Dolores focused hard enough, she could remember times when making love was satisfying, and times when they laughed long and loud. Every once in a while she thought back to the Aster-Paxton annual sales meeting of 1955, at the New York Hilton, the one and only time employee spouses were invited. She and Ken became mildly drunk at dinner and kissed so feverishly in an empty elevator that they missed their floor. After three more attempts, they finally made it to their room, took off their clothes, and rattled the hotel bed to the point where a guest in the next room had to rap on the wall. Something like that had never happened before, nor did it ever happen again. Also, every October, Dolores recalled the time when Ken tried to surprise her on their fifteenth wedding anniversary. He had purchased an expensive musical jewelry box and hid it so that Dolores would not find it before he had a chance to present it to her. But he was so nervous that she would find it in the morning that in the middle of the night he moved the little package from one hiding place to another one that he thought was better, and each time he picked it up, the jewelry box played a few bars of "Fur Elise," which woke up the entire house.

Dolores always smiled at the thought, mindful of the fact that the memory returned but once a year.

Ken was kind, supportive, and loyal. Was he also sad and disappointed? This is what Dolores came to believe, and one clue she had was his cigarette smoking, which had increased over the years from one pack a day to two-and-a-half and sometimes three. She always knew what kind of mood he was in by how many cigarette butts she found in the emerald green ceramic ashtrays scattered throughout the house. She worried about him and asked him to stop. He smiled and said he would try when he had more time. The irony, as Dolores saw it, was how he always made that promise while sitting in the den watching television.

• • • • • • •

Easter and Christmas were always special days at the Kelleher house. Everyone in the family chipped in with the decorating chores to make both the inside and outside look especially festive. Dolores and Ken were in good spirits and the children were particularly well-behaved.

Once, when she was a little girl, Caroline turned to her mother and asked, "Why don't you smile and laugh and kiss and hug us the rest of the year as much as you do on Christmas?"

"Oh, you silly..." Dolores chuckled, not knowing what else to say.

Dolores loved the way her house looked during the holiday season. Despite her family's eagerness to help, she did quite a bit of work herself when Ken and the children were away. That included using hammers and nails and splicing electrical wires. Many times, she commented on how she wished every house on the block could be decorated as nicely. She knew it would remind her of Sherborn, and that was a memory she cherished. "Couldn't the Stewarts and the Morrisons at least put up nice little white lights instead of those fat garish blue and orange ones?" she mumbled aloud as she stood alone in the front yard on a brisk December morning. She gazed at the reindeer on the Harris and Gilroy lawns and noticed their construction of cheap plastic. It was not carved wood, like hers.

"I know I can't hope for Beverly and Murray Hillman to do any Christmas decorating, and certainly not Rabbi and Mrs. Sheldon," she commented to Donna one day. "But would it be so terrible for them to put a wreath on their front doors and wrap their lampposts in red bunting? After all, you don't have to be Catholic to love holly and candy canes."

The next day, Donna had Darren put up holly and candy cane decorations on their own house.

Caroline was also the one who, much later as a teenager, asked during a family Christmas party why they couldn't sing aloud all the time, instead of just on the holiday. The three Kelleher girls sang well and were good at harmonizing. One morning, Ed Stewart, who lived down the block, passed by and overheard the girls harmonizing to "White Christmas." He gushed to Dolores, "They're like the Lennon Sisters on TV! They could be on *The Lawrence Welk Show*. You should let them audition!" Though Dolores smiled, she tried to disregard Ed's comment, for she harbored no such dream for her daughters. The next day, *The Lawrence Welk Show* was on television, with the sound low, while Dolores and Ken sat reading in the living room. The host introduced one of the show's older singers, known on the program as the "Champagne Lady." Ken saw Dolores look at the screen and he said, "Would you like to be the Champagne Lady of Westbrook Hills?" To which Dolores yawned, "I wasn't watching, Ken. I was just taking a break from the book."

Later that night, when Ken had gone to bed, Dolores sat alone in the living room with a glass of wine, singing to herself so softly that even Michael could not hear.

• • • • • •

Alexis married a man named Arnold Liebowitz in the fall of 1968. She had graduated from Nassau Community College three years earlier and was working as a waitress at The Birch Tree Cafe in Mineola when she met Arnold, who was sixteen years her senior. He was a New York

City stockbroker who frequented the restaurant on his way home to Plainview and asked to be served only by Alexis. Although terribly overweight, Arnold was sweet and attentive, and Alexis easily overlooked his size. She accepted his proposal after just three months of dating.

A week after the wedding, Douglas performed in "The Long Island Eight to Eighty Talent Contest," held the first Saturday in October at Salisbury Park, in a new band shell in front of a sweeping, gently rising lawn. Thousands attended. There were four celebrity judges. Ken left early from a pharmaceutical convention in Albany to join his family at the park, and still had on his suit when he arrived. Dolores had bought a new dress for the occasion. Bridgett was a senior at Molloy College and Caroline a sophomore at Hofstra University. Both attended the show to watch their fourteen-year-old brother perform. Dolores was pleased about that, though far less than thrilled that Bridgett wore a soccer jersey and sweatpants, and that Caroline had on a tie-dyed tee-shirt, no brassiere, and kept the shirt tucked tightly into her jeans, which made the outline of her breasts quite conspicuous.

A handicap-accessible van provided by the YMCA of Nassau County drove Michael to the park. Only Alexis was absent that day. She and Arnold were on their honeymoon in Las Vegas.

Ken stood with Douglas at the side of the band shell while Dolores and the girls set up a blanket and beach chairs near the bottom of the hill. One judge was a pretty and petite blonde television personality named Joey Heatherton. Ken and Douglas had seen her just the week before on *The Tonight Show* in a skin-tight leotard, trading sexual innuendoes with Johnny Carson.

"Which one of you two handsome gentlemen is performing?" Heatherton said to Ken and Douglas as she tiptoed up behind them. She commanded attention by her looks alone; people up and down the hill stared and murmured as she brushed back the short strands of her hair and then pulled at the front of her blouse to loosen the material that hugged tightly to her chest. On the hill, Dolores heard a teenage boy behind her say to his friend, "See that blonde? Pretty nice tatas on her, right?"

Douglas was the third act on the bill. He sang "Happy Together," with piano accompaniment by a music teacher from his school. His voice was in top form. He engaged with the audience. At the end of the two-hour show, Carl Yastrzemski, a Boston Red Sox first baseman and Long Island native, announced Douglas's name as the second-place winner, and then told the cheering crowd that a twenty-three-year-old flamenco guitarist from Massapequa took the top prize. After the show, Dolores, Bridgett, and Caroline rushed to the rear of the band shell, and Ken, who pushed Michael's wheelchair, arrived a few minutes later. They told Douglas how excited and proud they were. Carl Yastrzemski introduced himself and seemed to pay extra attention to Bridgett. He asked about her soccer skills. Bridgett's attention, however, was far more focused on the way Joey Heatherton continued to seduce the crowd from the band shell. Yastrzemski quickly lost interest.

•   •   •   •   •

At church that Sunday, three mothers told Dolores they had seen the talent contest at Salisbury Park and that Douglas should audition for television programs and Broadway shows. During the week, while shopping in town, Dolores ran into three other mothers of Our Lady of Mercy students, and each said something similar to her. "Someone with Douglas's talent, looks, and personality could easily get an agent," commented one of them.

That night, Dolores said to Ken, "You know, someone with Doug's talent, looks, and personality might easily be able to get an agent. In California, maybe."

"An agent?" asked Ken as he looked up sharply from his newspaper. "I thought you wanted him to be a trial attorney."

"I do. He will. But if he could make some extra money in television for a few years, that could help pay for a top law school. We're not rich, you know. Maybe it could also help us with Caroline's tuition, and maybe another wedding or two. It never snows in Southern California, Ken. You realize that, don't you? Michael wouldn't be stuck inside all winter long."

Ken was silent for the next few minutes. He appeared to be reading the newspaper.

"Barry Decker in accounts receivable told me the other day that Southern California is becoming the most lucrative territory for Aster-Paxton," he said as he put the newspaper down. "And there are holes in the sales force out there."

Dolores listened with interest.

"You didn't want to live in Boston," she said, with just a hint of mockery, "but you're okay with Los Angeles?"

"Los Angeles isn't Boston," Ken sighed. "More money to make, no goddamned snow to shovel."

"Well, since you're talking about it rationally, I wouldn't be a bit surprised if there were plenty of opportunities for me to get involved with an arts organization of some kind in Los Angeles. I'm sure there are dozens. Hundreds."

For the previous three years, Ken's income had barely increased. Between Alexis's wedding and the first few years of college tuition for their other daughters, the family savings account suddenly was less robust than either Ken or Dolores had expected it would be at this point in their lives. So with Ken's understated approval, and with the telephone help of a real estate agent in Los Angeles County, Dolores researched houses to rent in Southern California. "Just to test the waters," she said to family and friends whenever the topic came up.

One night, Dolores sat alone in the kitchen reading talent agency brochures that she had requested through the mail. Ken had been on a business call in New Jersey all day and was still a few hours away from home. Dolores poured herself a glass of wine. She wondered if she and Ken were doing the right thing. It was a major undertaking. A big change. She had a second glass of wine, and then a third, before dialing her sister Katherine. She needed to talk it out and knew that Katherine, who had been skeptical when she first heard the news, would lend an ear that was both honest and sympathetic. Katherine was surprised that Dolores had called so late, but attempted to sound unruffled. She asked Dolores to name all the reasons she wanted to move to California. Dolores spoke about the money that Douglas could make, about Ken's chance for advancement and the money *he* could make, and about the weather, which would be good for Michael.

"Also," Dolores added, "people won't look at me so oddly if I decide to do a little dancing or singing at some fundraisers—you know, just for fun. If I did that here, they'd throw me into a funny farm. But people in Hollywood wouldn't bat an eye. And who knows, maybe I could even stick a toe in some television and movie work myself, just for kicks."

"For kicks?" Katherine asked, gently yet uncertainly. "Just for fun? No offense, little sis, but this doesn't really sound like you."

"Katherine," Dolores snapped, "I have five children, twenty-three to eleven years old. One is missing a leg. One is married to a fat Jewish man. One loves to show the world her tatas. Don't I deserve to have a little fun?"

· · · · ·

A few months later, Ken and Dolores rented their house on Pearl Drive, with a one-year commitment, to a family named Goldstein. Ira and Lois Goldstein had twin boys, toddlers, and promised to keep the house immaculate. Most of the furnishings would stay, along with many of the decorations. Dolores decided to take just a few paintings, lamps, music stands, and all the crucifixes that were nailed into all the hallway and bedroom walls.

Douglas took a day off from school and traveled with Dolores to New York City, where they met with representatives of a Los Angeles talent agency called Bel-Ami Teens. The Bel-Ami rep, who had secured a 16-millimeter sound recording of the Salisbury Park talent contest, and who had also asked Douglas to read a few lines from a script, signed him to their roster of clients. The next day, after spending an hour on the phone with the Los Angeles real estate agent, Dolores felt as if she had found a suitable furnished house to rent in Sherman Oaks, also with a one-year commitment. The agent mailed photographs, which arrived three days later, and the images convinced Dolores to go ahead with the plan.

Ken planned to drive out to the coast in his own car, which he packed with as many belongings as he could. The rest would be shipped to California. Ken's brother Joe agreed to take care of Dolores's car for the year they'd be away; Dolores would lease one of her own once they arrived in Sherman Oaks. Joe also insisted on driving the family to the airport.

With all the arrangements made, and the start of the 1969 school year about to begin, the Kellehers of Long Island left for Hollywood.

SHERMAN OAKS, CALIFORNIA

"We ate like pigs, we sang like angels, and we spent obscene amounts of money on each other. It was a full family day, and now the family part must end! It's the natural order of things."

"I met a real-life Jeannie," Douglas gushed, "and she's beautiful and maybe I'll marry her one day and then she can grant me any wish I want. Wouldn't that be cool?"

The day after the Kellehers settled into their rented home in Sherman Oaks, Douglas began ninth grade classes at the Los Angeles County Children's Institute for the Performing Arts. The school, in West Hollywood, was geared to students interested in pursuing careers in television, motion pictures, music, or theatre. A nursery school for children of industry professionals was also part of the institution. Ken had dropped Douglas off in the morning on his way to the Aster-Paxton regional office in Glendale.

The school was a thirty-minute drive from Sherman Oaks, though Dolores, unfamiliar with the roads, took almost an hour to get to West Hollywood for the return trip. While he waited in the lobby, Douglas saw Barbara Eden, the pretty actress who played the leading role in the popular television show *I Dream of Jeannie*. She was picking up her four-year-old son, Matthew, at the nursery school.

In the car, Douglas said to his mother, "Maybe you can ask my agent if I can be on *I Dream of Jeannie*. Wouldn't that be neat? Barbara Eden smiled at me."

"We'll see," Dolores replied. "Did you enjoy the day? Do you think you'll like the school?"

"I guess... Wouldn't it be great if someone could really make wishes come true? Like on *I Dream of Jeannie*? I know what I'd wish for. What would *you* wish for?"

"A brighter house," Dolores mumbled as she nervously negotiated a difficult turn onto the freeway.

"A what?" asked Douglas.

"Nothing."

The rented house on Heidi Court was much gloomier, both inside and out, than implied by the photographs Dolores had seen in New York. A single garden along the front of the house was a mere strip of land no more than two feet wide; the photograph of the exterior made the garden appear much wider, perhaps because of the camera angle. Dolores remembered more windows in the photographs, as well. She had to wonder if perhaps she was just imagining that out of sheer hope and optimism. The windows that were there were much smaller than the ones in her mind.

With money still tight, and the prospect of spending so much time driving from Sherman Oaks to West Hollywood and back again, Dolores feared the rented house would have to remain the way it was indefinitely. To her, that was a pitiful reality, for she saw the house as nothing but dismal and inelegant. It had odd angles. It saddened her. She suddenly wondered what she had been thinking when she agreed to rent it sight unseen.

Dolores and Douglas made the rest of the drive home in almost total silence. Dolores realized the curious hush only after she pulled the car in front of the house, and that realization saddened her even more.

The two-story Southern-style stucco house had just three bedrooms, but Ken and Dolores deemed that acceptable, since the family no longer needed a house as big as the one back East. Their daughters, Alexis and Bridgett, remained on Long Island.

Alexis and Arnold Liebowitz lived in an apartment in Garden City. Alexis continued to work at The Birch Tree Cafe, and Arnold commuted daily by railroad to Wall Street.

Bridgett had graduated from Molloy College in May and accepted a job as a physical education teacher at Westbrook Hills Elementary

School. She found an apartment in Levittown and a roommate who was an English teacher. Things had been so hectic those last few weeks in Westbrook Hills that neither Dolores nor Ken had met her roommate or had even seen the apartment.

Following her sophomore year at Hofstra, Caroline transferred to Pepperdine University in Malibu to coincide with the family's relocation to Southern California. She used the second of the two upstairs bedrooms; Douglas and Michael shared the third bedroom on the main floor. The back door of the house led out to the ground-level patio, so Michael did not need a ramp to go outside.

Caroline liked Pepperdine, where she majored in communications. She enjoyed her new friends, who were wilder than any she had had on Long Island. Caroline kept her wild side a secret from her parents, although Dolores could always sense heady smells on her clothing and never believed her stories of working overnight on class projects in Pepperdine's closed-circuit television studio.

"I've never heard of that," Dolores said to Caroline one night in the kitchen, "a class that lasts all night long."

"Some television channels are on all night long," Caroline explained with conviction, "and radio is on all night long, and college teaches about real life and real jobs. So that's why the classes last all night long."

"And they let you go to school dressed like that? With no brassiere?"

"First of all, Mother dear, a brassiere isn't going to help me learn what I need to learn..." Caroline never got to second-of-all because Dolores walked out of the kitchen.

Still, Caroline kept her room neat, was polite in the house, and helped Michael whenever she could. So Dolores tried to suppress her own unease.

•　　•　　•　　•

Michael had turned twelve just before the move. He was enrolled at Gartner Junior High, a nine-year-old institution that was generously endowed by the state of California and dozens of wealthy donors, which made it California's most successful and progressive liberal arts school for students with physical disabilities. Michael enjoyed it. A specially outfitted bus picked him up at home in the morning and dropped him off in the afternoon. He made many friends, and the teachers liked him. The campus was on several acres of flat lawns and walkways, and he could wheel himself around with complete freedom and sheer delight. The same was not true of his own neighborhood; Heidi Court was lined with beautiful orange trees and palm trees, but was hilly (no one had mentioned that in New York), which made it difficult for Michael to self-propel his wheelchair for longer than a minute or two at a time. Fortunately, there was a park one block away from the house where he often spent hours alone, drawing nature scenes, cartoons, and portraits. Sometimes people stopped next to his wheelchair to admire his work. He scribbled *emkay* in the bottom right corner of each canvas, but refused to tell people who asked what it stood for. Nor did he tell anyone at home, although the moment Caroline saw a cartoon of his that the wind had somehow lodged in the front-yard garden, she deduced that *emkay* stood in for his initials.

Michael often brought a pair of binoculars with him to the park to study birds in flight and the distant hills, and would draw many of the birds and hills from memory as if he had taken close-up photographs.

One day, Dolores caught Michael staring at her with the binoculars in the house, even though she was only three feet away from him. She knew he was doing it to be silly.

"Why are you staring at me, Michael?" she asked. "Are you studying to be a spy?"

"Well, I did apply to the CIA the other day," he said, a relentlessly serious look on his face.

"Oh really? A twelve-year-old? What did they say?"

"They said I didn't have a leg to stand on."

For the first time in a very long time, Dolores laughed. She then had a cold, chilling sensation for doing so. She went to her bedroom, shut the door, and prayed to be forgiven.

Dolores hadn't been to church since she left Westbrook Hills, which by now was three months in the past. There had been no time. So she asked both of her neighbors if they knew anything about the local Catholic churches, and of the three mentioned, she decided to visit Our Lady of the Oaks, just three blocks away. She met the priest, Father Patrick Flannery, the next morning when she stopped by the church. She told him about the family, and returned later that afternoon for confession, where she asked if she was evil for having laughed at Michael's joke. Father Flannery told her it would be evil only if she had taken off his leg herself, "Which of course is absurd," he said, "since it was an accident. Therefore, I would have you committed to an insane asylum if you *didn't* laugh. Do you understand what I am trying to say?"

Dolores did not understand, or at least had no patience to try. She told Father Flannery she felt lightheaded and asked to be excused. She left Our Lady of the Oaks and realized as she got into the car that she had not been given her penance. That had never happened before on Long Island.

●   ●   ●   ●   ●

Aster-Paxton had helped with the relocation costs, but there were many other expenses that Ken and Dolores had not expected. Four months after they arrived in Southern California, Ken asked his supervisors to extend his territory. They did, and as a result, he worked nearly twice as many hours. His income increased, but so did his time away from home.

Meanwhile, Dolores joined the Outer Angeles Arts Org. As she was told several times during her orientation, its name ended with the one-syllable phrase "Org," not the word Organization. Dolores was a publicity volunteer, although between shuttling Douglas to classes and auditions, taking care of Michael, and trying whatever she could to make the house brighter and more cheerful, she had very little time for the group. She was chastised twice for saying Organization on the phone, instead of the required Org.

"It's called branding," the assistant director chided her, sounding quite annoyed. "Org! Not Organization. Anybody can be an organization. We're an Org. Do you understand? Org, Org, Org. Now let me hear you say it, Dolores. Say Org."

She quit that afternoon.

• • • • •

Douglas did not enjoy his classes. When he lived on Long Island, he was one of the most talented members of the relatively small music and theater groups to which he belonged. Other members were not nearly as capable. In West Hollywood, he was just one talented member in classes and workshops where every other student was just as talented, if not more so. The same was true at the auditions he attended. He no longer felt as distinctive as he did back home. As he wrote in a letter to his sister Bridgett, Hollywood was packed with people who listened but did not hear, people who looked but did not see, people who thought not of other people but only of themselves. (He later admitted to having borrowed those lines from a script he had to read in class one day — but agreed with them so wholeheartedly that he eagerly and assertively adopted them as his own.)

Not a week went by during which Douglas had more than a one-hour break from his activities. Between school and auditions, he had little time for friends, and even less for relaxation. Dolores raised the issue with Shiloh Green, his agent at Bel-Ami Teens. Shiloh insisted that such a grueling agenda negatively affected only those kids who had dysfunctional families, who had too much success too quickly, and who were predisposed to bad behavior. "But Douglas is Ken and Dolores's boy!" Shiloh said to Dolores, adopting the tone of someone who was an authority on the Kelleher family, "a normal kid from Long Island. Nothing to worry about."

Despite not yet having a union card, with the help and influence of Bel-Ami Teens, Douglas won a small, one-line role in a television show. One day at the CBS Studio Center, he and an eleven-year-old actress named Anissa Jones were caught smoking marijuana behind a trailer. The show was *Family Affair*, in which Jones played a leading role. When off the set, Jones behaved much older than her years. She was attracted to Douglas and befriended him quickly. "I got the weed from someone on *Hogan's Heroes* who I know," she told him. "He said it will help me relax, and my agent says I really gotta relax."

Dolores was called down to the studio and informed about the marijuana. Ken was out of town. Since Douglas had never been in trouble before, the studio said it would let the matter drop.

"He's a great kid," an assistant producer told Dolores. "When he was by himself the first half of the day he was fine. But when he hooked up with one of our regulars, well, I guess he got a little cheeky."

On the ride home to Sherman Oaks, Douglas tried to explain. "She said it helps her relax, Mom," he sighed. "And I don't get two minutes to relax. You know that. When do I ever get to relax?"

Dolores agreed, but was clueless what to do about it. She had no interest in talking it over again with Shiloh Green. Douglas took initiative on his own by putting in less and less effort, not only at auditions, but also in school. As Dolores and Douglas waited in the lobby at Bel-Ami Teens before a meeting, Shiloh, just inside the office door, overheard Douglas tell his mother that he was sick and tired of wasting his time, that he hated everyone he met, and that he was bored out of his mind. Shiloh walked into the lobby and told Dolores and Douglas that their appointment had to be postponed to a future date. When Dolores and Douglas left the building, the agent instructed his secretary to mail a termination letter to the Kelleher house.

On the day the termination letter arrived, Dolores also received a call informing her that Douglas's scene had been cut from *Family Affair*. She did not want to tell Douglas and thought of ways to postpone it. He was miserable enough. Dolores felt guilty for allowing events to unfold in Douglas's life the way they had. Without an agent, there would be no more auditions, so at least that part of the dilemma was solved. She drove him to school early the next morning, parked, went into the building, and arranged for Douglas to drop all but one performing arts class. She added three more academic classes to fill the open slots.

· · · · ·

Alexis phoned to invite the family to spend Thanksgiving with her and Arnold at their Garden City apartment on Long Island. She said there was a lovely hotel in town where they could all stay, and that Arnold would be happy to pick them up at the airport and drive them back and forth to the hotel and their apartment. Ken was dubious; the round-trip airfare for the five of them—he and his wife, the two boys and Caroline—especially around holiday time, would be an enormous expense on which he had not planned. In addition to that, they'd have to book a pair of hotel rooms for two or three nights.

"I guess we didn't think this thing through as carefully as we should have," Ken said to Dolores the day after Alexis called. "We never planned on having to go back East!"

A few days later, that oversight became even more painfully obvious; Peter Kelleher, Ken's seventy-eight-year-old father, passed away. Ken flew to New York for the funeral, alone, two weeks before Thanksgiving. It was a small, private affair in Rego Park, Queens. Alexis was there, Arnold was not. Ken stayed with his mother in her small apartment, a block from the cemetery. Over the next three days, Ken and his older brother Joe arranged for their mother to move into a senior citizens' home, also in Queens. Lucille did not handle the loss well.

"It's none of my business," Ken said to Alexis as they sat in a nearby diner for breakfast, "but why didn't Arnold come with you to the funeral?"

Alexis had difficulty finding the right words with which to respond.

"Troubles?" Ken asked gently. Alexis nodded. A few tears ran down her cheeks. "Well," Ken said, with the same tenderness as before, "we're here for you, if you need us. Understood? Listen—with Grandpa Peter gone, and with what Uncle Joe and I are going through with Grandma Lucille right now, and with everyone so busy out on the coast, and with whatever it is you're going through with Arnold... well, why don't we call off the Thanksgiving thing? We'll pick up the pieces later on. Together. Sound like a good idea?"

Alexis agreed and seemed grateful.

"Maybe you can come out to us for Christmas," Ken suggested. "You can get a few days off from the restaurant, can't you? You won't have to pay for a hotel. It's a small house, but we'll make it work."

Alexis said she'd talk it over with Arnold.

Back in California, Dolores decided to give Father Flannery at Our Lady of the Oaks another chance. She went to confession and allowed how terrible she felt about having paid so little mind to her husband's parents over the years.

"I should have invited them over more. I should have gone with Ken to New York for the funeral," she cried. "But on the other hand, there's Douglas and Michael to think of..."

Father Flannery asked Dolores if she felt that Peter and Lucille Kelleher had loved her and the family. Dolores admitted that despite their shyness, they did indeed seem to enjoy their visits to the Westbrook Hills house, and they enjoyed it even more when the family visited them in their small apartment in Queens. They adored their grandkids, she said, and seemed proud of the way she and Ken had built such a nice home life for the children.

"Well, then," said Father Flannery, "your contribution to their happiness is not insignificant. Whatever you did in regard to your relationship with them seems to have worked, because they were happy and proud. Isn't that enough for you?"

Dolores said she supposed it was enough.

"You suppose?" the priest snapped, startling her in the dark confessional. "Don't suppose. Know! After all, the love you take is equal to the love you make."

The remark confounded Dolores. She asked him to explain.

"Oh, well," he said, "it's from a Beatles song. I don't really know what it means, but I always wanted to use it somewhere. It sounds pretty hip and profound. Doesn't it?"

That troubled her. "Hip?" she repeated to herself irritably on the ride home (after realizing, once again, that she was given no penance). Father Flannery was so dissimilar to Father Woodward at Saint Matthew's in Westbrook Hills, and there could not have been a bigger difference in manner and disposition between Father Flannery and Father McDermott in Sherborn. To Dolores, the distinctions were astonishing.

She decided she would look for another church.

•   •   •   •   •   •

As the Christmas season arrived, Dolores decorated the Sherman Oaks house with wreaths and stockings that she had purchased two years earlier during a visit to Boston and had used once on Pearl Drive. She put Christmas songbooks on all the music stands—"The Holiday Up North" and "Sleigh Bells in the Berkshires"—and draped garland diagonally up and down each music stand in a candy cane design. She also placed a fully-ornamented miniature Vermont White Spruce in the living room and a larger one outside with glittery ribbons and cotton snow. In effect, Dolores turned a tiny piece of Southern California into New England. Although she found it somehow lacking, she felt it rose above the work of all her neighbors. The Coopers across the street had adorned their palm tree with dozens of small strobe lights, which Dolores found insidious to the holiday spirit; the Tanners, two houses down, had affixed to the trunk of their cottonwood tree a speaker that blared Elvis Presley singing "Blue Christmas" and "Santa Bring My Baby Back to Me" over and over, which Dolores found even more offensive.

Alexis and Bridget flew out west for a four-day visit. Arnold stayed behind because he claimed there wouldn't be enough room in the house for all three of them.

"You and Arnold could have stayed in a hotel," Dolores protested when they all sat down together in the living room.

"It would've been too much of a hassle," Alexis responded.

"Are you two having problems?"

Ken interjected. "Let's just concentrate on having a nice time," he smiled, then turned his attention to Bridgett. "How's your job? And how's your roommate?"

"Well, the job is only three months old," Bridgett said, "so it's too early to tell. Kim's fine. I'm sure you'll meet her soon. She almost came with me, but her family insisted she stay on Long Island."

"Why would she want to come all the way out here?" Dolores asked. "Isn't she just a roommate?"

Once again, Ken changed the subject.

"I may have to fly back east in a few weeks to attend a meeting," he announced. "Maybe I can see your place then, Bridgett, and meet Kim, too."

"Great," Bridgett said. "Unfortunately, you'll have to get a hotel room. It's just a one-bedroom apartment."

"One bedroom?" Dolores called out. "Why one bedroom?"

At that point, Ken insisted they all go into the dining room for the meal.

The dinner was delicious. The family sang "Santa Claus is Coming to Town" and "Have Yourself a Merry Little Christmas." Dolores, however, refrained from singing. Bridgett asked why.

"Oh, well, the acoustics in the house make my voice sound... I don't know—empty," Dolores explained. "Besides, I can't imagine Santa Claus ever coming to *this* town."

Everyone laughed. Dolores ignored it.

For presents, Dolores gave her three daughters elegant new clothes, which the girls said they liked. Douglas received a remote-controlled Jaguar that was advertised as being faster and able to go farther than any other model car. Michael's gift was a Nikon camera with five interchangeable lenses.

Ken loved his new leather briefcase, inside of which was the current issue of *Time* that began a magazine subscription Dolores had ordered for him. From the children he received ties, headphones, and a wood-framed 1880 map of the West Coast. His secret favorite gift was a silk bathrobe from Caroline. "Just like High Hefner's!" Caroline said when she presented it to him.

Among Dolores's gifts were jewelry, cookware, a coffee-table book about famous interior designers, and a subscription to *Horticulture* magazine. Her secret favorite gift was a fully-stocked wooden toolbox from Bridgett, upon which were painted scenes from historic Boston.

Alexis had also purchased gifts for her siblings. When she first landed at the airport in Los Angeles, she had urged her father to take her shopping. Ken said it was unnecessary for her to buy gifts, but Alexis insisted.

"Feeling a little melancholy?" he asked when they were alone. "Like you need your family maybe a little more than ever before?"

Alexis smiled and changed the subject, which indicated to Ken that his instinct was correct.

For Bridgett, Alexis bought a large-format book on famous female athletes that she had heard her sister talk about back on Long Island; for Caroline she picked up three record albums and sheet music by Herb Alpert, a musician she had heard Caroline talk about on the phone (and on whom apparently Caroline had a crush); for the boys she selected chronograph wristwatches. Everyone enjoyed their gifts.

After all the presents had been opened, Caroline said she had to leave, for there was another party at Pepperdine that she needed to attend. Dolores complained, but Caroline stood fast.

"We ate like pigs, we sang like angels, and we spent obscene amounts of money on each other," Caroline said with a grin. "It was a full family day, and now the family part must end! It's the natural order of things."

Later that evening, when she and Ken were alone in their bedroom, Dolores felt the need to discuss Caroline's behavior.

"Where does she get a mouth like that?" she asked. "Not from my side, that's for sure."

Ken asked Dolores what she meant by that; neither he nor anyone on his side of the family ever spoke rudely or tactlessly, he asserted. Dolores said it was his predictably indolent attitude that contributed to Caroline's behavior.

"Indolent?" he repeated. "Someone who works as hard as I do cannot be called indolent. If I were indolent, Dolores, which we both know means lazy, we wouldn't have a house to live in. We'd be out on the street."

"I'm sorry," Dolores conceded. "I misspoke. However," she added as she reached over impatiently to stub out a cigarette which Ken had only just lit, "where do you think she picks up her bad habits? For that, I *won't* apologize. You really should quit smoking, Ken. Not just because of Caroline, so that she won't start smoking, which I'm sure she will anyway. It's also bad for Douglas and Michael. The fumes, the smell… And it's bad for you, of course. You're coughing more than ever. Don't blame me if all our children end up smoking like chimneys."

Ken said he would try to quit. He did not want to arouse his wife's displeasure any further; it was, after all, still Christmas. By this point, he was getting ready for bed, even though it was only ten o'clock. He had to leave on a two-day business trip early in the morning.

Dolores had complained bitterly about the business trip when she first heard about it the week before. Ken explained he was visiting important Asian clients in Seattle who did not celebrate Christmas but would admire the fact that he had agreed to meet with them the day after the holiday. He said it could represent a lot of extra money, which Dolores knew the family sorely needed. So she buried her complaint and tried to forget about it.

•　　　•　　　•

The next day, Dolores took Alexis and Bridgett to Bullock's department store to exchange a few of the gifts. Caroline had never returned from her party. Douglas watched Michael at home. The boys played together, which was a refreshing change for both; they had never been terribly close, mostly because they were hardly ever home at the same time. They tried out Douglas's new remote-controlled car on the street, and Michael took pictures of it with his new camera. When they tired of that, they went back into the house to watch television in the living room. A children's show that had been on the air for just a couple of months came on, and although both of them were too old for it, Douglas and Michael sat on the couch and became absorbed with the program.

"I wish a was a kid again," Douglas murmured after fifteen minutes of *Mr. Rogers' Neighborhood*.

Michael looked at his sixteen-year-old brother and was tempted to make a joke, but decided against it when he realized just how tense Douglas had seemed over the past few months—at least on those few occasions when they were in the same room together. He realized how easily Douglas could be enchanted by the honesty and simplicity of a show far below his age level. After all, as Douglas himself believed, impatience and competition had taken away much of his youth. He saw shadows of his childhood in that televised neighborhood.

Michael, who was also far too old for the program, remained engaged with it for a completely different reason. During one segment, the amiable host built an unpretentious drawing easel out of four simple wooden parts and some string. It seemed to Michael to be a modest yet exceedingly useful contraption that he could take around with him on his wheelchair and set up almost anywhere. He memorized its construction and resolved to make it for himself one day.

When the show ended, Michael asked Douglas if he was happy living in California. Douglas said he missed his old friends.

"That's funny," Michael said. "I remember hearing you say that you couldn't wait to get away from them. Interesting."

"Interesting? What are you," asked Douglas indignantly, "a twelve-year-old psychologist? Maybe you should have your own TV show. Maybe *you* should be the actor in the family, and *I* should be the artist."

Sitting straight in his wheelchair, Michael gazed at his lap and said dryly, "Fine. Would you like to switch places?"

"Sorry," Douglas mumbled.

"That's okay."

When Dolores and the girls returned from shopping, Bridgett asked Michael if he'd like to go with her for a long walk; she wanted to explore the hills and valleys around Sherman Oaks and offered to push his wheelchair along the way.

'What about you, Mom?' Bridgett asked. "Would you like to come along?"

"Me?"

"Why not? You're in great shape. A jog will get you into even better shape!"'

"Thank you, dear, but a forty-eight-year-old woman has no right jogging in public."

"Why not? I saw the way the salesman at Bullock's was staring at you. I bet *he* would think you have a right to jog in public."

"I expect that kind of talk from Caroline, not from you, Bridgett. You're a teacher."

"Yes—a physical education teacher."

The next day, Ken drove Alexis and Bridgett to the airport for their return flight to New York. Douglas tagged along. Dolores stayed home with Michael. Michael spent most of the day taking pictures in the park, which gave Dolores an opportunity to go to Bullock's to buy some new clothes for herself. She spent ten minutes staring in the changing room mirror.

. . . .

In the spring, a few weeks before their first anniversary in the house, Dolores and Ken had several inconclusive discussions about whether to stay in Sherman Oaks or return to Westbrook Hills. Even though Douglas had given up acting, living in Southern California was not without its benefits. Ken, although on the road six days a week, was now earning a very handsome salary because of his high and frequent commissions. Douglas, much less stressed than before, was doing well academically. Michael remained captivated by his school, where he could draw, paint, and photograph as much as he pleased, and where getting around was easier than it was almost anywhere else. Caroline was hardly home, but when she was, she seemed animated and enthused.

As for Dolores, she read about several new organizations she thought she might like to join. So, after one last discussion with Ken, they decided to give California a little more time.

With that decision made, Dolores thought about the possibility of adding four new windows and two skylights to the house to bring in more light. She presented the idea to the homeowner, whose primary residence was in Beverly Hills, and offered to pay for all the construction expenses. The homeowner agreed to the plan. Dolores then visited half a dozen showrooms. At a window-and-door company called SoCal Brightness, she met a manager named Maurice, who was very friendly. Dolores noticed he bore a resemblance to the handsome actor Chad Everett from a television show she sometimes watched called *Medical Center*. She debated whether to mention the resemblance, but determined that Maurice had probably heard the comment a thousand times before.

Dolores decided to let SoCal Brightness help with her window and skylight project. On the way out of the showroom after her second visit, she saw herself in the reflective glass of a sample sliding shower door and heard Bridgett's voice echo in her head. What was it she had said? — something about the salesman at Bullocks staring at her?

Dolores went back over to Maurice to ask him a few additional questions.

Once she left the showroom, she drove over to Saint Mary's Church in Van Nuys for confession. She and Ken had recently joined the church after meeting with Father Martin Spencer, who Dolores considered much more reverential than Father Patrick Flannery. Her plan was to attend services every weekend with or without Ken, who she assumed would be too tired to join her, and with or without Caroline and Douglas, who she assumed would refuse to go. She was unsure of the church's wheelchair accessibility and asked Michel if he'd mind staying home when she went to church.

"It's fine. You can pray for me," Michael quipped. "You do it all the time anyway."

At confession, Dolores asked Father Spencer if she was committing a sin by being spirited with a complete stranger. She was, of course, thinking of Maurice. Father Spencer told her that all she was doing was fishing for a compliment. "In a world that can tend to beat us down at every opportunity, you may accept a compliment with humility and appreciation," he said. "You're human, and because you're human, you have a brain, and your brain will help keep you on the moral path, regardless of how many compliments you receive." He sent her home without penance, for penance, he said, was for those who sinned, and Dolores had committed no sin.

She went home and poured herself a glass of wine to think it over. While sitting on a wicker chair by a small glass table in the middle of the patio, her wineglass vibrated for a few seconds, as did the table itself. Dolores had consumed enough wine to insulate herself against any fear that a major earthquake might soon follow. Two or three times she had heard people in town talk about these minor quakes called tremors, and while sitting there by the table she decided that a tremor was simply a West Coast curiosity, and that there was nothing much to worry about.

Maurice called three days later and said he would like to stop by the house at noon to talk about the new windows and skylights. Ken was in Santa Monica on business, Caroline in Reno with the Pepperdine ski club, and Douglas and Michael were at school. Dolores spent over two hours showering, dressing, and cleaning the house. She wore a black sleeveless blouse tucked into white Capri pants. Maurice knocked on the front door just before noon. Dolores needed a few more minutes, but wished not to keep him waiting outside in the Southern California heat. She opened the door. Maurice, who stood there with another man who was wearing a fully-loaded leather tool belt, apologized for being early.

"Sal wants to take some measurements, and then he has to run off to a job in Irvine," Maurice said. "When he goes, I'll stick around and watch you sign all the paperwork." He winked.

Dolores said that was fine, then excused herself to finish primping. She told the men to do whatever they needed to do.

After she checked her image in the bathroom mirror one last time, Dolores walked back toward the living room. She overheard Maurice and Sal talking there. "Isn't that music stand adorable?" Maurice said. "We should have something like that at our place. And oh! — look at that sheet music. It's that Herb Alpert song we love so much, 'This Guy's in Love With You.' Can you believe it?" Dolores took another step toward the living room and saw Maurice tenderly rub Sal's back and then kiss him on the lips. She retreated to the bathroom while Sal took measurements of the walls.

When Sal finally departed, Dolores walked into the living room and told Maurice that she wanted to think it over a little more before signing any papers. Maurice said he understood and left the house.

A week later, Dolores called the SoCal Brightness number, late at night, and left a message on their answering machine saying that she decided against having the work done. The reason she gave was that she was no longer certain the family would remain in California.

That night, Dolores told Ken that she was having second thoughts about staying in Sherman Oaks. He said he was not opposed to the idea of returning to Long Island, which surprised her. He could visit twice as many clients in the northeast in half the time, he explained. They discussed it with the rest of the family. Douglas said that he had already reached that decision on his own. Michael was disappointed but said he'd use his experience at the Gartner School to make changes at whatever school he'd attend back east. Only Caroline was against the idea, for she loved the Southern California lifestyle and had many friends at Pepperdine. But she knew she could not stay behind, because dormitory living and cross-country airline flights would be too expensive for her and the family to manage.

Dolores called her real estate agent and told him they would not extend the lease beyond the year, and then she called the Goldsteins to talk about the lease on the Pearl Drive house in Westbrook Hills. It upset the Goldsteins that they had so little time to prepare to move out and find a new place, but there was nothing in the contract that forbade it.

When she walked into the Pearl Drive house three weeks later, Dolores was pleased to see that the Goldsteins had kept it immaculate. She felt no need to have the couches, chairs, and curtains steamed and fumigated, as originally had been her plan. Everything was just as she had left it—although the Goldsteins had put a mezuzah on the front door, which they took with them when they moved out. That left Dolores with the simple task to spackle, sand, and paint the holes where the mezuzah had been nailed. While she was at it, she also repainted all the other rooms.

* * * * *

"I think Alexis and Arnold are getting a divorce," Dolores said to Donna the day after the family returned to Pearl Drive.

Despite the distressing news, Donna could not mask her happiness over the fact that her friend and neighbor had decided against staying in California. Donna had seen Joe Kelleher's car pull up to the front of the house to drop off Dolores, Caroline, and the boys. Ken was not with them; Donna assumed he was driving his own car back to Long Island. When she saw Ken's brother drive off after helping with the luggage, she was tempted to go next door, but decided against it, for Dolores and the children looked weary. So she returned the following morning instead.

"I remember you telling me how Alexis and Arnold seemed so... so different from one another," Donna said as they sat down for coffee in Dolores's living room. "Didn't you try to talk Alexis out of marrying him?"

"I did, yes. A little," Dolores said feebly. "But I didn't want her to think that I'm trying to run her life. She was already mad at me because she thought I didn't like the fact that he's Jewish. Which of course is not true. I didn't want to make things worse, that's all. I wanted to tell her that the two of them... well... that it's just..."

"What?"

"The issue isn't only the fact that they have nothing in common. The man has no interest in *any* of us. The last time he visited, it was like we were invisible. He sat like an idiot right there where you're sitting, Donna. He sat there like that big Buddha in front of the Chinese restaurant on Hempstead Turnpike. I'll never forget it. So how nice could he be?"

Alexis finally confirmed the truth for her parents during an emotional visit when Ken finally arrived home from California. Arnold's favorite thing to do, Alexis admitted, was to play poker with his stockbroker buddies in the apartment almost every weekend. It was not only the liquor stains on the furniture and the lingering odor of cigar smoke in the apartment that bothered her, but also Arnold's complete disregard for her wishes and feelings.

Sensing that her daughter needed an identity of her own to weather the marital storm, Dolores, without Ken's knowledge, offered Alexis fifteen thousand dollars to invest in a restaurant of her own. She had been working at The Birch Tree Cafe for many years now. She was a bright woman, and with all that experience under her belt, owning a restaurant was not an unreasonable proposition.

"A restaurant of my own?" Alexis said indignantly. "Whoever said I wanted to own a restaurant? You don't even have that kind of money to spare, Mom. And Arnold would have a fit if he knew you were trying to give me money."

A week later, Alexis announced that she and Arnold had filed for divorce. It took an extra few weeks for Dolores to find the right way to tell her relatives in Boston. There had been only one divorce in Farrell family history, and that was a distant relative in the early nineteen-hundreds. It was an event sparked by the husband's alcoholism, which was caused by his eternal unemployment. But Dolores did finally tell her sisters and brothers, and then tried very hard to forget about it.

●　　　●　　　●　　　●　　　●

Dolores purchased a belated housewarming gift to give to Bridgett and drove over to her apartment unannounced. She used the key that Bridgett had given her during the Sherman Oaks Christmas visit to use for emergencies. Bridgett's living room was empty, so Dolores walked into the bedroom. The first thing she noticed was how dark it was because of the single tiny window. The second thing she noticed was that Bridgett was asleep in bed next to a woman with short black hair and a curvy figure barely hidden by scanty underwear. Dolores assumed it was Bridgett's roommate Kim, and she made a hasty exit.

Caroline, despite her protestations, returned with the family to Long Island. She still had her senior year in college to complete, but decided to take a year off before finishing her education elsewhere. That plan vanished when she landed a job with a radio station in White Plains, New York, that had a morning show called *Up With Adam*. At first, Caroline was a traffic reporter, but after a few weeks of bawdy banter with Adam, she was asked to become his regular sidekick. White Plains was on the other side of the Long Island Sound, and the radio station could barely be heard in Westbrook Hills. On certain days, though, Dolores could detect a faint, crackly signal on her kitchen radio. More often than not, she turned it off anyway, for Caroline and her co-host spoke about marijuana, wife swapping parties, and other unsavory topics. It made Dolores uncomfortable. She felt fortunate that Boston, too, was out of the station's broadcast range. Once, though, when her brother Randall was driving through White Plains, he unexpectedly heard the last moments of *Up With Adam* on his car radio. He called Dolores when he arrived home to ask a question that, for a moment, baffled her: why, Randall asked, did Caroline have a sudden interest in India? Dolores asked him what on Earth he was talking about, and Randall explained that the last thing he heard Caroline say before the radio show ended was something about how much fun it would be to work in New Delhi. Dolores, too, had heard that crackly exchange, but refrained from telling her brother that what Caroline was actually discussing with Adam was how much fun it would be to work at a nude deli.

· · · · ·

Douglas enrolled at Westbrook Hills High School instead of returning to Our Lady of Mercy. He was an exceptional student, but an argumentative nature had built up in him that concerned his teachers, a trait Dolores believed had sprouted in California. He squabbled almost every day with students and teachers alike. The principal speculated that it was his brightness that contributed to it—the intellectual excitement of a good debate and a spirited argument. The notion lost legitimacy when Douglas developed a habit of walking away from every debate and argument, muttering nasty words under his breath.

He was involved in the theatre club and joined the baseball team, but had few friends in either. He tried to start a club for enthusiasts of motorized go-carts and recruited Michael to draw a dozen posters for it. The school administration refused to let the club go forward, citing safety concerns. In response, Douglas collected information on all the students over the last few years who had injured themselves on ski club outings and in football games. Still, the school refused. Furious at the hypocrisy, Douglas went around the building and ripped up every poster into dozens of scraps, then showered the principal's office with the pieces. Dolores was called down to the school.

That night, at home, Michael asked Douglas, "Couldn't you have saved just one of the posters I made so that I can put it in my portfolio?" Douglas could not tell if his brother was truly angry or just making a joke. Dolores overheard the exchange from the kitchen and she, too, could not tell. She asked Michael about it at dinner.

"We shall never know, shall we?" Michael responded. "You have your secrets, I have mine."

Dolores, exhausted from the day, just let the comment pass.

•   •   •   •   •

Michael attended a private junior high school in Suffolk County called the Amsterdam Academy. It had a broad range of classes, a staff that inspired and motivated, and its own fleet of wheelchair-accessible vans. Even though the Academy was an hour from Westbrook Hills and had a high tuition, Ken and Dolores thought it well worth the travel and expense. Michael excelled at all his subjects. He was friendly and well-liked by all. One day in class, he mentioned the simple easel he had seen the host construct on *Mr. Rogers' Neighborhood* when the family lived in Sherman Oaks, and two instructors made one for him in the school's wood shop.

Some schoolmates, meaning no harm, nicknamed him the Watcher, for Michael had a habit of staring for long periods of time out of windows or at groups of students or even at odd arrangements of chairs. Teachers often would have to snap him out of it by shouting his name. This did not surprise Dolores when she heard about it, for she had caught him at home doing the same thing. When she questioned him about it, Michael said that he was committing images and ideas to memory so that he could draw or paint them later on. Dolores struggled to believe him.

"They call him the Watcher," Dolores complained to Father Woodward at confession. "The Watcher! Is that a sign of some sort of problem? An emotional problem, perhaps? Related to his handicap?"

"Must you always dig to find something negative—especially when the positive is staring you right in your Irish face?" Father Woodward admonished. "You said you came here today to repent for having negative thoughts about Michael, and then you tell me that this latest issue of yours is directly tied to his artistic talent. When he's not 'the Watcher,' he is entirely friendly, and funny, and bright, and happy. Is he not? Please, Dolores, please," Father Woodward urged, "do me a favor. Count your blessings, for crying out loud. Your blessings all have names. Their names are Kenneth, Alexis, Bridgett, Caroline, Douglas, and Michael. Your only sin is not counting your damn blessings, so if it makes you feel better, say three Hail Marys, then go home and have a glass of wine to help you count more of your blessings."

Dolores went home. Through the kitchen window she saw Michael on the back lawn, in his wheelchair, staring up at the clouds. He seemed frozen in time. Then she listened to a message on the kitchen answering machine. Bridgett had called to say that she and Kim would like to come over for dinner and share some news about a house the two of them wanted to buy.

Dolores suddenly heard crying upstairs. She went there. It was Alexis, who had decided to stay in Westbrook Hills until she could find a place of her own. Dolores tried to comfort her daughter as she wept on her old bed—but Alexis asked to be left alone. Dolores went downstairs to the living room to relax with Ken, who was reading the Sunday newspaper. In the paper was a column called "Around the Dial" that referred to Caroline Kelleher as "FM's answer to multiple personalities: one part Lady Godiva, one part Gloria Steinem, one part Linda Lovelace." Chuckling, Ken showed the column to Dolores, who became so incensed at the description that she grabbed the paper from him, tore it in half, and threw the pieces in the kitchen garbage.

"It's just a publicity stunt that the station orchestrated to get ratings," Ken said. "It doesn't mean anything, Dolores. Everyone gets it. No one cares."

"*I* care," Dolores replied. "It's disgusting, and I won't have it."

"You won't have it? What can you possibly do about it? It's business. It's marketing. It's freedom of the press. Come on…"

"*You* come on, Ken! I'm sick and tired of you not giving a damn that our family is going down the toilet."

"That's a little extreme, don't you think? Is that the kind of thing you say to Father Woodward? No wonder he always looks as if someone just gave him shock treatment."

"How would you know? You never come with me to church."

Ken knew their discussion was deadlocked, so he drove to the convenience store to buy another newspaper. He took a long route. Douglas came home from a baseball game. His face was scratched and caked with dried blood, and he had a swollen black eye. Dolores had no patience to ask how it happened. Douglas went straight to his room.

Through her living room window next door, Donna had seen Douglas ride up to the house on his bicycle and noticed the bruises on his face. She walked across the lawn, knocked on the front door, and asked Dolores if everything was all right.

"Oh, yes, fine," Dolores answered caustically. "Michael's in the back staring at absolutely nothing at all. Douglas has apparently taken up prize fighting as a new hobby. Alexis is upstairs crying her eyes out. Bridgett and Kim are buying a cozy little house together. And the newspaper is calling Caroline a porn star."

"Dolores, is there something I can—"

"I was just about to sit in the living room with a glass of wine and count all my blessings. Would you care to join me?"

PART TWO:
OFFICER DOUG KELLEHER

Doug received an acceptance letter from Fordham University's pre-law program in the spring of 1972. He had waited for the mailman each afternoon so that no one else in the house would intercept the envelope, and kept the news to himself for two days. He finally informed his mother in the kitchen one morning when she was sitting having breakfast with Michael. Ken had left for a sales call earlier than usual that day.

When she heard the news, Dolores nodded and said, "Thank you, Lord. What a glorious way to continue the Farrell heritage."

Doug walked to the library and left Dolores alone with Michael, who was now waiting for his school van to arrive.

"You do know," said Michael to his mother, "that his last name is Kelleher, not Farrell. I'm correct, aren't I?"

When Michael's van arrived, he wheeled himself out the back door and around the house. Dolores watched as an automatic ramp lifted his chair. When the van drove away, she poured herself a glass of wine, went outside to the backyard, and shook her head in wonderment at how fortunes can suddenly change.

She considered inviting Donna over to sit and chat, but decided against it. Instead, she wanted to welcome a pleasant daydream — and daydreams, she believed, were best enjoyed in solitude. In it, she saw Douglas dressed in a crisp new blue suit as he walked toward a magnificent court building in Manhattan, clinging a brown leather briefcase embossed with the gold initials DK. A Kelleher child who was wildly successful doing something important and honorable and wonderful… It was an inner vision that made her smile.

With the wineglass emptied, Dolores went into the kitchen and shared her delight over the phone, first with Donna, then with her sisters, and finally with her brothers. She saved Timothy for last. He was now a partner at the Providence law firm of Sedges, Buck & Birmingham.

When Doug had still been living in Sherman Oaks, once he had given up the auditions and cut back on his school activities he had more time to watch television and became captivated by the imaginary attorneys he saw on such programs as *The Lawyers* and *Owen Marshall, Counselor at Law*. He was equally impressed by the real ones he read about in the newspapers, among them F. Lee Bailey and Louis Nizer. Even before he moved back to Long Island, Doug decided to become an attorney. He began his studies at Fordham University the first week of September.

Ken and Dolores gave Doug their five-year-old Pontiac the day he graduated from Westbrook Hills High School so that he could commute from the Bronx, the New York City borough where Fordham was located. It was an hour-and-a-half commute to the school, and another hour-and-a-half back, mostly because of the dependable traffic near the Throgs Neck Bridge. To eliminate some of the stress, Doug made some friends at the university to see if he could stay with them two or three nights a week. He drove to Fordham twice to attend various departmental orientations and did, in fact, befriend other incoming freshmen who had apartments near campus. He spoke very little about his time in Los Angeles with his new friends. Once, when he became extremely inebriated at a party, he fabricated a story about having had sex with the stars of five hit television shows, including the mother and oldest daughter on *The Brady Bunch*. Nobody believed the story in its entirety, for Doug had become known as somewhat of a boaster and whimsical storyteller. Still, many of his friends assumed he did indeed experience his share of hedonism in the Hollywood hills. Despite sharing that over-the-top drunken tale and several others like it, Doug was well-liked around campus. Boys admired he was as comfortable singing a song as he was shooting a basket, and very good at both. Girls thought he was handsome and smart, for he did indeed take care in his appearance and performed well in all his classes. He tried out for the Fordham baseball team and was selected as a third baseman. He auditioned for the theater league's production of *Oklahoma* and won the part of Curly.

The entire Kelleher family attended the final performance of *Oklahoma*. It was on a Sunday afternoon. Dolores and Ken dressed elegantly and looked delighted. Alexis, who had finally moved into a small apartment of her own, came by herself and arrived just as the overture began, played by the university orchestra. She was unexpectedly delayed when she tried to leave The Birch Tree Café that afternoon, and had no time to go home to change. When Alexis walked into the campus theater in her brown and yellow Birch Tree uniform, her mother winced. Caroline drove in from White Plains, where she, too, had an apartment of her own. It pleased Dolores that her youngest daughter had dressed appropriately. She also wore a brassiere.

As Dolores and Ken quickly discovered, Caroline enjoyed a bit of fame among the many Fordham students who knew her from the *Up With Adam* radio program. Some recognized her before the show began and called out indelicate comments about oral sex and the allure of hard nipples. Campus security guards escorted some of those students out of the theater.

"Don't they like you?" Dolores asked, trying to sound tranquil.

"They love me," Caroline explained. "That's why they do it. They're my fans."

Dolores tried to disregard the exchange and buried herself in the playbill. It thrilled her to see that the second bio from the top read, "Doug Kelleher (*Curly*) is a pre-law student from Long Island who has won all of his cases in the mock trials conducted weekly on campus. He is also one of most promising third-basemen ever to play for the Rams." Dolores smiled.

Michael, too, attended the show. Bridgett had decided earlier on that her parents should enjoy the evening without having to worry about all the physical chores that went along with escorting Michael to public events. So she and Kim picked Michael up that afternoon, took him out for lunch, and drove him to Fordham for the play. Dolores was thankful for the consideration.

When the show was over, the audience roared its approval. Doug and his leading lady received a standing ovation. He looked thrilled. So did all the Kellehers. Since it was a long drive home, and Alexis had to go to work early the next morning, she excused herself right after the curtain calls. Bridgett and Kim left then, too, well aware that managing the wheelchair would be much easier if they beat the crowd to the parking lot. When Doug finally joined his parents and Caroline in the lobby, more students flocked to Caroline than to him. Many asked for her autograph. Some begged for a kiss. Doug cut his lobby appearance short and said he had a cast party to attend — although the rest of the cast remained in the lobby with their families and friends.

• • • • •

Doug dropped out of Fordham five months into his freshman year. He decided he no longer wanted to study law. Having had several opportunities as part of class exercises to shadow practicing lawyers in their daily activities, he realized that for much of their time lawyers sit around reading tedious legal tomes, wait in hallways and lobbies, and meet with odd and often difficult people. He wondered why he ever considered the practice of law in the first place; he recalled how his entire childhood was about the outdoors, about being active, about trying new things all the time, about acting on a natural wild streak that never should be held back by silly rules or meted out in stuffy rooms.

Just before he made his final decision, Doug discussed it with a Fordham friend named Steve, who tried to talk him out of it.

"As a successful lawyer, Doug, you'll be someone's hero all the time," Steve counseled.

"Whose hero?" Doug replied. "Some drunk-driving asshole who will probably stiff me on the bill anyway? Who needs that shit?"

"You're being a jerk. *You're* the asshole. And I'm not the only one who thinks so, by the way."

Doug despised Steve's response. In retaliation, he seduced Steve's pretty girlfriend, Trisha. He walked across campus to intercept Trisha, and convinced her to go out with him on Valentine's Day. He made sure that Steve was aware of the tryst. Doug and Trisha dined and then went back to her room to have sex. The next day, when Steve questioned him about the date, Doug said that he was simply trying to see if he was persuasive enough to talk Trisha into going out with him, and then going to bed with him. Success would be a clue, he quipped, whether he should reconsider his decision to drop out of law school. Steve punched him in the face, kicked him in the groin, and threw him against a cement wall. Bruised and bloodied, Doug was humiliated by his inability to see it coming and to defend himself. He drove home and never returned to Fordham.

When Doug shared his decision with his parents, it surprised him how little they said about it — at least to him. Later on he imagined that his mother and father must have discussed it for hours afterward, perhaps even fought about it, in the privacy of their own bedroom. But there was not much time for Dolores to belabor the news, for it was later the same day when she learned that her eighty-one-year-old father had passed away.

• • • • •

The entire family drove to Massachusetts to attend the funeral of Alexander Farrell and spend some time with Mary Ann. They slept over that night in the Sherborn house. While driving back to Long Island, they stopped at a restaurant on the Connecticut border, where Alexis announced that Arnold Leibowitz, for some inexplicable reason, had decided to sue her for money he claimed she owed him. It had something to do with a small savings account he had opened for her when they first married to enable her to attend graduate school one day. The details were murky. Dolores listlessly picked at her salad and insisted that her brother Timothy be told about it so that he could deal with Arnold, "first informally, then legally." She glanced quickly and cautiously at Doug when she said it.

Back in Westbrook Hills, Doug submitted to his parents his second profound revelation of the month: informing no one in the family, he had applied to and was accepted at Nassau Community College, and following his graduation from the two-year school he planned to take a test for entrance into the New York City Police Academy.

The next day (after she had vented to Donna), Dolores said to Doug, "Are you absolutely sure that you want to be a policeman in New York City? Have you thought this through?"

"Yes," he stated.

"Donna has four policemen in her family, but all here in Nassau County. They like it. It's another story entirely in New York City, Douglas. It's so..."

"Dangerous? That's why they need policemen. Don't worry," Doug added quickly, as he grabbed a handful of walnuts from a bowl on the table. "Maybe one day I'll make detective, and then I can wear a suit and tie every day. You'll like that. That's what you've always wanted, right?"

Dolores did not appreciate his tone, and told him so in no uncertain terms. Doug apologized and seemed genuinely contrite. Then, as he stood up to leave, he used a comically officious voice to promise his mother that he would have himself arrested if he ever used that tone again. That made Dolores cry, but Doug was unaware of that, for he had already left the house.

●　　　●　　　●　　　●　　　●

Doug graduated from Nassau Community College in June 1975, which was the same week he was accepted into the New York City Police Academy. His police training began that summer. Eleven-and-a-half months later, at twenty-two years of age, Doug Kelleher became a rookie officer, assigned to midtown Manhattan. He still lived at home, but was hardly there.

One Saturday when he could sleep late, he gave a photograph to his mother during breakfast that showed him in his new police uniform, crisp and blue and embellished with official insignia and a shiny name badge. Dolores put the photograph on the fireplace mantle next to the only other one there, a faded image of her father that was taken at his retirement party from Boston College many years before.

Bridgett stopped by for a visit that afternoon.

"Why does she do that?" Michael asked quietly when only he, Bridgett, and Doug were in the living room.

"Why does she do what?" asked Bridgett.

"Put M.M.C. pictures all over the house."

"Are we supposed to know what M.M.C. stands for?"

"Make Me Cry pictures. She's what you call a real glutton for punishment."

"Maybe you should replace them with other pictures when she's not looking," Doug suggested.

"Okay," Michael grinned. "I'll get one of me in my wheelchair, one of you holding your Fordham Law acceptance letter, and one of Bridgett and Kim smooching by the fireplace."

* * * * *

Doug's first assignment as a New York City police officer was to keep Forty-Second Street and the Broadway theater district safe for tourists. That was a tall order, given the prevalence of live peep shows, x-rated movie houses, drug dealers, prostitutes, pickpockets, and con artists in the area. He was one of two dozen officers given the responsibility of chasing the miscreants away and arresting the most egregious of the lot. His partner was another rookie, a twenty-five-year-old woman named Rosalie Parker. Doug and Rosalie developed a romantic relationship shortly after they began working together. By mutual agreement, they kept the liaison simple and informal, since both were aware of how difficult life could be as police officers, let alone adding an emotional component to it. In the first few weeks, Rosalie was subdued in manner and plain in looks; it was only after Doug accepted an invitation to join her for dinner one night that he realized how funny and quirky she was—and also how attractive. He had not even known that she had long red hair until, for the first time since they met, she unleashed it from her cap and a series of barrettes. He had also been unaware of how shapely she was. "The damn uniform hides about a hundred-twenty-five percent of your gorgeous body," he said when he took her to bed.

Doug brought Rosalie to Westbrook Hills for a Saturday night dinner that Dolores had planned for the family at the end of the summer. The only family member unable to attend was Bridgett, who had to travel to a physical education conference in Albany.

Alexis and Caroline were there, as was Caroline's new boyfriend, Howard, an automobile salesman. Even nineteen-year-old Michael had a friend with him, Lisa, a girl his age who worked at the community center where he volunteered as a photography instructor. Lisa was quiet but friendly. She always wanted to help Michael navigate his wheelchair when she was with him (even though Michael hardly needed the help), and was adamant about doing so at the Saturday night dinner. She insisted that Michael's parents and siblings be free of that responsibility for the night.

Everyone sat around the dining room table and chatted amiably for the first half hour. Doug and Rosalie were sensible enough to avoid describing some of the more salacious details of their assignments. Caroline, however, deliberately invalidated their caution by asking both of them about all the "tittie bars and two-dollar hookers on Forty-Second Street." Howard laughed. He was the only one who did. Dolores was aghast and left the dining room. Ken glared at Caroline, who excused herself and went to find her mother to apologize. When both returned, everyone sat quietly once again and resumed their chatter.

Dolores attempted to remain cordial and good-natured for the rest of the evening. She glanced around the table from guest to guest as the conversation mandated, and smiled at each face she saw, including Rosalie, Howard, and Lisa. At one juncture, when Dolores's eyes landed upon Alexis, she saw the ache behind her daughter's eyes. Despite being the oldest, Alexis was the only one of the Kelleher children not currently in a relationship, and apparently it burdened her mind. Everyone else felt the awkwardness, too, including Doug, who, for the first time in a long time, tried to engage his oldest sister in a thoughtful conversation as the evening came to a close.

•   •   •   •   •

A few weeks later, Doug rented an apartment in Riverdale, one of the nicer sections of the Bronx. Living in the borough enabled him to avoid the long commute from Long Island. He could take a subway from Riverdale to the midtown Manhattan station house where he was based. On his last night in Westbrook Hills, he stayed awake in his bed long past midnight, unable to sleep. With the house so quiet, he could detect his mother tossing in her own bed. The next morning at breakfast, she was exhausted. As Ken slept, Dolores made a cup of coffee, took it into the backyard, and invited Doug to join her there. He declined and explained how he wanted to pack up the rest of his belongings to take with him to the Bronx. Moments later, from his bedroom window, Doug heard his mother chatting with Donna outside.

"I wonder what everyone would think if for the next family dinner I didn't invite all my children," Dolores muttered. "It might be a little easier, on me and on everyone else. I'll have two dinners instead. Maybe three." She looked at Donna. "Silly, right?"

"Well, I don't have children," Donna said, "so maybe it's not fair of me to say anything. But it just sounds like a lot of hard work, Dolores. Like one of those can-of-worms things. You know what I mean?"

"Unfortunately, my family *demands* hard work. My family *is* a can of worms." She looked at Donna forlornly. "That's cynical, isn't it?"

What Doug overheard made him feel remorseful, but it also strengthened his resolve to leave the house as quickly as possible.

• • • • •

One year after Doug joined the police department, he and Rosalie were transferred to the Bronx, to a less agreeable section than the one in which Doug lived. As he was already aware, far too many New York City neighborhoods were in terrible shape, with some of the worst offenders in the Bronx, such as Morrisania, Hunts Point, and others in the southern end. They stood as decisive symbols of the urban nightmare. Officer Douglas Kelleher, at twenty-three, was thrust into a routine that even fifteen-year veterans of the force found brutal, and not a shift went by when he did not have to arrest young black men who had beaten their pregnant girlfriends, or teenage Dominican boys who had sold cocaine to even younger boys. Several times a week he had either to escort a frightened Korean grandmother who wished not to leave her sweltering apartment alone just to buy groceries, or break up a bloody fight between rival Mexican gangs. He had to help

Orthodox Jews find sacred silver ornaments that had been ripped from their ramshackle synagogues. He constantly had to dodge broken glass and puddles of urine and sometimes even bullets just to get from the beginning of his shift to the end.

Doug was busy on the beat and equally busy trying to build a decent and modestly stimulating off-duty life for himself. He did that by surreptitiously taking women other than Rosalie Parker out on dates, and by going drag-racing upstate with fellow cops and a small coterie of female admirers. Between his work and social lives, Doug was so busy that he had to struggle to find the time simply to decide if being a police officer was living up to his expectations. He even had to wonder if his leisure life was living up to his expectations. For his work life, sometimes the answer was yes, particularly when someone on his beat told him how safe they felt when he was nearby. Sometimes the answer was no, mainly when he was moments too late to stop an innocent bystander from getting robbed or assaulted. For his social life, sometimes the answer was yes, such as when he'd win a drag-race and be honored by his pals with dinner, drinks, and a sexual favor by one of the pretty hangers-on. Sometimes the answer was no, usually when he had an erstwhile date with a woman who would then make unreasonable demands on him, including the threat of violence.

But going from yes to no and back again as often as he did made him anxious. Doug soon discovered that one way to ease the anxiety was by showing no mercy to the worst of the perpetrators on his beat, by having feverish sex with some women he knew who were too weak to make any demands at all, and by spending dozens of hours in a Bronx bar with buddies from the force and beers from the tap. His work suffered. He was late for several shifts, which earned him a reprimand. He was disciplined for using excessive force on three separate occasions, put on probation, and compelled to take a special course at the Academy two nights a week.

Certainly Doug shared none of this with his mother or father, nor with his Grandma Lucille, his father's mother, who lived nearby in Queens. He visited her at least once a month. Grandma Lucille considered Doug almost superhuman, thanks to his brawny good looks and because she believed he had one of the most important and heroic jobs known to mankind. Grandma Lucille and Grandpa Peter had lived in the same Queens apartment their entire married lives, and now his widowed grandmother was in a nursing home just two blocks from there. In the past, the elderly couple had been harassed by neighborhood toughs, landlords, even some neighbors, and they had always considered every police officer they encountered a divine presence. Lucille enjoyed Doug's monthly visits, and Doug loved the adulation. Whenever he was there, he would walk around the block to see if anything was amiss, and check the locks on the doors and on the windows, and test the smoke detectors and radiators in Grandma Lucille's room at the nursing home.

"Do you visit your mother and father as much as you can, Douglas?" she asked him one day. "Because that's important."

He said he did, although he knew it to be a lie. He visited his parents far less than he visited Grandma Lucille. Doug knew deep down that he was angry with his mother because of how little an effort she made to hide her disenchantment with his choice of career and with his life. He tried desperately to hold on to the love and respect he was taught to have throughout his childhood. His wish was that Dolores would at least be proud of the fact that he listened to his own heart when he changed directions, and that he sailed through Nassau Community with honors and through the Academy with commendations. He wanted her to be delighted that he had saved five lives and put thirteen criminals behind bars, and that his salary was good enough so that he could buy expensive presents for his sisters and his brother on their birthdays. But he never sensed that delight in her.

"Maybe it's because of the Bronx," Doug said to Rosalie Parker one night at her Brooklyn apartment, as the two of them discussed their respective families. "Maybe it's because my visits home are so few and far between. Oh, what the hell," he concluded, "she is what she is. And anyway, it's not just me. She's annoyed at everyone. She's annoyed with my father for never being home and for smoking pack after pack when he *is* home. She's annoyed with Alexis for working at a restaurant. She's annoyed at Caroline because she joked to a magazine reporter that when she was a kid, she was forced to take baths fully clothed. She's annoyed at Michael for not being angrier about living in a wheelchair..."

Rosalie was a good and compassionate listener. She said she totally understood why that kind of constant tension would cause him to want to stay away from Westbrook Hills. When it was her turn, Rosalie recounted for Doug many of her own family issues. She had just one brother, so her stories were fewer, though no less maddening.

"Well," Doug said, just before he took her to bed, "at least I'm not alone in my complete misery."

But he sounded miserable when he said it, and that bothered Rosalie. She loathed that kind of attitude. She explained to Doug that she had had a relationship two years earlier with a man who was miserable, and little by little this man's misery revealed itself in self-destructive and, eventually, violent ways. "Promise me you'll try not to be miserable," Rosalie said to Doug that night as they removed each other's clothes. "It's just not worth it."

Doug said he would try. Rosalie was unconvinced. As much as she liked him, she was never entirely certain if he would abide by his promise. She drifted away from him, and he sensed it. She even asked her captain for a transfer, claiming that her skill at speaking Russian would come in more handy on another beat. A few weeks later, Doug and Rosalie met one last time for coffee at a donut shop in Brooklyn. They ended up at Rosalie's apartment building. "Want to go up, for old time's sake?" Doug suggested with guarded optimism as they stood at the bottom of the stairway.

Rosalie consented, but Doug felt her emotional distance while they made love, and he quickly excused himself, feigning exhaustion. On his way home, Doug stopped off at the Bronx bar where fellow officers could always be found. "Well, I fucked a mannequin once more tonight," he said after several drinks. "Another relationship down the tubes. Just like my career. Just like my family." He followed his comments by throwing three beer mugs against the wall. This incensed the manager, who demanded that two of Doug's colleagues escort him home to his apartment.

$$\bullet \qquad \bullet \qquad \bullet \qquad \bullet \qquad \bullet$$

Doug attempted to curb his aggressive lifestyle by being more discerning. He would do everything in his power to stop himself from beating a drug dealer to a bloody mess. Or he would say no to a sexual threesome suggested by prostitutes he had arrested. He started having two instead of six double shots of vodka at the Bronx bar. He would also work hard to recall the happy dreams of childhood and the infinite possibilities that had been part of those dreams. Sometimes he cried when he remembered the dreams and the possibilities. One day, as summer drew to a close, he saw an audition flier taped to the brick wall of a building as he was walking home to his apartment. It was for a musical. He thought something like that might ease his troubled mind. So he tried out for *West Side Story* at the Garnett Community Theater in a relatively quiet section of the South Bronx called Melrose. The director assured him that, if he received a part, the production would accommodate his schedule.

Doug won the leading role of Tony, the American Romeo who falls in love with a girl named Maria, the Puerto Rican Juliet of the modernized tale. A beautiful twenty-two-year-old girl named Maria Chibas was cast as Doug's leading lady. "This gives typecasting an entirely new significance," commented Garnett Community Theater's publicity director in an interview with the local newspaper. "A pretty Puerto Rican girl named Maria playing a pretty Puerto Rican girl named Maria! Where else but in New York City?"

From the first read-through, Doug was smitten with Maria. Not only was she beautiful—with long black hair, high cheekbones, clear olive skin, and a glorious figure—but also extremely bright, with a hint of mischievousness in her personality and more than a touch of modesty. It was a combination of traits Doug found alluring. He liked the fact that, despite her beauty, she was not perfection personified, for that made her even more interesting; the outer corner of her left eye dipped just a trace lower than the right—completely unnoticeable unless one stared intently at her for a long time, as Doug was sure to do whenever he could. He asked her about it in a gentle way, but she quickly changed the subject.

Doug wooed Maria relentlessly for the first two weeks of rehearsal. She worked as a waitress at the Four Corners Diner, but had plans to become an administrative assistant. Once a week, she took free secretarial courses at a local community center. Doug showed up often, both at the diner and the community center. His persistence and solid physique were irresistible to Maria. Once they finally became comfortable enough to hug and kiss, Maria said she felt completely safe in his arms, a feeling she said she was not used to. He was the kind of American, she said, that she had secretly fantasized about since she arrived in New York just before her sixteenth birthday. Doug told Maria that she was the kind of girl he fantasized about ever since he saw *West Side Story* on Broadway when he was six.

Doug and Maria spent many hours together after rehearsals in the evenings and on weekends. While Doug's schedule as a police officer, and Maria's as a waitress, often posed a logistical challenge, they were happy to find a few hours here and a few there to see each other, to embrace, to talk. They packed much into that time, and once the lovemaking began, they spent many more hours in bed.

Maria had a restless spirit. Even their lovemaking was interrupted many times by her suggestions that they take a break and walk around the neighborhood, or visit shops and museums, or sit in the park to observe people and their pets. To Doug's wonderment, there was hardly a topic that Maria did not enjoy. She liked to hear about his work on the police force, his love of drag racing, and his family.

"Your sister Alexis is probably a much better waitress than I am," Maria said in the park one day. "She will own the restaurant one day. You will see." To which Doug replied that if anyone could take over a restaurant and make it thrive, Maria was the one, not Alexis, because of how bright and charming she was. Maria denied it.

"But I *could* be the mayor of New York!" she tacked onto the denial.

At first Doug thought it was a silly joke, but when he looked into her eyes, he noticed an earnestness that suggested otherwise, and a wisdom beyond her years. With his curiosity and affection piqued, he asked her to explain what she meant. Maria told him that if she could become a senior administrative assistant in a New York City government agency, there was a mostly unknown chain of events, highly unlikely though they would be, that could conceivably position her as an interim mayor until a new election could be held.

"Last year, some boys threw rocks through the window of the diner," she explained. "We were closed for two days. I could not work. There were no classes at the community center those two days. But I did not tell anyone. I did not tell my family or my friends. I went to the library. I spent two days learning about the government in New York City. I thought it would help me when I apply to be a secretary at City Hall, or someplace like that. That is when I found out who becomes mayor if something happens, and then if something happens again, and again, and again."

"Wow," was all Doug could say in response. He was now even more impressed and bewitched by her.

"Of course," Maria added quickly with a smirk, "before I become mayor, twenty-three people will have to die."

One day, Doug walked to the community center to pick up Maria after her class. They went behind the building to kiss. Maria took a small bottle of White-Out from her purse and wrote **Doug + Maria 4 Ever** on the brick wall. She encircled it with a heart and some Spanish phrases that Doug could not decipher, and which she refused to translate.

"I could arrest you. Graffiti is illegal."

"Good," Maria smiled. "I like handcuffs."

After four weeks of rehearsal, no one in the cast or crew of *West Side Story* was unaware of the fact that Doug and Maria were deeply in love. So inspired was Doug by the romance that he told his mother and father about it during an exuberant visit to Westbrook Hills. Despite his exuberance, he provided only the sketchiest details about Maria, while making it seem like a fully realized narrative.

At the Garnett Community Theater, fellow cast members affectionately made fun of the way Maria pronounced the name Douglas in her thick Puerto Rican accent; she was perhaps the only one Doug knew who always used his full first name, and he made no objection to it. Once, by mistake, she called him Douglas on stage during rehearsal. "Tony!" called out Kurt, the director, "Tony! Not Douglas. Please, Maria. I beg of you..."

"Tony, Douglas—it all sounds the same to my Puerto Rican ears," Maria said with a wry smile, and a heavier-than-normal accent. No one knew if what she said was a joke or if she said it with complete sincerity. That's the way she was, and Kurt didn't know how to handle it; he handled it by giving Maria more leeway than others in the cast.

Doug, so happy with Maria, and so pleased to be happy at last, was in a good mood almost all the time and gave Kurt no problems at all. The director was delighted with the path he was taking for the role. During the song called "Maria," Doug sang the most revealing line with such emotion and conviction that it brought tears to Kurt's eyes: "Say it loud and there's music playing, say it soft and it's almost like praying. Maria, Maria, I'll never stop saying Maria."

Backstage, Maria whispered to Doug, "I have never seen Kurt smile so much, Douglas, and I have never seen him cry. Tonight, maybe you should make love to him instead of to me."

* * * * *

The community center where Maria took secretarial courses had purchased a computer called the Apple-1. One night after hours, just before a late-night blocking rehearsal at the theater, Maria slipped Doug into the building to see the new computer. Earlier that day, after class, she had unlocked a window at the back of the building; it was through that window that she and Doug entered the community center.

"Now I'll *really* have to arrest you, Maria. This is breaking and entering, plain and simple," Doug said.

"I told you," Maria winked. "I like handcuffs. Very sexy."

Doug had never seen a personal computer up close before. The police department had several, but no one he knew had one at home. When Maria showed him the Apple-1, he said that it looked like an overweight typewriter with a television stuck on its head.

"Watch what this overweight typewriter can do," Maria said. She showed him several complicated mathematical calculations and card games. Then she created elaborate and colorful graphics of lines and shapes. Finally, she added artful letters that transformed into the words Say it loud and there's music playing.

"Where did you learn how to do all this?" asked Doug incredulously.

"I just started playing around with it," Maria answered. "Like I started playing around with you one day, Douglas. And I got good at that, too!"

"You sound more like an American every day."

The spirit of the moment filled the vacant classroom with excitement, and an innocent computer demonstration turned into an illicit lovemaking session. Doug wished for it to never end. He asked God to extend those moments into hours, for he felt happier and more alive than he had in years.

"Maria, Maria," he whispered.

"Yes?"

"Let's skip the blocking rehearsal."

"No. That is not a good idea, Douglas." She convinced him that there would be plenty of time for love, but that time was limited to make the show as good as possible. So they went to the rehearsal and arrived twenty minutes late.

"Real life is not our show and our show is not real life!" Kurt bellowed, as Doug and Maria sprinted to the stage. "You can't run away together until *after* the final performance. Do you understand?" It was the first time the director had been angry with them.

·   ·   ·   ·   ·

Life *was* like the show for Doug and Maria. Even though he had a badge and a gun, Doug had to cope with the hate and mistrust he saw in the eyes of young Puerto Rican men who watched him walk down the street or dine in restaurants with Maria by his side—just as Tony had to cope in *West Side Story* with his parallel relationship. Also, often Doug had to climb the fire escape to sneak into his beloved's apartment bedroom, replicating Tony's covert visits to see his own Maria with no one noticing.

Maria Chibas lived on the fifth floor of an old brick building that resembled hundreds of others in urban canyons throughout the Bronx. She shared the apartment with her parents and two younger sisters, Risa, twelve, and Olivia, nine. The two younger girls slept on an old, broken trundle couch in the living room that the previous tenants had left when they were evicted. Maria had her own room, as did her parents.

Doug and Maria had to keep their trysts secret because Luis and Rosa Chibas discouraged their oldest daughter from socializing not just with American boys, but with any boys at all. Doug could not understand why, since Maria was such a sensible and courteous girl at home.

Luis was a janitor at a small YMCA in another part of the Bronx. He took the subway to work every morning. Rosa was a housekeeper at a tattered motel near the Throgs Neck Bridge. She, too, depended on mass transit. They had no car. Between Maria's salary at the diner and her parents' combined paychecks, the family earned just enough money to pay the monthly rent and buy food for the five of them. If one girl took ill and needed medication, or if an appliance broke, or if someone in the family was mugged on the way home from work or school, there would not be enough money to last the month. Doug heard these details little by little over the course of his relationship with Maria and felt terrible for the Chibas family. He tried to give Maria money, but she steadfastly refused. She explained that if her father found out, he would be furious with her.

"I spent many years making my father angry," she told him. "I do not want to do that anymore."

Doug craved more details about Maria's past (as well as many parts of her present of which he still unaware), but neither did he wish to upset her, and she often seemed to be on the verge of being upset whenever he asked questions about her life in Puerto Rico. He knew the pain of family distress, what with Michael growing up with one leg, his sister Alexis's divorce, and the much more recent news that his father was coughing up blood. (Dolores had shared that news with him during their last phone conversation.)

Doug wanted no more stress—he felt he had had enough over the past few years to last a lifetime—so to avoid it, he tiptoed around Maria's emotions. He talked himself into believing that just being close to her was enough. He felt privileged when he was with her and adored it when she said how happy and safe she felt in his arms. She said it many times. He considered their lovemaking to be sincere, and nothing less than breathtaking. He believed good luck had come his way at last, all of it well deserved, and he wished not to jinx it by upsetting the beautiful Maria. So he asked her very little. That did not, however, stop him from wanting to know more.

Doug asked Maria to move into his apartment in Riverdale. She said that was out of the question. In a moment of blind courage, he asked her to marry him. She said no—at least not yet. She did not deserve to be taken care of by someone else, she said, without first proving that she could take care of herself. That's when Doug's unrequited curiosity returned, and he yearned once more to learn about his lover's life, as it was, as it had been, and the way she hoped for it to be in the future. So he asked again. Still, Maria would explain almost nothing.

"Why aren't you happy?" he inquired as gently as possible. "You should be. You're beautiful and talented, and healthy and free, and glowing and alive..."

Maria responded to him almost under her breath, with what seemed to be an ache in her heart. "Yes, I am alive. But I should have been dead several times by now."

Then, swiftly, she smiled and hoped that Douglas would not demand an explanation.

"Goddamnit, Maria!" he wailed. "What the hell does that mean?"

Instead of providing an answer, she kissed him passionately. That effectively stayed his frustration. For the time being, at least.

· · · · ·

As the rehearsal schedule reached its final weeks, Doug found himself being annoyed with Maria more often. Whenever he attempted to find out about her past, she deceived him into dropping the pursuit by a kiss, a hug, or a spicy whisper. But after the fact, he didn't like being deceived. It gnawed at him. He found it very hard to tread softly over her evasiveness. Doug now saw Maria as a contradiction. An enigma. A hypocrite. A beautiful and captivating specimen of... what? Nonsense? Craziness? In the last days of rehearsal, he wondered if he worshipped and loathed her at the same time. He drank after every shift, though by now it was without the companionship of other police officers. He drank because he did not know how to adore and detest someone at the same time. That made the dress rehearsals exceedingly difficult—but Doug knew the role so well, and was so highly functioning even after a few drinks, that he got through them without incident.

One night, before the last rehearsal, he tried one last time to make sense of Maria's nonsense by grilling her with questions about specific times in her life, all of which she sidestepped in her patented way. He snapped and slapped her. She said she deserved it, and that infuriated him even more.

"If you have such a low opinion of yourself, why did you try out for a show?" Doug beseeched her just before rehearsal began. "You're the goddamned star!"

"I like to sing," she said, almost without emotion. "I live close. I can walk to rehearsals. It gives me something to look forward to. That is why I tried out for the show, Douglas."

"And what about me? Can't you look forward to *me*? If you can, then why are you driving me crazy with your stupid non-answers and all these goddamned secrets about who you really are?"

It was at that precise moment when Maria had to go onstage to sing "I Feel Pretty."

. . . . .

West Side Story was well-received by every audience at the Garnett Community Theater. Those who came to see the eight performances overwhelmingly approved of the acting, singing, dancing, sets, and all other aspects of the amateur production. Luis and Rosa Chibas, who didn't have enough money for four five-dollar tickets, refused to accept the complimentary seats or loans offered by Kurt and Doug, and therefore did not attend. Ken and Dolores Kelleher drove in for the final performance. It was a chilly Sunday afternoon in the middle of October. Dolores had earlier warned Doug that they would leave the theater as the final curtain came down simply to avoid having to travel through the Bronx when it was dark outside. Doug told them it was all right, since he had plans to celebrate with Maria.

Kurt had planned a cast party for later that night, several hours after the last show, at his apartment in Pelham Gardens. When Doug saw Maria backstage after the final bows, he told her to go home, put on her best dress, and meet him on the fire escape. They would drive into Manhattan, he said, to dine at the Waldorf Astoria Hotel. There would be plenty of time to get back to the Bronx for Kurt's party. Maria said no; she could not see herself at the Waldorf Astoria.

"Too fancy for someone like me," she whispered. "I do not deserve it."

"Why the fuck not?" Doug yelled. "What the fuck is the matter with you? Why are you so fucking strange? What the fuck..."

He could not stop himself. Three other actors had to drag him outside to the alley behind the theater. Maria ignored the pleas of two other young women from the cast to stay away from Doug, and she went outside to the alley to be with him. She asked the other actors to leave the two of them alone, insisting that everything was all right.

Doug and Maria stood facing each other in the back alley, Doug like a prizefighter who had neither an iota of strength nor the slightest desire to fight anymore, Maria like a wounded yet indestructible prey. There were tears in her eyes; he had yelled at her in the past but this time it was so harsh and unrestrained that tears were inevitable. Maria took a deep breath as a way to halt the drops, for she wished not to lose all control. She stiffened her arms—this, too, a maneuver to manage her emotions. His venom spent, the victim willing, Doug enveloped Maria in his arms and apologized. Without asking permission, he drove her to his apartment, where they made love. Maria was quieter than usual.

With the play over and both their work schedules suddenly expanded, Doug rarely saw Maria over the next few weeks. He wanted to and eagerly tried to. They met for a cup of coffee less than a handful of times, but opportunities for walks, or talks, or lovemaking, seemed to disappear. Two weeks turned into two months. Doug wondered if the relationship had initially moved too fast. Perhaps that had scared Maria. Or maybe her parents gave her a hard time. Could it be that she made excuses simply because she had lost interest? Did she find someone new? Doug swirled these thoughts around in his mind, and each time he did, they stung like a wet towel whipped against bare skin; not knowing the truth was a nearly physical pain, and certainly an emotional one. One morning, he stared at himself in his bathroom mirror and in a flight of fancy said aloud, "Hey, you want to be a detective, right? So... detect! Here's your chance, pal. Be like Lieutenant Columbo and figure out what her motives are, why she's like the way she is, why she's doing what she's doing—and what the fucking hell is going on..."

•   •   •   •   •

Doug went about his snooping cautiously, for he did not want Maria to find out he was doing it, nor did he want Mr. and Mrs. Chibas to grow suspicious and then take it out on their daughter. Guardedly, almost clandestinely, he spoke to former *West Side Story* cast and crew members who had been friendly with Maria even before the auditions. With judicious spying, he was able to figure out her schedule and went to the diner when she was not at work to chat casually with cashiers, busboys, and other waitresses. With the help of a buddy on the police force, he ran Maria's name through the department database and confirmed that she had no arrest record, at least not in New York. He briefly dated a woman who worked at the New York office of the Puerto Rico Federal Affairs Bureau and with her help obtained photocopies of the few Chibas family records that were stored there, including several handwritten notes. He spent hours in Maria's Bronx high school by showing up in his police uniform and pretending to do what he called "a city-sanctioned school grounds security sweep." While there, he identified six teachers who had had Maria in class and spoke to each one. He made believe he was a crossing guard one morning, two blocks from her apartment building, and traded a few words with Risa and Olivia Chibas. He told them he knew their sister because he had helped build the set for *West Side Story*. Having never seen the show, the girls had no clue who he really was.

As 1978 was just about to arrive, Doug urged his captain to put him on Times Square duty for the New Year's Eve celebration, for which he had not originally been scheduled. That would help him avoid thinking about Maria on that special night; it would be too noisy, too crowded. He knew he would be able to think of nothing but keeping the peace.

Other than two close friends on the police force, Doug told no one about his secretive detective work. Finally, a story of Maria Chibas emerged that was as perplexing as it was disturbing. Maria had been a wild youth in Puerto Rico. As young as thirteen years old, she was having sex with men and boys and smoking marijuana. She became pregnant and had a back-alley abortion that almost killed her. Her parents had no clue how to control her, so they simply prayed and cried. Then Maria saw the error of her ways and tried to be a good girl and a good student and to make her parents proud. And her parents *were* proud, but also very poor, and Maria was tired of seeing them so poor, tired of seeing them struggle so hard, tired of having no decent clothes to wear and often no food to eat. So she used her beauty and her charm to get things from stores without paying for them, sometimes by teasing and cajoling, other times by offering her body. She took clothes and food at first, then jewelry and electronics. After a while, when she tired of the teasing, cajoling, and debauchery, she relied on pure thievery. She was arrested twice. After the second time, she was sent to a juvenile facility in the town of Ponce, where she was beaten by other girls and where she herself beat up several inmates to the point of hospitalization. One time, just before she was to be released, Maria was beaten so severely that she almost lost her left eye. She needed plastic surgery, but her parents mistrusted the local doctors, so they sold everything they owned and traveled to New York so that Maria could have the surgery performed there. Luis Chibas worked three jobs to help pay for the procedure. The Chibas family stayed in New York. Though Maria was just fifteen, she was mature enough to realize what she had done to her parents and to understand the sacrifices they had made for her. So she changed her ways yet again, but this time she resolved to stay on a reputable and trustworthy course.

Doug's investigation, which began three months after the last performance of *West Side Story*, took him three months to complete. Once concluded, he spent another two months trying to reconnect with the woman for whom he still had an infatuation, perhaps even more than he had before. Maria remained elusive. The shade of her bedroom window had been pulled down and kept that way throughout the day, every day, and the fire escape staircase had been pulled up to its highest position. She was never where she was supposed to be. Doug failed to cross her path even once. That only added misery to misery, for he now had to consider himself a poor detective. Sure—he found out more than he originally thought he would, but now? Now he couldn't even locate a Bronx resident whose name, appearance, residence, and work location were already known! Almost daily he wondered aloud, but only to himself, and *about* himself: Just how much of a failure can one person possibly be?

Doug became convinced that Maria had serious emotional issues. He was clueless about what to do. Even if he had access to her, he knew he would be ill-prepared to deal with it on his own.

It was a miserable time for Officer Doug Kelleher. He hated his job. The hollow sexual trysts he instigated with secretaries at his precinct and with women in his apartment building he now considered abhorrent, though he felt powerless to stop. He hated lying to his family about life as one of New York City's most eligible bachelor cops, but too ashamed to tell the truth.

He hated loving someone who was all but an apparition now.

One afternoon in July, while he stared into his bathroom mirror to get ready for another miserable shift, there was a knock on his apartment door. There in the hallway were Risa and Olivia Chibas, now thirteen and ten. They had on what appeared to be school clothes—nice, but tattered. Risa clenched in her arms what looked like a package rolled up in light green terrycloth. Olivia held a large canvas bag, the strap of which seemed to dig uncomfortably into her small, bony shoulder.

"Maria told us where you lived," Risa said. Then a flash of recognition crossed her face. "You were the crossing guard at our school. She didn't tell us that."

"What's the matter? Is she all right?"

Risa, followed by Olivia, walked past Doug and placed the package on the floor by the couch. The girls turned to look at him. Doug gazed first at their faces, then at the package, and that's when he noticed, in a small opening in the light green terrycloth, a tiny face with swollen eyes shut tightly. It was a sleeping baby girl with chubby cheeks and olive skin.

Doug had no clue what to say.

Risa, the older sister, filled the void.

"She's four weeks old," she said.

"Whose baby is it? Maria's?"

"And yours."

Risa took the strap from her sister's shoulder, put the case on the floor in front of Doug, and informed him that the case was filled with baby care items. Enough to last about a month, she said.

"You're not leaving her here, are you?"

Risa nodded.

"Maria went away," she said, "and now we're all moving away."

The girls went back to the door, which was still open. Doug remained by the couch, staring at the swaddled package.

"What's her name?" Doug called out. There was no answer. He looked toward the door, but the girls had already disappeared. Returning his gaze to the child, he saw in her face mostly Chibas, but also some Kelleher. He picked up the package, an easy chore because of how firmly swaddled it was, went to the door to close it, then walked back to the center of the living room.

"Maria Chibas Kelleher," he said as he held the tiny baby in his arms. Moments later, while still staring at the chubby brown face, he felt his lips curl into a smirk as he murmured:

"Well well well... Dolores Kelleher's granddaughter."

•　　•　　•　　•　　•

Maria grew from a cranky newborn to a good-natured infant, though the transition might not have happened as well as it did if not for three people. One was Officer Rosalie Parker, who came back into Doug's life as a friend, having bumped into him at a police department seminar. They knew by mutual acknowledgement that they were better friends than they were lovers. Rosalie still cared for Doug, and he for her, though both agreed that their relationship had to stay platonic in order to remain genuine. Rosalie's schedule allowed her to watch the baby when Doug was on duty. While Maria slept, Rosalie often napped on Doug's couch. She strolled through Riverdale Park with the baby, and twice a week took her to a playgroup at the homes and apartments of young mothers and nannies she met during her strolls. Rosalie didn't mind the distance she had to travel between Staten Island, where she now lived, and the Bronx; her mothering instinct was strong, and now that she was twenty-seven-years-old without a serious relationship in sight, that instinct drove her to want to spend as much time with little Maria as possible.

When Rosalie was unavailable, a resourceful couple from the apartment above Doug's had more than enough time and skills to pitch in. John and Jon, both in their forties, made Maria laugh and soothed her with their singing when she was irritable. With a credit card that Doug had loaned to them, John and Jon continually stocked Doug's apartment with diapers, baby food, formula, toys, and ointments. They set up a new playpen in the living room and a crib in the bedroom. They even wheeled Maria to a pediatrician down the block for checkups and whenever the baby seemed under the weather. When Doug was off duty but wanted to play basketball or go drag-racing with friends from the force, John and Jon were usually able to babysit. They felt forever in Doug's debt because of how well his presence in the building insulated them from the nasty taunts they used to receive before Doug moved in.

Over the phone, Doug told his parents about little Maria. He said that the baby's mother had kept the pregnancy a secret from him and then, for a reason of which he was unaware, decided that she no longer wanted the child. Doug said he had decided not to pursue the matter because, as a police officer whose constituency included many single mothers and unwanted children, he knew that his taking on the responsibility of little Maria would ultimately be better for the child. He told his mother and father not to worry because he had plenty of friends and neighbors eager to help, practically every day of the week and every hour of the day. He knew that driving out to the Bronx was an undertaking his mother would loath, so he insisted she not even consider it. Doug promised to visit as soon as he felt comfortable enough to drive to Westbrook Hills with the baby in tow.

Doug drove to Westbrook Hills twice by the time Maria was eight months old. John and Jon had purchased and installed the car seat for him. Ken and Dolores were guardedly engaged and amused by the little girl. Doug's sisters and brother played with the bright, sweet-natured baby and spent some time alone with her to build the bonds that would otherwise be difficult to establish. Almost nothing was spoken of how she came to be part of the family, although it was fairly obvious to everyone that the young lady who had played Maria in *West Side Story* was the mother. (Michael found the playbill in his desk drawer and read it cover to cover several times.) Doug knew it was Maria's adorable expression and good nature that encouraged the Westbrook Hills visits to be pleasant ones, rather than the uncomfortable ones he had initially expected. He was pleased about that.

* * * * *

It was a completely new and complex life that Doug had in the Bronx, divided as it was into unequal and changeable thirds: work, recreation, and little Maria. Along with it also came a sort of death — a death of spirit. Doug truly loved Maria, but wondered how much of that love masqueraded the longing he still felt for her mother. He loved the child, but disliked the gloomy notions that invaded his brain almost every time he gazed upon her angelic face. Looking at her made it far too easy for Doug to count the errors and disappointments in his life. He could hardly look at his daughter without wondering if her very existence represented yet another terrible and irreversible blunder.

One night in the summer of 1979, just after Maria's first birthday, in the middle of a week's vacation from police department work, Rosalie Parker visited Doug at his apartment. She noticed how tense he was and insisted that he relax while she took care of the toddler. She said she would feed and bathe Maria and put her to sleep, and that for those few hours Doug could do whatever he wished, even if he just wanted to stay in the apartment and sleep. Doug had a few beers, and then a few more, and while Rosalie walked back and forth with Maria snuggled into her shoulder, Doug reclined on the couch and asked if he could tell her a story. Rosalie thought he meant he wanted to try his hand at Dr. Seuss or Mother Goose. She worried, though, that Doug was too drunk to hold the baby. "Tell it from there," she cautioned as she looked at her former lover reclining in a near-motionless trance. "I'll hold Maria while you tell it."

"When I came home from California," Doug began, "I started using the fingers on my right hand to count the mistakes I've made." At that point, Rosalie realized it wasn't a children's story he wanted to tell. "When I celebrated my first anniversary with the NYPD, I started using the fingers on my left hand. Last Saturday—it was a beautiful afternoon, the last day of June, I think—I was off duty, watching Maria. You had been called away for those lootings in Brooklyn, and John and Jon were at some wedding in Jersey. A buddy of mine from the Academy called. Frank Lepore. Do you know him? Anyway, he asked me if I wanted to spend the day with him and a couple of other cops up at the Pocono Raceway. They were having a special event where you get to drive stock cars owned by some of the famous stock car drivers. Five laps each."

Maria had fallen asleep. Rosalie placed her in the playpen on her stomach, with her face to the side, looking very peaceful.

"That's when I realized," Doug continued, "that I had said 'no' five times that month alone to people who wanted to do things with me. Five times. When I hung up with Frank, Maria threw up all over the playpen and had the biggest poop I've ever seen in my life. That's when I ran out of fingers to count on."

Rosalie listened, but stayed silent. She knew Doug was in no condition to understand or accept anything she might say to make him feel even the tiniest bit better. Mostly she wanted to say how unjust, how potentially damaging it would be to consider Maria a mistake, how reckless to say it out loud and to let that notion fester internally.

But she knew Doug would not have been able to weigh her criticism accurately. Not in the condition he was in.

"She has such an adorable face, doesn't she?" Doug continued after a short breather, during which he sipped his beer, shook his head, and wiped away a tear. "Sometimes I look at her face and wonder if I'm being blessed or punished."

At the very least, Rosalie was glad to hear him say the word blessed.

"What do you mean?" she asked.

"You can't *not* love that face, and yet, I can't help thinking that she shouldn't even be here. It's not fair to her. No mother. A shit-for-brains father. Bad cop. Bad son. Bad brother. Bad friend. But maybe that pretty face is also God's way of telling me that I did something good. I mean, she's so smart, and so sweet." The beer took its toll on Doug's insides, and he paused a moment to release some of the pressure, loudly. Maria stirred in the crib, but remained asleep. "Who knows, maybe she'll be the one to fix this stupid, fucked-up world. Maybe she'll work her way into lots of other hearts. Of course, for that to happen she'd probably be better off with someone else. Not *this* guy, who should probably go far, far away—"

"Please don't say that, Doug," Rosalie whispered, biting her lip.

"I'm sorry. I know I sound pathetic. But you gotta give me points for that great speech, huh? I would've made a terrific lawyer."

Doug sat on the couch and seemed to almost instantly doze off in a sitting position. Rosalie stayed the night. She helped Doug stretch out on the couch, and she went to sleep on the bed in his room. In the morning, satisfied that Doug was sober, Rosalie left the apartment. She would have preferred to stay, but was scheduled for a shift later in the morning and had no choice. Doug said he was fine. Before she left the building, Rosalie knocked on the door of John and Jon's apartment, but there was no answer. With a measure of anxiety, she drove home to her apartment on Staten Island.

When Maria awoke, she was crankier than usual. Doug, still lightheaded from the night before, handled her less delicately than he knew he should. The phone rang. It was Frank Lepore. He said he had been invited to a classic roadster rally in Delaware that afternoon and wanted to know if Doug could join him.

"I have a friend down there who owns a BMW Z1, and he's gonna let us drive it," Frank gushed.

Doug was silent.

"Doug? Are you there... Doug?"

"I'm here. I can't. I don't have anyone to watch Maria."

"Jeez, buddy. Again? Isn't there anything you can do?"

"I don't think so."

When Doug hung up the phone, Maria vomited and then had a large and very loose bowel movement that seeped out of the diaper and onto the floor of the playpen, which in a way duplicated the story he had told to Rosalie hours earlier. Doug changed Maria's diaper, halfheartedly attempted to clean the playpen, took Maria outside, put her in the car seat, and drove to Westbrook Hills.

⦁　⦁　⦁　⦁

Doug's next scheduled visit to Westbrook Hills was still more than a month away, which is why Dolores was so surprised to see him walk into the house carrying the baby. Only Dolores and Michael were home when Doug arrived. Ken was playing golf with a client. Michael wheeled himself from his room to the foyer and took the crying baby in his arms.

"She seems hungry," he said. "I'll feed her. The highchair is all set up in the kitchen."

"Sorry, Mom," Doug said when Michael disappeared. "I would have called ahead, but something came up suddenly and I'm in a bit of a bind. Police business, and I can't find anyone to watch her."

"Did you bring the diaper bag?" Dolores asked. "You came in empty-handed, other than the baby."

"Damn. I forgot."

"Forgot? Douglas.... Well," she said, calmly yet frostily, "it's a good thing I thought to stock up on supplies, just in case. I suppose this is one of those 'just in case' situations, isn't it? But you know, I just as easily might not have been prepared. Then what we have done? We would have been in quite a bind, wouldn't we, Douglas?"

"Yes. I'm sorry."

"Please have a little more respect—not just for me, but for your daughter."

"I will," Doug said. "I promise. Listen—I really gotta go. I'll be back tonight, and we'll talk some more."

Doug left the house and hopped into his car. He never returned.

PART THREE:
DOLORES AND MARIA

1. FIRST BIRTHDAY PARTY

Aside from yearly barbecues with the immediate family, Maria had her first real birthday party on Saturday, June 16, 1984, when she turned six.

Nine of her friends had been invited. All nine showed up, along with their mothers, to help Maria celebrate. Dolores was pleased; it had been at least fifteen years since she had planned a birthday party, for Michael's twelfth, and she worried that she may have missed a detail or two. Once all the guests had arrived and smiles and laughter filled the yard, her nerves abated.

Earlier that morning, as she decorated the backyard patio, Dolores sensed the weather would be comfortable and mild and considered that a good omen for it would enable her handiwork to be thoroughly enjoyed by all the guests. She began the work outside at five forty-five, just after sunrise, before Michael and Maria had awakened. Ken was not at home; against his doctor's advice, he went on an overseas business trip to Texas to help train a new Aster-Paxton sales team just established in Austin.

Maria woke at seven, made herself breakfast, washed and dressed, and at eight o'clock took S. E. Hinton's *The Outsiders* to the patio to read. It was a book that she had checked out of the library the day before. She had been unaware that her grandmother was already setting up for the party, so instead of reading, she offered to assist with the decorations.

Dolores told her that nearly all the work was complete.

"Besides," Dolores added, "Donna said you wanted to help her bake the cake. She's probably starting now. Why don't you go next door and see?"

Maria put the book back in her bedroom and walked over to the Kelsey's house. Donna had just set out all the cookware she needed to bake the cake, and Maria helped her pour and mix the ingredients.

"I assume your grandmother knows you're here," Donna stated.

"Yes, she told me to come," Maria responded with an assured smile. "She finished setting up for the party even before I woke up."

Donna bent down to kiss Maria on the head.

"Your grandmother can't sit still," she said.

Back at the house, Michael had gotten out of bed, wheeled himself outside, and he, like Maria a bit earlier, asked his mother if she wanted his help. All that was left to do, she told him, was to hang some balloons up in a tree, and that she would get Darren to do it later on.

"I can do it," Michael said. "I'd love to try to ride my chair up a tree."

"Stop it, Michael," Dolores said with an irritated edge to her voice. "I don't find that funny at all. I spoke to Darren yesterday. He's bringing his ladder."

"Don't we have a ladder?"

"No. Not for years."

"How come?"

Dolores walked away to straighten the benches by the picnic table on the patio. Michael was actually pleased that there were no more party chores to do, for he had wanted to plan out a few magic tricks for the kids at the party and needed some time to do so.

Donna and Maria finished baking and decorating the cake an hour later, and walked over to the Kelleher house.

"Can I help you now, Grandma?" Maria begged, as Donna stood by. "Isn't there *anything* left to do? Please?"

"I really don't need any help, Maria," Dolores said sternly. "Besides," she added, attempting to soften the charge, "it's your birthday party, and you of all people should not have to do any work."

Having heard the exchange from the kitchen, Michael called out, "When did they pass a law that says that people can't help decorate their own parties? Is it in the U.S. Constitution? The Magna Carta? The King James Bible?"

"Quiet, Michael," Dolores said, just loud enough for him to hear. She was angry, but also embarrassed in front of Donna—though she let only the anger show. "Fine, Maria. Why don't you set out the rest of the napkins on the table? That's really all that's left to do."

"Okay!" Maria began her job. "Rojo, azul, amarillo, morado," she said each time she set another colored napkin on the table.

"Where did she learn to speak Spanish?" Donna asked quietly.

"I have no idea," Dolores replied.

"Well, the cake and I will be back when the party starts," Donna said. "Need me for anything else until then?"

"No. Thank you, Donna."

Donna departed. Dolores went into the kitchen to make two pitchers of lemonade. As she worked, she looked out the kitchen window and saw that Maria had completed the napkin task and was now running around to the front of the house, having heard a car radio blasting. Dolores heard it too. It was Caroline.

Dolores turned around to go to the front door and was startled to see Michael in his wheelchair just two feet away.

"I told you never to sneak up on me like that, Michael!" she admonished him.

"It was because of me," he said.

"What are you talking about?"

"Last year I told Maria a little bit about her mother," Michael explained. "As much as I knew, at least, which wasn't a whole hell of a lot. About Puerto Rico."

"Why? Why would you do that?"

"Why not, for crying out loud? No one else wanted to. I thought it was important. It's her mother, for God's sake. Anyway, she got interested in Spanish. I knew a few words from school. Maria told me that she asked her kindergarten teacher if she could learn more."

"Spanish? In kindergarten?"

"Mrs. Reiner told her that no one takes language classes until fourth grade. But for whatever reason, she decided to give Maria private lessons during rest period. She told Maria it would be their little secret. Or as Maria put it, their pequeño secreto. They've been doing it for months."

"Oh, for goodness' sake, Michael. I hope she wasn't a nuisance to poor Mrs. Reiner."

"That's all you have to say? Nothing about how awesome Maria is?"

"What do you want me to say, Michael? That my granddaughter is smart *and* a showoff?"

Michael did not wish to argue a point he had unsuccessfully argued with his mother many times in the past. He went into the house, wheeled to his little studio at the side of the living room, took out a large piece of sketch paper, and quickly drew a caricature of Maria as a toddler. In the drawing, the toddler wailed uncontrollably. He placed a dialogue bubble above her head and in it wrote: "¡Waaaahhh!" In the next panel he drew a caricature of his mother standing over the toddler, and in her dialogue bubble he wrote, "Can't be mine! I don't speak Spanish." Michael smiled — but then crumbled up the paper and threw it in the garbage.

Michael worked as a cartoonist for the Suburban Gazette Newspapers, a company that owned eight weeklies across Long Island, one of which was the *Westbrook Hills Gazette*. Though he still lived at home, he craved his independence and paid his parents a small stipend that he urged them to consider as rent. He had tried living elsewhere on two separate occasions, but neither time was to his liking. At one house, which was shared with other handicapped people and professional aids, he was told to avoid telling dirty jokes and using saucy language when discussing politics, both of which he liked to do. At the second house, he was required to be properly dressed at all times, whereas at home he could wheel himself around without pants, if he so desired. He told his parents that always having to wear pants seemed to him to be an admission of embarrassment about his handicap, whereas it didn't embarrass him at all. Dolores never wished to pursue that line of conversation and forbade it to be discussed in the house.

· · · ·

"I'm glad you're wearing pants today," Caroline said to Michael when she finally made it into the house after letting Maria show her the backyard decorations. Caroline had driven in from Philadelphia, where she now hosted a popular morning radio show.

"Well, I'm glad *you're* wearing pants today," Michael said to her in return. Caroline laughed. They both knew he was referring to her peculiar yet lucrative reputation as Philadelphia's raunchiest deejay — the one who often talked about the joys of shopping and bowling in the nude.

"There's no one here from Philly, is there?" she whispered to her brother.

"Just the Archbishop," Michael joked. "But he's your biggest fan."

Alexis and Bridgett arrived within minutes of each other. They, too, went first into the backyard to chat with Maria and their mother. Then they went into the house to say hello to Michael and Caroline.

Alexis had been divorced for five years. She was the assistant manager of the expanded Birch Tree Cafe, a position she had been offered and refused several times. Last year, at thirty-eight years of age, she finally accepted. Along with the responsibility and success came a new air of confidence. Dolores could not decide if she liked it very much.

Bridgett, now thirty-seven, was a physical education teacher at McArthur High School in Levittown and still lived with Kim, a guidance counselor at East Meadow High School.

Maria's friends arrived with their mothers. Donna came over with the cake. The children played on the swings, slide, and seesaw at the back edge of the yard — the same playset that Maria's father, aunts, and uncle had played on when they were little. Ken had set it up when Caroline was born, and over the years Dolores had changed some rusted nuts and bolts, replaced a few chains, and gave it several new coats of waterproof paint. After twenty minutes of swinging and sliding, Maria motioned to Michael to begin his magic tricks. Michael called the kids together and performed a disappearing penny trick, then a crying quarter trick, then two card tricks, and topped it off with a drawing game. He selected a child to scribble five lines on a large pad. He then chose someone else to shout out the name of a famous cartoon character. Finally, he would turn those five lines into that character. The children enjoyed it immensely.

Dolores paced from the kitchen to the patio, and from the patio to the garbage cans stored by the green door at the back of the garage. Donna told her to please sit down and enjoy the party.

"You're making me mad, Dolores," she said. "Relax, for crying out loud. If anybody needs anything, *I'll* get it. It's the least I can do. You've helped me out plenty of times when Darren was down at Cape Kennedy."

Grudgingly, Dolores sat with Donna by the food table on the porch. One mother after another came up to her, almost as if they had all been clued in that this brief break would be the one and only respite Dolores Kelleher would take during the party.

Patricia Morrison, whose daughter Jeannie had had her sixth birthday party the week before, walked over to Dolores. "He's really good, your son Michael," she said, "with all the games for the kids. He could do this as a sideline. Children's parties or something."

"Oh, I don't think that's a very... It probably isn't something he'd care to do," Dolores said in response.

"It's such a lovely party," commented Adrian Burke moments later. "Such an interesting family you have, Dolores. And Maria is so smart. She was teaching Chrissie Ann about the planets the other day. Imagine! A six-year-old who knows about the planets!"

"I think her Uncle Michael tells her a lot of things."

"Oh, don't be modest. When I was picking up Chrissie Ann on the last day of kindergarten last week, Mrs. Reiner said both Chrissie Ann and Maria are the smartest students she's had in years, and that she wouldn't be surprised if Maria skipped a grade or two. Listen, Dolores," she whispered. "I wanted to ask... Is it true that you never met Maria's mother?"

"It's true," Dolores said with a pursed-lip smile. "She was hardly in the child's life."

"I see." Adrian then went to find her daughter.

Next came Linda Bindi, who lived three blocks away and whose daughter Debbie was Maria's best friend.

"It's nice that you know her real birthday, Dolores," Linda said. "I mean, after all..."

"Oh, we don't know her real birthday, Linda," Dolores interjected, a bit more brusquely than she had intended. "We never did. We're not even sure if it's in June. But she *has* to have a birthday, doesn't she? And birthday parties."

"What does she call you, Dolores? I'm just curious."

"Grandma. What *should* she call me?"

"I'm so sorry. I didn't mean anything by it. My kids call my mother—"

"No need to be sorry, Linda. I *am* her grandmother."

"Well, you look very young, Dolores."

Dolores excused herself and went into the kitchen to get the cake that Donna had put on the counter. Candles had already been placed on top.

Donna walked in from the backyard.

"The pizza just arrived, Dolores. I'll help serve. I insist. Then I'll bring out the cake and cut slices."

"Donna, I'm sixty-three, not ninety-three. I may be older than everyone else here, but I'm perfectly capable of serving pizza and cutting a cake."

Donna, who knew Dolores better than anyone, looked at her quietly and waited an extended moment for her neighbor's frustration to subside.

"Though I *could* use a very tall glass of wine," Dolores added, with the tiniest smirk on her face. She probably would not have said it in front of anyone else.

• • • • •

The afternoon moved on. By two-thirty, many of the girls and their mothers had departed. Just one slice of pizza remained. The pretzel and potato chip bowls had only crumbs inside. The lemonade pitchers were empty. Alexis made a pot of coffee.

The three mothers who remained drank coffee and talked among themselves, while Maria and their daughters played in the backyard. Maria, the shortest of all her friends, was well-liked and got along with everyone. Dolores and Donna stayed inside. Michael rested in his room.

Outside, Alexis, Bridgett, and Caroline stood by the table, chatting. Two of the mothers, Anita Tobias and Jane Hibbler, walked over to them.

"You're Maria's aunts," Anita observed.

"Yes. I'm Alexis, and these are my sisters, Bridgett and Caroline."

"Nice to meet you," Anita smiled. "And what do you girls do? Are you in pharmaceuticals like your father? Or cartoons, like your brother Michael?"

"Alexis is a hospitality tycoon," Caroline said. "Bridgett owns a sports franchise. And I guess you can say I'm a psychotherapist. We're an extremely boring family."

Anita and Jane, not sure what to make of Caroline's odd exchange, smiled and walked away.

"Hospitality tycoon?" questioned Alexis.

"Sports franchise?" said Bridgett.

Caroline whispered to her sisters, "Well, I *could* have said that my sister Alexis gives people food poisoning at a restaurant, that my sister Bridgett watches sophomore girls take showers, and that I tell people to drive around Philadelphia totally naked. But I think what I said was a lot safer. Don't you agree?"

·   ·   ·   ·   ·

Meanwhile, Linda Bindi had gone to the front yard to retrieve something from her car, then returned to the kitchen.

"Such a lovely party," she said to Dolores. "But you hardly sat! If it wasn't for Donna, you'd be worn down to a frazzle. Is Ken away?"

"Yes. He's been in Texas, but he'll be home tonight."

"Oh! Well, Frank gave me something to give to him. Can I leave it with you?" Linda's husband, Dr. Frank Bindi, was one of Aster-Paxton's biggest customers. Frank had given Ken 'thank you' gifts once a year for the past six years. Linda handed to Dolores the large paper bag she had brought in from her car. Dolores reached inside and took out four cartons of Lucky Strike cigarettes.

"Thank you, Linda. Oh—matches, too. I'm sure Ken will be so pleased."

* * * * *

Michael came out of his room and wheeled himself to the backyard. Two of Maria's friends were still there.

"Did you have a good time, girls?" Michael asked.

In tandem, they shouted a resounding 'Yes!'

"What happened to your leg?" asked one girl, with such sweet innocence that Michael could only smile.

"I had a really bad accident when I was a baby."

"Does it hurt?" asked the other girl.

"No. I just can't do some things that other people can do. But I make up for it by doing other things."

"Does it make you sad?"

"Not really."

The first girl turned to Maria.

"Your grandma is always sad," she said. "My mommy told me."

Maria promptly changed the subject by suggesting they all play basketball in front of the house. Ken had set up a toy plastic hoop that echoed the real one fastened to the top of the garage. Michael watched Maria and her friends run around the side of the house.

"Out of the mouths of babes..." he muttered quietly.

* * * * *

By late afternoon, the house and the backyard were spotless. Maria's presents were put away neatly in her room. Maria rested on her bed. Dolores sat outside with Donna. Michael worked on a drawing in his studio. The small studio had once been a secondary coat closet, but a few years earlier Dolores had the idea to turn it into art alcove dominated by a drawing table, a flexible lamp, and a small desk to hold all of Michael's supplies. It provided easy access to the living room, the kitchen, the bathroom, and Michael's bedroom. By herself, Dolores had removed the coat rack, taken off the door, and started to widen the opening. The job ultimately proved too difficult for her to do alone, so at Ken's urging, she finally agreed to use a contractor to complete it.

Kim, who could not attend the party because of a dental emergency, stopped by the house a few hours after the party ended. Michael was in his alcove studio, filling in a cartoon with a colored pencil. He saw Kim enter the foyer through his open doorway.

"Hi, Kim," he called out. "We missed you. How's your tooth?"

"The dentist thinks it has to come out. Can you draw me a new one?" She peeked her head into the studio.

"Sure," he said, holding up the pencil. "But it will have to be bronze."

"Not a problem. Where are your sisters?"

Michael nodded toward the living room couch. Alexis, Bridgett, and Caroline were all there, reclining deeply, their six legs indiscernibly intertwined. Kim turned to look.

"Interesting composition," she smirked. "Don't you think?"

The three of them yawned their hellos.

"Where's the birthday girl?"

"Upstairs resting," Michael said. "It was her first birthday party ever. So she got more presents than ever. She probably has sticker shock."

"Bridgett and I were talking about that just the other day — that it's her first party," Kim said. She walked further into the studio and peered over Michael's shoulder. "My God, Michael, that's fantastic."

He was finishing up a drawing on his easel that showed a dinner table upon which sat six little cups and saucers, a copper kettle, and four miniature brass trumpets. The caption read, "Oh, for heaven's sake, Marvin, I said tea and *crumpets*!"

Kim laughed.

"Michael, you should leave the *Gazette* and work for the *New Yorker*," she said. "You have to see this, you guys," she called to the others on the couch. "Michael, do you submit your drawings to magazines?"

Before he could answer, Dolores walked into the living room from the kitchen.

"Where's Maria?" she asked. "I need to ask her something."

"Upstairs," Caroline said. "Resting."

Dolores noticed Kim in the alcove with Michael. "Kim, you're here," she acknowledged. "Did everything go well at the dentist?"

"Yes and no. Thank you for asking."

Dolores went upstairs.

Kim walked over to the couch and squeezed in between Alexis and Caroline.

"So how was the party?" she asked. "Did you talk to any of the mothers?"

"I spoke to Mrs. Hibbler for a few minutes," Alexis said. "She wants to fix me up with her brother. I think his name is Wolfgang, or Rudolph, or Adolph. Something weird like that."

"Go out with him!" Bridgett quipped. "It might be fun being Mrs. Adolph Hibbler?"

"I spoke to Patricia Morrison," Caroline said. "She knows about my show. She took me to the side of the house to tell me how she danced topless at Woodstock. If I didn't know better, I'd swear she brushed her boobs up against me."

"Lucky you," Bridgett said. Kim slapped her arm.

"What about you, Michael?" Kim called out. "Any good party news?"

He thought about it.

"No tengo nada que decir," he said. The four women on the couch looked at each other quizzically and shook their heads.

●　　　●　　　●　　　●　　　●

Dolores drove to Saint Matthew's.

The church had changed little from the time when the Kelleher children were small. Thanks to its diligent preservation committee, of which Dolores was a member, the building's Belgium block facade was still white and its wooden steeple untarnished. Father Woodward, however, had visibly aged. Still, he kept his mind active and dealt with Dolores the way he always had.

Dolores and Ken continued to attend Sunday worship, though the number of Sundays when Ken insisted on sleeping in had increased in recent months. Dolores and Maria went alone on those days. For confessional, Dolores went on average once every other month, informing no one in the house where she was going. It was hardly a secret, though.

Father Woodward sighed after hearing Dolores question her role both as a mother and a grandmother. "A bad grandmother?" he said. "How can you possibly make that judgment when, number one, you never even knew your own grandmothers, and number two, your family situation at home, through no fault of your own, is completely unlike that of every other family in the neighborhood?"

"I know, Father. It's just that—"

"So in addition to being a wife, a mother, a grandmother, and a volunteer here at church, you also want to be judge, jury, and executioner about your role as a mother and a grandmother? You take on too much, Dolores. You think you've sinned? You think you need punishment? If you really deserved punishment, trust me, you'd know it."

"But sometimes I feel—"

"That you've already been punished? Why? Michael again? That funny, brilliant artist of yours? Maria? That incredible little girl? Who, Dolores? Who? Instead of being punished, you should celebrate. Go home, Dolores. I'm sorry—I'm getting nasty in my old age. Get out of here. Your penance is to go home and have a celebratory glass of wine."

She did, but hardly found it celebratory.

2. CHILDHOOD HOME

"Michael, you won't mind babysitting Maria while we're at the wake and the funeral. We'll be gone just two days."

"First of all, commandant," Michael replied to his mother, who stood in the entranceway to his studio, "was that a question or a decree? Second of all, Maria's not a baby. Third of all, isn't 'babysitting' a superfluous word for me? What else can I do but sit?"

"Do you really think this is a time to joke around?" Dolores said frostily.

Mary Ann Farrell, Dolores's mother, passed away at eighty-eight years of age on July 14, 1984. Despite her advanced age, Mary Ann's death was sudden and unexpected; she had been entirely coherent and robust in body and spirit until the last moments, active to the end with walking groups, flower groups, and charity groups. She had stayed busy ever since her husband Alexander's death, and claimed never to have felt isolated or abandoned, as she knew was the case with so many elderly people. As she often liked to say to her grown children on the telephone, she was "far too busy being far too busy to feel alone." That's why she insisted on staying in the house, even though her aging body found it difficult to keep up with the housework and the shopping. Timothy Farrell arranged for an aid to come to the house three times a week. The aid, over the course of the two years she had been employed, had grown very attached to Mary Ann. The loss devastated her. She told Dolores's sister Katherine that the last thing Mary Ann said as she got into bed the night before she died was, "I think I'll put a built-in pool in the backyard. It's great physical therapy and you won't have to drive me to that smelly Jack LaLanne anymore."

Mary Ann did not awaken the next morning.

The multiple rounds of phone calls by the Farrell siblings to plan for Mary Ann's wake and funeral began the morning of her death. There were calls made between Massachusetts, where Katherine and Patricia lived, Rhode Island, where Timothy practiced law, Virginia, where Randall taught at Norfolk State University, and Long Island.

When Dolores had asked Michael to babysit, Ken was on the living room couch reading *Newsday*, and Maria was on the floor of Michael's studio reading Madeleine L'Engle's *A Wrinkle in Time*. She looked up forlornly at her grandmother.

"Why can't I come?" Maria asked. "Your mother was my great-grandmother, and if *you're* sad, I want to be sad with you."

With the newspaper in front of Ken's face, Dolores could not see her husband smile. And with Michael's wheelchair turned toward his desk, neither did Dolores see her son's broad grin.

"Don't you trust Michael?" Dolores asked Maria. "It will be far easier for him to stay here with you than dealing with his wheelchair at the funeral home and the cemetery."

"Of course I trust Michael. But I'd really like to come. Besides, it's summer vacation."

"Exactly. It's summer vacation. Do you really want to spend it at a cemetery?"

"We'll be gone just two days. Vacation lasts two months."

"Fine," Dolores conceded, too weary to argue.

• • • •

Alexis joined Dolores, Ken, and Maria for the trip to Sherborn. Bridgett and Kim, resting up before the new school term, had already begun a vacation in the Florida Keys that had been planned many months before. Caroline was on jury duty, in the middle of a rape trial. She chose to continue with the trial rather than ask for bereavement dismissal. She swore she had heard Grandma Mary Ann once say that she despised funerals, and that she would much rather her grandchildren celebrate life instead of acknowledging death. Caroline said she wanted to honor her grandmother by remembering *only* her life, and not the day she was buried. Dolores did not recall such a comment from her mother, but didn't have the strength to argue with Caroline's resolve to skip the funeral.

Instead of staying home alone, Michael accepted an invitation to a two-day event specifically designed for the physically handicapped at an Eastern Long Island Indian reservation.

"Chief Missing Limb will see Old Squaw in just two days! Don't worry about a thing," he said to Dolores the morning of the trip. Dolores found his comment distasteful and told him so.

Two days before the wake, Ken had to travel to Colorado Springs to give a speech at Aster-Paxton's annual National Sales Meeting. Dolores begged him not to go. She was worried about him returning to New York just a few hours before they were to leave for Sherborn. Also, she loathed having to drive to La Guardia Airport late at night to pick him up.

"You won't have to drive to the airport," Ken explained. "I can share a taxi with Toni Moore."

"Who's that?"

"A new sales rep. Lives three miles from here."

There were almost a hundred people in attendance at the McKenzie Funeral Home in Sherborn, and most of them also traveled to Pine Hill Cemetery. Dolores's sisters and brothers, along with their spouses and grown children (some of who were married), were among the mourners, as were several of Dolores's aunts, uncles, and cousins, and friends of the family. The Kellehers—Dolores, Ken, Alexis, and Maria—were invited to stay overnight at Katharine's spacious home in nearby Wayland Township, where Katharine lived with her husband John. Their children had homes of their own.

The next morning, Dolores spent some time alone with Father Harkey, the priest who had taken over the pulpit from Father McDermott at Saint John's Catholic Church in Sherborn. Father McDermott had died nine years earlier.

Later that afternoon, without stopping by to see the old Farrell house on Oak Street, Ken drove the family back to Westbrook Hills.

•   •   •   •   •

Dolores made a second trip to Sherborn two weeks later to help clear out her mother's house and prepare it for sale. Once again, Maria tagged along.

The first thing Dolores noticed when they pulled up in front of 618 Oak Street was a motorized antenna on the roof.

"When I grew up here, we didn't have any antenna at all, let alone such a fancy one," she murmured as she turned the car into the driveway. "Besides, there wasn't even a television in the house until ten years after I moved out."

Dolores noticed, too, that the blue shingles on the house were a different shade than the ones she recollected from her childhood.

"Those poor gardens," she said as she gazed at the sparsely populated beds that at one time had been so lush.

Other than those few changes, the rest of the old Farrell house looked much the way Dolores remembered it as a child. But she sensed that soon the rest would change.

She had not planned to take Maria along on this second trip to Massachusetts, preferring to avoid the extra pressure of watching over the child while also going through the emotional turmoil of helping to settle her mother's estate. Eventually she consented, though, thanks to Michael's intervention.

When they first began the trip, they got as far as the end of Pearl Drive when Dolores remembered she had forgotten Maria's suitcase in the house. She turned the car around roughly, sped back, retrieved the suitcase from Maria's room, and started up the car again.

"I'm sorry," Maria said. "I should've taken it downstairs myself."

"It's not your fault," Dolores said impassively. "I blame your father. I mean your grandfather," Dolores said. "He was supposed to do it."

They drove in silence for a while. Maria brought with her a cassette tape of songs from old Disney movies, which she had received as a birthday present. Dolores asked her not to play it on the car's cassette player, at least for a little while.

"You understand, don't you? I have a lot on my mind. A bit of a headache. Maybe later."

Once in Sherborn, Dolores had to park on Oak Street because four cars already crowded the driveway when they pulled up in front of the house.

"Last one to arrive," she muttered under her breath.

"I'm sorry," said Maria.

"I told you, it's not your fault," Dolores sighed behind closed eyes.

Katherine—Kat, as she was called by her friends and many of her relatives—was sitting on the living room couch as Dolores opened the front door. When she heard the front door open, Dolores's other sister, Patricia—more commonly called Trish—came in excitedly from the kitchen.

"My goodness, look at you!" Trish said to Maria. "Such a big girl. I hardly got a chance to talk to you last week." She turned to Dolores. "Why don't you come up with her more often?"

"Or invite us to Long Island, at least," Kat said in a low, sarcastic, but good-natured whisper.

"Let's not start in, girls, shall we?" Dolores said, in what she tried to make a lilting voice. "Mother's not around anymore to break it up."

"I told you Dee would be fine, Kat," said Trish, "She might be our baby sister, but somehow she's also always been the oldest."

"You thought I wouldn't be able to handle this? Mother's death?" Dolores said with much more gravity than before. "I've handled a lot in my time. Believe me."

Maria sat next to Kat on the couch while Dolores looked for a place to put her pocketbook.

"Aunt Kat?" Maria asked.

"Yes, honey?"

"Who's Dee? You said that 'Dee' would be fine."

Kat and Trish laughed. Dolores sighed. She put her pocketbook on the bureau and sat on the easy chair.

"You know how people shorten my name Katherine to Kat, and how they shorten Aunt Patricia's name to Trish? Well, Trish and I shorten your grandma's name to Dee."

"Nobody else does," Maria said.

"I never liked it," Dolores chimed in. "Where are Timothy and Randall? I saw their cars in the driveway."

"They're upstairs in Dad's old study, going over papers," Trish explained.

"Is Uncle Randy a teacher?" Maria asked. She had never been told much about Dolores's family, but recalled having heard that one of her great-uncles was a professor.

"Yes," said Trish. "He teaches history at a college in Virginia, and Uncle Timmy is a lawyer in Rhode Island. They'll come out soon to say hi. They've been so busy up there."

"So many files. So much paperwork," said Kat. "I'm sure it's not easy."

"Speaking of school, Maria, aren't you starting first grade in about a month?" asked Trish.

"Yes. But I wish it could be third grade."

Trish and Kat chuckled.

"Our mother just died and you two are laughing like children," Dolores snarled.

"Died *peacefully*," Kat assured her in a voice sharper than she had planned. "She died peacefully, in her sleep, after living a life more active than anyone I know! Sorry, Dee. I'm sad, but I'm just finding it hard to be miserable. Besides, she'd *want* us to laugh."

Randy called down from the study upstairs. "Stop fighting, girls, or I'll send you to your rooms," he said.

"Why do you wish it could be third grade, Maria?" asked Trish.

"Because I have a friend whose sister just finished third grade, and it sounds a *lot* more interesting than first grade."

"Dee, she's got Timmy's brains and Randy's sense of humor," Trish said. "A real Farrell through and through."

Dolores stood up.

"Well..." she said, "I appreciate the sentiment."

There were a few moments of silence during which Dolores made her way to the bureau to get a tissue from her purse.

"It was a hot ride and we hit a lot of traffic," she said to no one in particular. "I need a drink of water. Can I get you anything from the kitchen?"

"Timmy plans on picking up some takeout food for lunch in a few minutes," Trish said.

"How is that supposed to quench my thirst right now?"

Dolores disappeared into the kitchen.

"I was talking to your Uncle Michael on the phone the other day," Kat said to Maria in a quiet voice, "and he told me how you love hearing stories about when you were a baby. I want to tell you something that sticks in my mind. Once, when you were about two years old, your grandma and grandpa and Uncle Michael came here for a visit. Nana Mary Ann thought you were the most adorable thing. She had a wonderful time with you. But Michael wasn't happy. If I remember correctly, he was having a hard time at the place he was living in at the time. Nana Mary Ann tried to talk to him, Unfortunately, she didn't help much. But whenever Michael played with you, right here in this room, his smile could not have been bigger, Maria. It didn't matter that he was having problems. He was a changed man whenever he played with you. It was so nice to see."

Maria enjoyed hearing that story very much.

"I have another," added Trish. She took a seat on the floor beside the couch and, like her sister, kept her voice low. "I was at your house one day. You weren't much more than a year old. There was some kind of seminar I had to attend on Long Island, and I surprised everyone when I stopped by. Alexis was also there unexpectedly. She saw you in a playpen for the very first time and she said, 'What the heck is going on?' And your grandfather said, 'It's our miracle baby.'"

"He did?"

"He sure did! You are one lucky little girl, Maria. You have so many people who love you so much."

Dolores walked back into the living with a glass of ice water.

"What are you talking about?" she asked.

"Just telling some old stories," Trish said. "About Ken and Michael, mostly."

"Michael? Why?" She looked anxious.

"Why not?"

"By the way, how *is* Ken, Dee?" Trish asked.

"Busy. But slowing down a bit, thank goodness. He has his doctor and me to thank for that."

"I gotta tell you, Dee," Kat said, "he smoked maybe half a pack of cigarettes at the funeral alone. The fumes made me nauseous. You should really get him to stop."

"Don't you think I'm trying, Patricia? I've been trying for years. Sometimes it seems as if all I do is try try try on behalf of everyone in my family."

"How are the girls? Did Bridgett get over that virus she had when she was in Florida?"

"Yes. Thank you for asking."

"Aunt Bridgett tells me stories, too," Maria interjected.

Dolores, surprised by that revelation, looked up sharply from her glass. "Stories? What about?" she asked.

"Lots of things. Like about how we both feel different."

"Different?" Dolores sounded more alarmed than surprised, and struggled to change the subject; carelessly spilling a drop of water on her lap helped.

Timmy, from upstairs, unwittingly came to her rescue. "We're going out to get a couple of pizzas for lunch," he shouted down. "Call out your toppings!"

*   *   *   *

"Chinese? Pizza for lunch, and now Chinese food for dinner?"

"What's the problem, Dee?" Timmy asked.

"It's just a little—"

"A little nothing. None of us are fat. We had to throw everything out from the kitchen fridge. We're hungry. And it's not gonna break the bank. Besides, I heard that what used to be the Good Ol' Sherborn Bookstore is now the best Chinese takeout joint in all of New England."

So that evening, after hours of work in their father's old study, Timmy and Randy went to China Wok and took Maria with them. As they told Dolores when they pulled the little girl away from reading *The Chronicles of Narnia* on the living room floor, they had seen Maria only four or five times previously and wanted to get to know her better.

"I think you should just leave her here with us," Dolores insisted.

"Oh, stop worrying, Grandma," Timmy smirked as he lifted Maria and held her upside down. "We'll have her back in one piece, right side up, and covered in duck sauce."

While her brothers were out with Maria, Dolores drove to St. John's for a chat with Father Harkey. Instead of taking confession, which he rarely did at this hour, Father Harkey agreed to sit with Dolores in his study. After twenty minutes, he commanded her to go back to her family.

Over dinner, Timmy and Randy continued to fawn over Maria. They mentioned how bright and funny she was. Dolores wanted to intervene, lest it build in her some undue vanity. Dolores had had enough of that years earlier with Douglas and Caroline. She even ran some words of caution through her head to say to Maria, but held her tongue, wishing not to be criticized in front of her granddaughter, nor in front of anyone else. Finally, she let it pass. Trish saw the unease in her younger sister's eyes.

"Are you enjoying the food, Dee?" Trish asked.

"It's fine," Dolores answered. "Thank you."

"Don't you want any soup?" asked Randy. "You're the only soup-less one here."

"I'm not a fan of wonton soup."

"Just pretend it's chicken soup. Just like you're pretending the rice is… well… rice!"

"I'm fine, Randall. I don't have to pretend anything."

After dinner, Tim and Randy went back upstairs to go over more papers, and Maria stretched out on the living room couch.

"I'll wake her in a few minutes and drive her to your house to put her to bed," Dolores said to Katherine. "John's home, right?"

"Oh, let her sleep," Kat insisted, staring at the child whose deep, rhythmic breathing revealed how comfortable she was at the moment. "She'll be fine. Timmy or Randy will carry her out to the car later on."

"You're the only one who didn't read your fortune cookie after dinner, Dee." Trish asked suddenly. "How come?"

"I don't believe in that nonsense."

"Do you know what mine said? It said 'Sometimes the truth hurts before it heals.' I thought it was yours."

"What are you implying, Patricia?"

"That sometimes I get the impression you think you're living a life you never expected to live. "

The comment baffled Dolores. Her brow furrowed, though she said not a word.

"You seem to be on edge all the time," Trish declared. "Like you can't believe you have the family you have. A son like Michael. A granddaughter like Maria —"

"Am I *supposed* to have a granddaughter who has no parents and a son who's missing a leg, Patricia?" Dolores said sternly. Her voice was shaky. "I love them. I love them both dearly, and they're wonderful. But yes, sometimes it's hard to believe. Is that a crime? Is it a crime, Patricia?"

"Let's drop it, Trish," Kat intervened. "We're not therapists. Or priests. This isn't the place or time."

Maria grunted and rolled onto her side. The sisters ceased their talk to avoid waking her, unaware that Maria had been awake the entire time.

•   •   •   •   •

Timmy and Randy began the next day by meeting with their mother's banker, insurance broker, and eldercare attorney. Trish and Kat gave a tour of their mother's house to three real estate agents. Dolores tended to the gardens. She wanted to bring them back to respectability for potential buyers who would come by to see the property. Maria played in the basement, enamored with the ancient toys that Mary Ann had built for her children and had kept for all her grandchildren.

After lunch, with the real estate agents gone and their brothers still away, Kat and Trish insisted on taking Maria for a drive around Sherborn to show her where they used to go to school, where they swam in the summer and ice-skated in the winter, and where they built gardens out of empty lots — only one of which remained. Dolores, whose first inclination was to say no to her sisters' request, relented. She used the opportunity to spend some time by herself in the house. She told Kat and Trish that she was tired.

Dolores found herself in a small alcove upstairs off the master bedroom, surrounded by nothing but silence and memories. Mary Ann had built that alcove on her own, for her own use and her husband's. In the alcove were a wide desk with two sets of side-by-side drawers, a chair, and a few shelves of old books. As Dolores recalled, her mother sometimes referred to the alcove as the Idea Shop. Dolores had always thought it was merely a lighthearted name her mother had given to the space; Mary Ann often gave silly names to random things as her children grew. Dolores and her sisters and brothers had not been allowed in the Idea Shop, and she had a fleeting sensation that her presence there even now was forbidden.

Curiosity won over fear, and with careful, reverential movements, Dolores lifted notebooks and shoeboxes out of the two top drawers. She delved into those items just as carefully and reverentially. In one shoebox was a pair of ballet shoes; Dolores remembered seeing her mother dance once or twice, but never did she know her to own a pair of ballet shoes. In a notebook Dolores found nine or ten handwritten short stories that her father had composed when he was a young man, as shown by the dates scribbled on the first pages of each story. She never knew about that, either. The stories had curious titles such as "I'll Follow the Sun" and "The Best Policy." Dolores realized that the former was also the name of a Beatles song her children used to listen to, and she momentarily delighted in how the Beatles composed their song forty years after Alexander wrote his story. The latter was a bit more cryptic, which compelled her to glance at the first page. Alexander wrote: "Young Benjamin Franklin — and mind you, this was twenty years before he coined the phrase 'Honesty is the best policy' — looked squarely at the ill-tempered customer in his brother's Boston print shop and said to him, 'Sir, a lie stands on one leg, truth on two.' Benjamin then turned around and left the customer speechless." Dolores closed her eyes and, as if it stung her fingers, placed the short story on top of the desk.

But she wasn't finished in the Idea Shop. She looked into one of the two bottom drawers and saw what appeared to be a blueprint. Slowly, she opened the large, brittle, multi-folded piece of paper and saw that her parents had illustrated a series of buildings. Her father and mother's distinctive handwriting on all the edges of the blueprint indicated with arrows where a 'little theater' would be and where a 'piano studio' should go, and how far back in the woods the 'camper cabins' should be built. At the bottom of the page, in firmer, darker letters, her mother or father had written Camp Skerries, Berkshire Mountains. Had Alexander and Mary Ann Farrell planned to build a sleep-away camp in the mountains of western Massachusetts? Devoted to children who enjoyed the arts? It was all very intriguing to Dolores, and wholly bewildering. What other surprises might be hidden in the Idea Shop? Cautiously, she opened the second bottom drawer. Inside were two dusty, crudely constructed scrapbooks made from two sheets of cardboard held together with shoelaces – the mark of her father, who was sloppier and more casual in his projects than Mary Ann. Dolores picked up the two scrapbooks and opened one. In it were black-&-white photos and discolored postcards. She pulled out a postcard. It was from a place called Sky Farm, in Liberty Corner, New Jersey. On one side was a photo, faded and in the shape of an oval, that showed two men and two women in front of a lake, all four completely nude, and one couple generously endowed. Above the photo were the words, "America's Newest and Most Relaxing Nudist Colony." At the bottom of the postcard, in almost miniscule type, it said, "Garden State Stationers, Newark, NJ. 1932."

With her hands quivering, Dolores put the notebooks, stories, shoeboxes, and folders back in the desk, closed the drawers, walked out of the bedroom, and sat on the old majestic Queen Anne chair that watched over the hallway and the staircase. Her breath was shallow. It took her a while to regain her bearings. She was unaware of just how long she had been sitting there. Moments later, she was startled out of her trance when Timmy, at the bottom of the stairs, called up to her.

"Hey, Queen Dolores," he warbled, "wake up! We're back."

•   •   •   •   •   •   •

Randy drove to a Mexican restaurant to buy takeout food for dinner.

"Mom dies, and we eat like pigs," Timmy said amiably as they all sat around the kitchen table.

"I don't think that's very funny," Dolores complained.

"You have to learn to relax, Dee," her brother retorted. "We've still got about a million hours of stuff to do to settle Mom's estate and empty the house. A little comfort food, especially in a basically empty kitchen, is... well..."

"Comforting!" offered Maria.

Everyone but Dolores laughed—but neither did she wish to remain the object of ridicule, so she managed a smile and continued to pick at her food.

Randy assumed the bulk of the formalities, since he had the legal training to make the most sense of it. The family trusted him to make the right decisions. The physical labor fell to the others. Most of the household items had been packed and divided among the five siblings by the time Kat, Dolores, and Maria went back to Kat's house for the night. They gave Maria the task of writing the appropriate names on the boxes in magic marker. She enjoyed writing "Kat" and "Trish," and without her grandmother's knowledge, she wrote "Dee" on several of the boxes.

Dolores had originally intended to leave for Long Island early the following morning. Her unexpected adventure the previous day in the Idea Shop changed her mind. When they were all in the living room to say goodbye to each other, Dolores asked Randy to pull down the attic ladder so that she could take a quick look up there.

"The attic? Why?" asked Randy. "I've been up there. There's nothing but spiders playing musical chairs on clumps of mouse poop."

"I'd like to take a quick look," Dolores insisted. "For old time's sake. Just indulge me, Randall. Is that asking too much?"

"I swear to you, Dolores, it's empty up there. Mom and Dad never really kept anything there in the first place. Did you look in the Idea Shop yesterday, by the bedroom, before we boxed everything?"

"Yes."

"Did you see anything interesting?"

"Dad used to go up into the attic from time to time," Dolores said, completely ignoring Randy's specific question. Maria listened with interest.

"But he hadn't gone up there in the last twenty years of his life," said Timothy, who was nearby. "He moved everything that was up there into the basement. We packed it all."

"Besides," added Kat, "don't you think we already know everything we need to know about Mom and Dad? Everything *they* wanted us to know? I mean, you don't want to find something you *don't* want to know. Do you?"

Dolores didn't like being outnumbered, nor did she enjoy finding herself at a loss for words. So she gave up.

"Fine. Let's forget it."

Timmy and Randy loaded a few small boxes into the trunks and hatchbacks of the five cars out front. (The larger boxes would remain in the garage until shipping arrangements could be made.) Then Timmy and Trish took Maria outside to help her climb the giant White Spruce they had all climbed as kids. Dolores saw one small box of photographs that was left in the foyer and put it in the back seat of her car. They made their goodbyes, as well as promises of more visits in the future and wishes for no traffic on the way home.

Shortly after Dolores merged onto the interstate, Maria looked pensively at her and said, "I wish they didn't stop you from looking in the attic."

A diligent driver, Dolores kept her head forward, but the comment was just too curious for her to let pass. She diverted her eyes ever so quickly to Maria when it was safe to do so."Why do you say that?" she asked.

"I'm sure Uncle Randy and Uncle Timmy could have missed something," Maria said. "It's sad when you don't know your parents as much as you want to," she added.

Dolores nodded and then told Maria that she could play her Disney tape if she wanted to.

3. A NEW ROOM

"I think it would be okay. I'd even dip myself in duck sauce on the very first day if that happened," Maria said in answer to her grandmother's question about possibly skipping a grade.

While Dolores no longer found herself stunned by Maria's witty and clever retorts, neither was she grateful for them. She still had an urge to rebuke the more impertinent replies, but also knew that her sermons hardly sculpted her own children into the images she preferred; why would Maria be any different?

Dolores had posed a hypothetical question to Maria, as the two sat in the living room reading books.

"Maria," Dolores began, "I suppose it's possible that after school starts next month, your teacher might—just *might*, mind you— recommend that you actually go into second grade instead of staying in first. How would you feel about that?"

That's when Maria said she would not mind, and would even be excited about it.

"As long as my friends don't think I did in on purpose to show off," she added.

"Why—do they think you show off now?" Dolores asked.

"No. But people change."

Dolores had been well aware for some time that Maria was beyond her schoolmates in intellectual ability. She thought of her relatives, of Ken's, of the lineage on both sides from way back and far off. Certainly there were many gifted relations, not just academically, but culturally and artistically, as well. Maria was different, with a quality and character that was distinct from anyone else in the family. Dolores could not put her finger on just what it was; then again, how could she possibly measure Maria against the maternal side of her granddaughter's own family? That was impossible and probably would remain so forever.

"How would *you* feel about it?" Maria asked. "Would it be okay with you?"

Dolores was completely unprepared for the question. As if by divine intervention, Ken and Michael walked into the house at that moment, from the kitchen door. They had spent all of Saturday afternoon at a vintage car show at the Riverhead Raceway.

"I didn't expect you back for another hour," Dolores said when they arrived in the living room. "Anything wrong?"

"Dad started coughing like a 1925 Model T Ford," Michael explained. "I didn't like the way he was breathing, so I insisted we come home early."

"I'm fine, Dolores," Ken insisted. "Please don't start in."

"Don't start in? Are you kidding me? You missed out on our children growing up because of your job. You want to miss out on Maria growing up because you're dead?"

Ken looked wounded and defeated. He knew Dolores was speaking from the heart, but was ill prepared for the harshness that went along with it.

"You're right. You're absolutely right. Starting right now, I'll take better care of myself. I promise."

Ken went into a coughing fit. Dolores helped him onto the couch. Michael wheeled himself to the kitchen to get his father a glass of water, and Maria ran upstairs to grab his pillow and reading glasses. The coughing subsided as Ken's wife, son, and granddaughter stared at him with concern. He was comfortable now, at least, and Dolores sat on the easy chair beside him. She had a scowl on her face.

"Michael, Maria—" she began.

"Let me guess," Michael interjected. "You two would like to speak alone. Fine. But don't talk about Maria or she'll let out her secret."

"What secret?" Dolores said wearily.

"That she's actually a thirty-year-old Asian doctor hiding inside of a six-year-old Puerto Rican body who will monitor her grandfather's health on a daily basis." Dolores and Ken were dumbstruck at the randomness of the remark. "Come on, pipsqueak," Michael said to Maria. "While they rack their brains trying to make sense out of my nonsense, I'll show you the gigantic present I found for you at the racetrack. It's outside. Let's go."

The two exited through the back door and left Dolores and Ken alone.

"Did he really buy her a present?" Dolores asked.

"It's an empty candy wrapper printed in Spanish. He found it in one of the vintage cars."

"You know, Ken," Dolores said, "I didn't want to say anything in front of the children, but I've been noticing how you can barely climb the stairs to our bedroom anymore. You're always out of breath when you get there. I'm very happy about what you said—about turning over a new leaf. But I think we also need to make some changes in the house. Temporarily, at least. To avoid aggravating the problem."

"What are you suggesting?" Ken said, a sudden bitterness to his tone. "You want me to make believe I'm thirty years younger? Shall I play basketball with Maria? Push Michael's wheelchair up a hill? Want to have six hours of wild sex?"

"Ken! What's gotten into you? I'm being serious."

"I'm sorry." He meant it; Dolores could tell. "I guess I'm just..."

"Worried?" She finished the sentence for him, and he assumed she was correct. "And you want to take it out on me? My father would have quoted Shakespeare right now."

"To be or not to be?"

"No, that's not the quote I had in mind. It's about protesting too much. Listen to me, Ken. I think we should turn your study into a bedroom for you, so that you don't have to go up and down the stairs so many times. You know the way you are—up and down a thousand times a day, for one reason or another. This way, all your clothes, your toiletries, your papers, your books, all your things will be right in your own room down here, on the same floor as the kitchen, the living room, the garage, and just a few steps away from the bathroom..."

Ken did not object. He rather liked the idea. And so Dolores went about transforming Ken's study into a bedroom. She purchased an expensive, well-made lounger that switched easily between a couch and a bed, constructed a dark-wood vanity in the corner with a mirror on the wall, installed a clothing bar in the closet, put down a large area rug, and ordered track lighting, which Ken had always said he liked. The room already had a desk, a filing cabinet, and several well-stocked bookshelves. Dolores created the new room by herself, except for the track lighting. For that, she hired a young electrician named Gary who had been a friend of Bridgett's when they were children. When he came to the house to discuss the job with Dolores, Gary said he remembered that the room had once been a study.

"Did you make all the changes in this room yourself, Mrs. K? Why'd you stop at the track lighting? Why didn't you do that, too?"

"I don't like heights."

"Really? I remember you on ladders all the time when we were kids. A bunch of us used to love seeing you do all that stuff around the house. That's why we came over! It was pretty cool."

Dolores excused herself and walked to the bathroom. She leaned against the sink, closed her eyes, then took a washcloth to dab her face.

The room was ready for Ken on the first day of September. Preparing to retire for the evening that first night, he looked around and admired the cozy little space that was all his own now, in which he could work, read, think, sleep—all without the need to go upstairs. He glanced at the desk and realized that some Aster-Paxton notebooks and files that he usually kept in the master bedroom, materials he often glanced at before going to bed, were still upstairs. He mentioned it to Dolores, and she insisted that she'd bring the notebooks and files down herself. She didn't want him to climb the stairs.

In the master bedroom, Dolores looked for the material that Ken had asked for, grabbed a three-ring binder and half a dozen manila folders, and walked toward the hallway. A few folders fell to the floor. Out of one slipped some greeting cards. On the front of one card, the name 'Ken' was written in large, flowing, red-ink letters. She picked it up. Under Ken's name was a photo of a flowerpot and a watering can. Dolores opened the card. Inside it said, "You are more than a mentor. You are a friend. Thanks for everything. And that little corporate recognition package I have at home? It's yours as well as mine. See you in the salt mines. Toni."

Dolores backed up slowly and sat on the edge of the bed. She could not move and was unable to decide what to think. She stared at the wall — the one with the framed photographs of all her children when they were teenagers — but saw only blankness. Maria stepped into the room., but Dolores did not notice.

"Grandma?"

"Oh! Goodness. You scared me."

"I'm sorry. I just wanted to ask you something."

"What is it, Maria?"

"Grandpa didn't go to work yesterday or the day before. Is he going to be all right?"

"Grandpa has been the most dedicated salesman at that company for forty years. Hardly ever missed a day. He just wanted a little time to rest. That's all. No one at the company will mind. He'll be fine."

"Since he doesn't have to climb the stairs anymore," Maria said, "he'll get better very quickly. Right?"

"Yes. I'm sure he will."

"And that will make everyone happy. I just hope you don't get too lonely up here all alone."

"What?"

"I want you to be happy, too."

Not knowing what to say, Dolores attempted a smile, stood up, straightened out Ken's material into one neat stack, and took it down to him. Maria went to bed early. First grade was to start on Monday.

4. RECOGNITION PACKAGE

The weather was unseasonably warm; every window at Westbrook Hills Elementary School had remained open all day, and the dismissal bell was heard up and down Timber Lane. Michael had gotten a late start and was not yet at the school by the time a hundred fifty students said goodbye to their first full week of class. The boys and girls ran out to their mothers and fathers, and a few to their grandparents. Dolores was not among them. She had to rush to Philadelphia and asked Michael to pick up Maria that day. Michael heard the bell from half a block away and wheeled a little faster, but was barred from navigating his wheelchair to where Maria could easily see him because of all the adults standing on the sidewalk in front of the school. Hardly anyone stepped aside to let him pass. But Michael was certain that Maria would remain unruffled if she did not see a familiar face right away.

"Uncle Michael!" she called out when she saw him in the distance. She ran over to him so that Michael wouldn't have to plot a treacherous course on the hilly lawn in front of the school. "Hi! Where's Grandma?"

"Aunt Caroline had a little accident in Philadelphia," Michael explained. "I'm sure she'll be all right. Grandma and Aunt Alexis drove down there, and Grandpa Ken is gonna meet them there a little later. Bridgett and Kim are coming over to our house after work."

"What happened to Aunt Caroline?"

"I really don't know. We'll find out later. I'm sure it's nothing bad."

On the walk home, Maria commented it was funny how she had lived on Pearl Drive her entire life and knew almost no one on the block.

"Just my best friend, Debby Bindi," she said. "No one else, really."

"I know," Michael responded. "I've yelled at your grandmother many times about that. Maybe she pulled a few too many muscles pushing me around the neighborhood when I was your age and just doesn't have the strength to take you around."

"Guess what. I can walk by myself!"

Michael laughed.

Maria asked Michael to tell her a little bit about the families on Pearl Drive as they walked and wheeled along. With each house they passed, Michael painted stories of the people who lived there, and made some of the mental pictures a little more cartoony than others. He described for Maria which families he knew, which ones remained mysterious, the tales and rumors he had heard over the years, who used to date whom, who used to hate whom, which houses had the scariest parents and the best backyards, and who gave out the best Halloween candy.

"That one on the right — those are the Hillmans," Michael said, as they approached the house that was directly across the street from their own. "There was a boy who lived there named Daniel who was a friend of your father's. They used to make believe they were Batman and Robin, Superman and Inspector Henderson, the Green Hornet and Kato, all kinds of crazy things like that. I vaguely remember hearing Daniel call your father a jerk one time for never letting him be Batman or Superman." Michael chuckled. "It's funny what sticks in your mind, isn't it? Anyway, the last I heard, Daniel was a big-shot reporter in New York City."

"You mean he finds out things about people? Even people who are missing?"

"I guess so," Michael said. "Why do you ask?" He looked at Maria, who was lost in thought. "Never mind. I know why."

· · · · · ·

Dolores, Ken, and Alexis were with Caroline in a room in the intensive care unit of Thomas Jefferson University Hospital. Sergeant Carrey, the first officer on the scene, had explained to them a few hours before that a disturbed fan had attacked Caroline just outside the radio station after her morning show. It seems the young man, who was in his twenties and clean-cut, was obsessed with her. As the sergeant put it, "He was apparently fixated on someone he had a crush on and who he was convinced was teasing him on the air. I'm guessing he was sexually frustrated and thought Caroline was giving him permission to assault her — probably because of some of the things she says on her show. He dragged her into an alley at the side of the building."

"Was she raped?" Dolores asked quietly, her head down.

"No. She put up a fight. But she was pretty badly beat up. The doctor will be here in a few minutes to explain."

"Did they catch the guy?" Ken asked.

"Yes. Almost immediately. Your daughter gave a good description, and other people saw the guy a few blocks away all disheveled and acting strange. He had some pretty bad bruises, too."

"It's that job of hers," Dolores muttered angrily. "She should never have left Sherborn."

Ken looked at her.

"Sherborn?"

"I meant Westbrook Hills," she said.

"Mom," said Alexis as gently as possible, "you do know she's thirty-four, right? An adult."

"Please, Bridgett. Not now."

"You're right. I'm sorry."

The doctor later explained that Caroline had a slight concussion, two broken ribs, a few punctured blood vessels near her right eye and above her cheek, and several acute though non-critical external lacerations. She would have to stay in the hospital for four or five days.

Caroline's Philadelphia roommate stopped by the hospital. She was a young woman from Ireland named Sally, who was a home healthcare nurse. Sally convinced Dolores and Ken that she could take excellent care of Caroline and that they should not feel obligated to stay in town. After she consulted with Ken, Dolores thanked Sally and accepted her offer, mostly because of the need to look after Maria at home. She said they would stay overnight, visit Caroline in the morning, drive home, but return to Philadelphia the day that Caroline was discharged from the hospital.

Alexis drove home alone that night. Dolores and Ken checked into the Penn's View Hotel. They were exhausted when they finally settled into their room after an anxious dinner in the hospital cafeteria. Almost immediately, Dolores used the telephone on the small desk next to the TV cabinet to call the house, where Bridgett and Kim were with Michael and Maria. She explained Caroline's situation first to Bridgett, then to Michael, and asked them to deemphasize the severity of the injuries when they talked to Maria.

After the phone call, Dolores had a great urge to once again rail against Caroline's choice of profession, but knew that Ken would have sensible counter-arguments. For Ken's part, it was not a specific topic that was on his mind, but the need for a cigarette. He had by this time cut back to one pack a day, and his coughing fits had lessened considerably. "I know I already had a few today, but if there's any time that deserves it, it's now," he said quietly. "You have to agree." He took out a cigarette and lit it.

"You know I can't stand it, right?" Dolores asked. "You know I think it's a disgusting habit."

"My daughter was violently assaulted today," he snapped. "I need one."

"If I smoked every time something bad happened, I'd have been dead of cancer forty years ago," Dolores lamented.

"What is this—a goddamned contest? You're equating having to move out of Sherborn with our daughter getting the crap beat out of her?"

"What about when Douglas ran away leaving us with his motherless daughter? What about when the damn garage door fell on Michael?" She refused to look at Ken. "Don't talk to me about bad things. Don't talk to me about regrets. Don't talk to me about anything."

Ken knew the guests in the rooms on either side could hear them, but that was not why he let Dolores have the last word; he simply did not wish for an extended fight or a sleepless night. He was nervous about seeing his beaten and bruised youngest daughter once again in the morning, and equally nervous about the three-hour drive back to Long Island with Dolores that would follow the hospital visit. As far as work was concerned, although his bosses and colleagues knew beyond any doubt that for Ken Kelleher, family always came first, he could not help but wonder about the professional consequences of having walked out on a multimillion-dollar sales call in Princeton. That meeting was cut short when Dolores and Alexis tracked him down by phone to tell him about Caroline. He hadn't even explained anything to the potential clients; he just walked out. He knew deep down that a quick word or two to them would have been a wiser move.

In short, he needed at least a few hours of sleep at the hotel.

But that was not to be, for after she washed up and put on her nightgown, Dolores had more on her mind to discuss with her husband.

"I have to ask you something, Ken," she said as she sat down stiffly on the chair in front of the desk. Ken was already in bed.

"What?" he asked.

"Did you have an affair with someone named Toni?" She said it as calmly as she knew how.

"What?" Ken asked. He turned his head to look at her.

"Did you have a child with her?"

Now he turned his entire body around to face her.

"What are you talking about, Dolores? Are you insane?"

"No," she said, maintaining as much composure as possible. "I'm not insane. I found a card in one of your files at home. It was from someone named Toni. It said something about you being more than a mentor. She thanked you for something—for everything, really. She had a very peculiar term for the baby. I think she called it a recognition package. Isn't Toni that saleswoman you helped train?"

It was Dolores's self-control that annoyed Ken nearly as much as the accusation itself. It proved to him that she believed the story to its core and was waiting for him to break down and confess.

"Dolores..." he said, struggling to find the right words. "Dolores... Yes, she's a saleswoman, and yes, I trained her. She's done very well in her territory. Every once in a while she thanks me with cards, or sometimes tiny little gifts. A book. Dinner on the road. Now stop it, Dolores. This is silly."

"A book? Dinner on the road? That sounds very personal to me."

"How does a book sound personal, Dolores?"

"And what about the so-called package she has at home?" Dolores said harshly. "She wrote that it's as much yours as it is hers. What else could that possibly mean? What else could it be but a baby?"

"For crying out loud, Dolores, most salespeople get little incentives from Aster-Paxton. Usually cheap pieces of crap. Paperweights. Pens. Plaques. Picture frames. Shit like that. They're called recognition packages. She's gotten a few, and she says they're as much mine as hers because I goddamn trained her!"

Dolores looked down and took a deep breath.

"Ken," she said quietly, "remember—I saw the note. Such beautiful handwriting. She took her time writing it. There was love in that handwriting. She loves you. Do you love her?"

Ken could no longer control his volume.

"She does not love me, and I do not love her," he screamed. "I was her mentor. All salespeople at Aster-Paxton have mentors. Yes, she likes me, and I like her, but we only like each other as colleagues. We get along nicely, which isn't always the case in sales. She's happy to be successful, and she's thankful that I helped her get that way. Is there anything wrong with that?"

"I'm sure you get along," Dolores said, rather frigidly. "Maybe you're too naïve to know that it's called flirting. And I know as well as anyone that flirting can lead to—"

"Fine!" he said. "Do you want me to admit to a little flirting? Yes, there's a little flirting. I have news for you, Dolores. It happens all over the goddamned country. The difference is—and it's a huge difference, and I'm furious with you for not knowing it—the difference is that with me it stops at the flirting. Nothing more. That's the truth. Now you tell *me* the truth, Dolores. You never, ever flirted with anyone? Anyone at all? In Westbrook Hills? Sherman Oaks? Not even once?"

The silence was just as disquieting as the yelling.

"Let's forget it, Ken," she said. "We're both tense. We're both angry. Let's just go to bed."

They did, though neither slept well.

•   •   •   •   •

"Did you make any new friends this week in first grade?" Bridgett asked Maria when she and Kim were at the house after the accident.

"Yes," Maria said, "but Grandma asked me not to invite anyone home."

"Ever?"

"Maybe just for a few weeks," Maria assured her aunt. "She'll change her mind when she gets tired of me following her around the house asking questions and then more questions."

Bridgett looked at Kim, and Kim looked at Michael, who was in his alcove studio working on a cartoon.

"The *real* problem," Michael said, knowing full well that Bridgett and Kim were thinking the same thing, "is that Maria might get kicked up to high school before she makes any friends at all."

"Maria," said Kim, "you must have been surprised to see Michael instead of your grandma picking you up at school today. Were you?"

"How could she not be surprised?" Michael piped up instead. "Every other kid had a Yuppie parent waiting by a fancy car. Maria had an ugly uncle in a beat-up wheelchair."

"Shut up, Michael," Bridgett said, laughing.

Bridgett, who had spoken to her mother on the phone an hour earlier, told Maria that Caroline was in the hospital because a bad man who listened to her on the radio tried to hurt her. "She'll be fine," Bridgett said. "She just has a bunch of really bad boo-boos."

"Bad boo-boos?" Michael scoffed. "Are you kidding me, Bridgett? You're talking to Maria! You can say acute abrasions instead of boo-boos."

"You want us to stay over tonight, Michael?" Kim asked. "Just to help out a little? I can make breakfast in the morning. Your mom and dad should be back around lunchtime."

"Thanks, but that's not necessary," Michael said, as he wheeled himself out of the studio. "I may only have one leg, but I have two arms that are very good at making pancakes in the shape of Snoopy. After breakfast, Maria and I are gonna continue our 'who's who' tour of the neighborhood."

"I heard it might rain."

"Then we'll do what they do in Philadelphia."

"What's that?"

"Let it rain."

Bridgett, Kim, and Maria all shook their heads pitifully.

"I guess I should stick to cartoons, huh?"

"Which reminds me, Michael," said Kim, "last time I was here, your father was going nuts looking for a pencil. I did him a favor and borrowed one from your studio. While I was in there, I caught a glimpse of some of your cartoons. Unbelievable, Michael! When in God's name are you gonna submit them to *The New Yorker* or *Harper's* or *The Saturday Evening Post*?"

"I do," Michael said.

"Often?"

"Not too often."

"Why not? Don't you know that the more stuff you send out, the greater the chances are that something will sell?"

"I know that, Kim. But the more I send out, the more that come back rejected, and my mother's usually the one who takes in the mail. It upsets her because she thinks it upsets *me*, even though it doesn't. It's just easier not to send anything out."

"That's the most ridiculous thing I ever heard."

"I know. Welcome to *my* world."

·　　·　　·　　·　　·

When Ken and Dolores returned from Philadelphia, Maria was on the front stoop of the house reading E. B. White's *Stuart Little*. It hadn't rained after all. She and Michael had made their neighborhood tour after breakfast, and now Michael was in his studio, working.

"Where did you get this book?" Dolores asked.

"My teacher. Miss Besher," Maria responded.

"I remember Alexis and Bridgett reading this book in school," Ken said, "but not until fifth grade, I think!"

"Fourth grade at my school," Maria said nonchalantly.

"You *do* know you're in first grade, right?"

Maria smiled.

"Miss Besher said she thought I'd like it and that I could read it if it didn't interfere with my other schoolwork."

Ken entered the house. Dolores, gazing absently at the paving stones that bordered the garden, called out Maria's name.

"I'd like to apologize to you," she said as she used her foot to straighten out one stone.

"For what?" Maria asked.

"For not picking you up yesterday. I know that the first week of school is a big deal for most people, and I wasn't there. I feel badly."

"It wasn't your fault. I mean... Aunt Caroline..."

"I know. But still..."

"Will she be all right?"

"Yes."

"I had a good time with Uncle Michael."

"Did you? What did you do?"

"We walked around the neighborhood. He told me there was once a big snowstorm when he was little, and that everybody walked in the middle of the street because cars couldn't drive on it, and that everybody who walked by looked at the Christmas decorations on our house and said nice things."

"Michael told you that?"

"Yes," Maria said. "He said you're an expert."

Dolores left the paving stones behind to sit on the stoop next to Maria. She suddenly felt a little faint, what with Caroline's bruised face still fresh in her mind, a stressful drive home from Philadelphia with Ken, and yet another surprising and mystifying comment from her granddaughter.

"I wonder how they celebrate Christmas in Puerto Rico," Maria said.

A car turned onto Pearl Drive. Dolores and Maria watched it pass.

"I'm glad you had a good time with Michael. Let's go inside and have lunch."

"Michael also told me about some of my daddy's friends. Like Daniel Hillman, who lived right there." She pointed to the house across the street.

"Yes," said Dolores. "He was a nice boy."

"Did you know that he's a writer? Michael said he writes for a lot of famous magazines."

"Yes, I think I heard about that."

"Sometimes he finds things. For his articles. Like Stuart Little does in the book. The parrot runs away, and Stuart Little finds her. I just read that part right before you got home."

Dolores felt another dull ache working its way back into her head and knew that indecision was the cause: should she engage in what was obviously an attempt by Maria to find out more about her father and her mother, or would that merely result in more questions with precious few answers? Could it lead to some sadness? Did the family need any more sadness? All these thoughts swam through Dolores's mind in the seconds after Maria described the investigative efforts of Stuart Little.

"Would you like to take a walk with me across the street?" she asked Maria.

"Sure," Maria said.

They went to the Hillman house and knocked on the door. Beverly Hillman answered and was surprised to see Dolores. After a pleasant if subdued reintroduction—the two had very little occasion to socialize over the years—Beverly said she had never met Maria, although she had seen her plenty of times in the front yard. "Active little girl!" Beverly said. "In the front, on the sidewalk, in the garage—"at which point Dolores suddenly changed the topic to Daniel, Beverly's son, who had been a friend of Douglas's.

"Does he have any children?" Dolores asked.

"Daniel? No, he's not married. Maybe one day. He's seeing someone, I think."

"What about your daughter?"

"No, I'm afraid Lori's not married, either. Although she's in a relationship, so... well... you never know. Hope springs eternal! I still have time to be a grandmother. The prayer of every Jewish mother, right? Well, *all* mothers, I suppose."

Dolores smiled.

Beverly invited Dolores and Maria into the living room.

"I can't believe how big she's gotten, Dolores. I remember seeing her from my living room window when you wheeled her down the block in her carriage."

"Actually," Maria said, "I'm the smallest one in my class."

"And the prettiest, too, I bet."

"My Uncle Michael says that good things come in small packages. And he said that he's always right!."

Beverly laughed.

"Pretty *and* smart, Dolores," she said, still giggling. "Then again, your whole family was like that, from what I remember. Douglas was very bright. And so talented!"

She saw Maria's face light up.

"Oh, please, Beverly," Dolores said. "That's not why I stopped by. I wanted to ask about Daniel. Did I hear that he's a reporter?"

"Yes, he is. He's very busy, and he seems to enjoy it very much."

"Which magazine?"

"Different ones, from what I understand. He doesn't have a boss or an office, which to me sounds like he's unemployed. But what do I know? He calls it freelance. I hope that doesn't mean he does it for free. From what I remember, he's written for *Vanity Fair, Esquire, The New York Times Magazine, The Saturday Evening Post...*"

"*Playboy,*" Maria added.

The women looked at Maria with baffled and embarrassed looks.

"Michael told me," she said.

Beverly was unable to stifle another laugh. Dolores was glad, for she didn't know how to respond on her own.

"What's he doing now?" Dolores asked.

"Actually, Daniel is out of the country right now. In China. He's working on a series of articles, though I can't remember for which magazine."

"China! That's quite an assignment."

"I don't understand why they can't get a Chinese writer to do it. He's been gone a few months but comes home in a week or so. I just don't get it. Who will make him chicken soup in China if he gets sick?"

"He can have won ton soup and just pretend it's chicken soup," Maria said.

Beverly covered her mouth to hide yet another giggle.

"Well, Beverly, I don't want to take up any more of your time. You must be busy."

"Actually, a real estate agent is stopping by in a few minutes. Murray and I are moving to Florida. We never thought we would—but we are. Not right away, but soon."

"Oh! Good luck with that, Beverly. Please say hello to Murray for me."

"I will. He's at the hardware store. Would you like a cup of coffee?"

"No thank you. We should be going. We have a lot to do at home. I just wanted to say hello. It's been so long."

The women rose from the couch. Maria followed close behind. They walked to the door.

"It was so nice to see you, Beverly. Please keep in touch."

"I will, Dolores. Say hi to Ken for me. I'll tell Daniel that you and Maria stopped by. I'm sure he'd have wanted to see you both."

Dolores and Maria left the Hillman house and crossed the street. On one hand, it felt to Dolores as if she had accomplished a mission of some sort, based merely on the fact that she had acted on an impulsive idea. She was uncertain, though, exactly what the mission had actually accomplished.

· · · · ·

When Maria watched Michael work, he knew it was to learn and admire; when his mother watched, he felt it was to pass judgment on his choice of occupation. That's why he was comfortable only when Maria watched.

Michael felt that his circumstance embarrassed his mother: a twenty-seven-year-old man living in his parents' house, earning a salary of just eight thousand dollars a year as a local newspaper cartoonist. Ken, though, never seemed embarrassed, nor did Michael's sisters. He broached the subject to his mother one day, and she insisted she was just concerned for him and in no way embarrassed. Still, the look of grief on her face whenever she passed by the alcove studio muted Michael's creative juices, and so he stopped working in the alcove whenever she was nearby. He soon stopped working entirely whenever she was in the living room, and then whenever she was on the main floor of the house.

Maria stood in the opening of Michael's alcove. Dolores and Ken were next door chatting with Donna and Darren Kelsey.

"If they have Show and Tell in first grade, I'm gonna bring in some of your cartoons," Maria asserted. "We didn't have Show and Tell the first week."

"I'd be honored, Maria. Just don't let your grandmother see you taking my cartoons to school. She'll give you a music stand made in Boston instead."

Maria took a step closer to Michael's drawing table and peeked over his shoulder. With a pencil, he had sketched shirts draped over hangers, each shirt missing a shoulder and a sleeve, lined up one next to the other on a retail clothes rack. A sign above the rack said, "Half Off!"

"I get it!" Maria laughed.

"Of course you do. But keep your voice down. It could be dangerous."

"Why?"

"Laughter in the Kelleher house? It's a sign of something terribly wrong."

"Why?" she asked.

Michael put his pencil down, wiped his hands, and spun his wheelchair to face Maria. The colorful Afghan that flowed from his lap to the floor got caught in a wheel. He pulled it out with a loud grunt.

"Why? Maybe because I'm always yelling at Afghans, and too much yelling makes your grandmother tense." But as soon as he said it, he sensed that Maria would have much preferred an actual answer.

"Can't get you to crack a smile, huh? I used to make my sisters laugh all the time. Grandpa too."

"What about Grandma?"

"Not so much, to tell you the truth. But don't let it worry you, kid. She's just had a lot on her mind — for about twenty-seven years or so. Probably a lot longer. The rumor is that she never even wanted to live on Long Island. So maybe for all these years she's just been learning how to deal with the cards she was dealt. I'm not even gonna ask if you know what that means because I'd bet my left leg you do. And that's the one I *can* bet."

"So it isn't me that makes her sad?"

"You're too smart to think that, Maria. Granted, she's probably a little pissed at your father," Michael said, "but how can she possibly be sad about you? If anything, it has more to do with me."

"That was an accident."

"Which doesn't make it any less shameful. To her, at least."

"I once heard her tell someone on the phone that *I* was an accident."

Michael touched Maria's arm.

"Well, if that's true, what you have to remember is that wonderful things come from accidents. You're a whole person, with a fascinating past, an interesting present, and an exciting future. If that's what an accident is all about, then God bless accidents."

Maria stared at the colors of the Afghan. She was deep in thought.

"I know, I know," Michael conceded, "you wish you knew more about your fascinating past. I'm right, right? Because frankly, I usually am."

Maria nodded.

"Your grandmother and grandfather never told me or your aunts much about the whole thing, Maria. I don't even think *they* know too much. I know they tried to find your dad for a while. The police helped for a few months. I think they even considered hiring a private detective. But nothing ever came of it." A thought occurred to him. "Hey, let me show you something." He pivoted his wheelchair once more to face the desk, opened the single drawer, and took out the playbill from *West Side Story*.

"Look," Michael said. He handed the playbill to Maria.

Maria looked it over cover to cover with quiet fascination. It had no photographs, and the biographical paragraphs about her mother and father were terribly scant:

"Maria Chibas (*Maria*) works at a diner and is studying to be a secretary. She was a member of the chorus in last year's Garnett production of *Carousel*. She says that what is most important to her is her family... Douglas Kelleher (*Tony*) is a New York City Police Officer. He has appeared in over 10 musicals on Long Island. This is his first at the Garnett Community Theater."

"It's not much," Michael said, "but at least you can see their names on the same page."

"Chibas," Maria whispered. She had been told her mother's name two or three times before, but it sounded fresh to her each time anyone mentioned it.

Maria continued to study the small booklet by glancing at the advertisements, the director's note, the names of other cast members, and the lists of scenes and musical numbers.

"There's a song called 'Maria' that Tony sings!" she said excitedly.

"'Say it loud and there's music playing'" Michael sang, "'say it soft and it's almost like praying. Maria, Maria, I'll never stop saying Maria.' I memorized it when I was a kid. We had the album from the Broadway show."

"You're a good singer, Michael."

"Compared to a turtle, maybe."

"I mean it."

"Listen, kiddo. I forgot how little meat there is on this bone," Michael said as he took the playbill back from her and returned it to the drawer. "But I have another idea."

"What is it?" she asked eagerly.

"Listen carefully: I can't get upstairs without twelve burly men and an act of God. So I can't go in into your room, which used to be your dad's room. Are you with me so far?"

"You mean to look around? For what?"

"And since I can't go into your room, I can't help you reach up to the top shelf in the closet to see what, if anything at all, might be pushed up against the wall. Following me?"

"I think so... but..."

"And since I can't go up to your room, I can't help you take out the drawers from your desk, which used to be your father's desk, to see what, if anything at all, might be stuck underneath, if you catch my drift. Maybe nothing, but maybe... well... who knows? Some ghosts from the past, perhaps. Am I making myself crystal clear?"

"Sort of."

"But here's the catch. Since I can't go up there, I *certainly* can't help you clean it all up afterwards, which you'll have to do all on your own. But I think you can handle that. Am I right? Of course I am. I'm always right."

•   •   •   •   •

Maria did all that Michael had suggested through his amusing hints, working fast so that she could straighten up before her grandparents returned from their next-door visit. Using a stepstool that was stored behind the attic steps, she reached up to the shelf in her bedroom closet. At the back of the shelf, up against the wall, she found a New York Mets baseball cap, three Matchbox cars, a small felt banner from Howe Caverns, and a crumbled centerfold from *Playboy* that, when straightened out, unveiled a color photograph of the naked Playmate of the Month from April 1967. As Maria exited the closet, she saw seven names carved into the wall where no one could see them if just looking in: Bonnie, Susan, Rosemary, Jodi, Karen, Helen, and Annette. Around all the names, in red crayon, was a big heart.

Then she took out the desk drawers. Behind them Maria found half a dozen baseball cards, a Hershey Bar wrapper, nearly a dollar's worth of change, and a piece of lined paper, crumbled like the *Playboy* centerfold. Once unfurled, the paper revealed an angry handwritten scrawl: "I hate your guts. I'll beat the crap out of you after school tomorrow." Maria was unsure if the handwriting belonged to her father or to someone else.

Although the results of her quest were far less than what she had hoped for, Maria felt as if she had taken a baby step forward in her quest to find out more about her parents. At least about her father. And that, she knew, was better than standing still or falling backward.

She went downstairs to tell Michael about her trivial findings — and also to thank him for the idea. Then she returned to the bedroom to put away the stepstool and return the desk drawers to their proper places. She deposited all the items she had found into a shoebox and placed the box on the floor at the back of her closet. Finally, she looked around to make certain that her room was just as it was when her grandmother last saw it. After all, as everyone in the family knew, Dolores's face always took on a look of annoyance whenever things were out of place.

5. WOODHULL AVENUE

Alexis accepted a proposal of marriage.

As part of her increased responsibilities at The Birch Tree Cafe, she had to meet from time to time with James Crowley, assistant director of client relationships at Vista Corporate Resources, the company that administered Birch Tree's health insurance policies. Jim was a friendly and personable man who gallantly aspired to appear dapper despite his shiny scalp, slight paunch, and tousled appearance. He and Alexis met twice for meetings at the restaurant and then Jim asked her out on a date. They went to dinner and saw a movie, and quickly discovered they had much in common, from their leisure-time pursuits to their emotional baggage. They also made each other laugh.

Alexis and Jim talked about their families and about themselves. As Alexis discovered, Jim was twelve years her senior, had been married once before, and had two children in college. Alexis told him she, too, had been married before and had not counted on getting married again.

"My motto in life, Alexis? Never say never," Jim told her amiably.

The next week, a few days before Thanksgiving, Jim took Alexis to the Westbury Music Fair to see Olivia Newton-John, and when the singer performed one of her popular songs, "I Honestly Love You," Jim turned to Alexis with a serious look on his face.

"I honestly love you," he said. "I think we're perfect for each other. Is that crazy? Let's just get married and say to hell with anyone who says we're crazy."

He purchased an engagement ring the next morning and gave it to Alexis during her lunch break at The Birch Tree Cafe. Alexis visited her parents after work.

"Twelve years," stated Dolores after Alexis shared the news with her in the living room. "He's twelve years older than you, Alexis. Even if you have children right away, he'll be ready to retire before they even get to high school."

"Is that your only complaint, Mother dear?" said Alexis, who lately had developed a much more confident way of talking to Dolores.

"Frankly, no. I'm also concerned that he was married before—"

"So was I!"

"And I'm concerned that you said he was an *assistant* director. Does he earn a good salary? At his age, Alexis—"

"Dad," Alexis interrupted, now addressing her father, who was reading the newspaper on the couch, "how many assistant directors are there at Aster-Paxton, and how old are they?"

Ken put the paper down.

"A dozen. Between the ages of twenty-five and sixty."

From his studio Michael called out, "Kenneth Kelleher, crisp and concise."

"Stop it, Michael," Dolores complained.

"The fact is, Mom," Alexis explained, "that Jim could have been a director, but preferred to be able to get out of the office and meet with people, instead of being trapped in the same building day after day. He turned down a director's position."

"Was that wise? Did he not expect to have a family one day?"

"Not a second one, no."

"I think that's admirable, Alexis," Ken offered, determined to let his daughter know her announcement fell on at least one set of approving ears. "I'd probably have done the same thing if an office position had been offered. Who wants to push papers around on a desk and never see new people or new places? Not me."

"Of course not," Dolores said sarcastically.

Maria came downstairs from her bedroom and sat next to her grandfather. She grabbed a section of his newspaper, though that may have been just a simple rouse to get him to raise an eyebrow.

"Congratulations, Alexis," Michael added. "I can't wait to meet Mr. Jim Crowley. And at least there two things are for certain. Two *good* things."

"What two things, Michael?" Alexis asked.

"One, he's old enough so that he'll never have to run away to find himself. And two, you'll always have good health insurance."

"How will you raise your children?" Dolores asked. "Didn't you say he was Protestant?"

"We'll raise them well," Alexis said.

"Let's have a toast," Ken announced. "I'll get the champagne."

"Can I have some?" asked Maria.

"Sure. Why not?"

"Ken!" Dolores objected.

"She has a lot to celebrate, too. She got an excellent report card yesterday, she pushed Michael's wheelchair halfway down the block all by herself, and maybe one day soon she'll have a cousin!"

"Dad!" Alexis protested with a smile. "Can we get through the wedding first?"

•   •   •   •   •

Later that evening, after Alexis had gone home, Maria overheard her grandmother tell Donna on the telephone that she hoped Alexis knew what she was doing. "She's taking such a risk, Donna," she fussed. "So much could go wrong." When she heard Dolores hang up, Maria walked into the kitchen with a copy of *The Tales of Hans Christian Anderson*.

"Aunt Alexis reminds me of something in my book," she said.

"What are you talking about, Maria?" Dolores sat down at the kitchen table, closed her eyes, and rubbed her temples.

"In one of the stories, there's a duck who's sad and lonely. She flies with the swans, even though the swans could hurt her. But she wants to take the chance. And then, one day she finds out that she's a swan, too! So she made the right choice after all."

Dolores took the book from Maria's hands and looked at the cover.

"Are you reading this for school? Or did your teacher loan it to you?"

"She loaned it to me. It's really a third-grade book."

"Of course it is."

As was almost always the case, Dolores had much on her mind. She had made it to Saint Matthew's only twice since the summer and felt guilty about that. Also, she worried about an upcoming trip that Ken had to take to North Dakota. Finally, she was angry with Caroline for deciding to stay at the Philadelphia radio station when her contract was up for renewal. And now, on top of all that, there was this news about Alexis getting married to a much older man named Jim Crowley. With these concerns swirling around in her head, Dolores nearly forgot that Maria was right beside her.

"An ugly duckling and a swan... Where in God's name did you come from, Maria?"

Maria took the book back from her grandmother.

"I came from my mommy and daddy," she said as she left the kitchen to go upstairs to bed. "And you and Grandpa."

•   •   •   •   •

Alexis and Jim planned their engagement party for the second Saturday in December. Dolores thought it was ill-advised and cited unpredictable weather as her primary concern.

"We're getting married in May, Mom," Alexis explained during another visit. "That's only five-and-a-half months away. There's not much time for an engagement party, but we *want* an engagement party. So we're gonna have one! Not only that, but Jim has a client who gave him an absolutely unbelievable deal on this gorgeous place for the party, in Connecticut. New London. The whole place is available that day. It's perfect. New London is about halfway between here and Boston, so all our Massachusetts relatives will be able to come. Jim's family is in Albany, except for his brother Gavin and his wife, so it will be good for his Albany family, too." So animated was Alexis about the engagement party plans that Dolores could hardly get in a word. "It's an amazing place, Mom. You won't believe it. It's like a crystal cathedral. All glass. If it snows a little, it will be even *more* spectacular. They import hundreds of flowers, and they fill the place with them. You can even stay overnight. They have guest rooms."

"I don't think that will be necessary."

As the day of the party drew near, several important decisions had to be reached, such as the advisability of letting Michael and Maria attend. Michael settled the matter. It would be a long day, he acknowledged—two-and-a-half hours to get to New London, two-and-a-half hours to get back, and about five at the party. "Probably a little too much for me and Maria. Anyway, it's the wedding that counts, and we'll both be there. So I say let the two of us skip the engagement party. Besides," he added, "I'm allergic to crystal."

Caroline, fully recovered from the assault, told Alexis that she would drive to New London by herself. She had considered bringing her new boyfriend, she said, but ultimately decided against it.

"He's fiercely bright, impossibly handsome, loads of fun, and rich," Caroline told her sister on the phone.

"So what's the problem?" Bridgett asked. "Why don't the two of you just drive up together?"

"Because his name is Lawrence *Katzenberg*," Caroline responded, emphasizing the last name. "You don't want your engagement party to be the site of another Dolores Kelleher meltdown, do you?" She waited for a response and heard only a muted chuckle. "Maybe I should say his name is O'Katzenberg. It's just a teeny tiny stretch. What do you think?"

The day before the party, Bridget and Kim slept at the Pearl Drive house. They arrived just as a brief snowstorm swept over Long Island, not severe enough to jeopardize the festivities, but nuisance enough for Dolores to feel validated in her original criticism of the date. For a short time, the wind gusts that came along with the storm were fairly strong. Dolores claimed to have heard wind seep in through microscopic cracks in several window frames throughout the house. She began spackling the frames that afternoon.

"You're doing this because you're angry," Ken insisted, as he watched his wife move from one window to the next with caulk, scrapers, mallets, and some other tools from the basement workroom. "It's a psychological thing, Dolores." He wasn't pleased.

"Just stop it, Ken," she protested." Do you want us all to catch pneumonia?" .

"None us have yet, and these windows have been here for forty years."

"Things change," she snapped.

"Not all things."

Jim Crowley stopped by the house to see if everyone was all right. He told them that the weather was expected to clear overnight, and that he had hired a professional limousine driver to take Dolores and Ken, and Bridgett and Kim, to New London. No one in the family would have to drive, he assured them.

"That's so nice, Jim," Kim said, as she and all the others sat in the living room watching the snow swirl across the picture window. They were all in pajamas and bathrobes, except for Dolores, who still had on her clothes from the day.

"What about you and Alexis?" Bridgett asked.

"I hired another limo for me and Alexis, and for my brother and his wife. Since Gavin's my best man, I thought he'd like a little treat. He's always been a little jealous of me for some reason, so this is a good way to make him even more jealous!"

Dolores paid little attention to Jim's story, but seemed pleased that he had stopped by. She told him it was very considerate of him. "Do you think you can lend me a hand while you're here?" she asked.

"Of course. What's up?"

She asked him to help her spackle the moldings at the top of the tallest windows.

"Oh, for heaven's sake, Dolores," Ken yelled. "He has more important things on his mind right now. He doesn't have to help you patch window cracks that don't really exist."

"I don't mind, Ken. Really," Jim said.

"Dolores, you've been fixing things on your own for years. All of the sudden you need help from a guy who's having an engagement party in a few hours?"

"I don't climb ladders," Dolores grumbled. "And the windows have to be done. I don't want you to do it with all your aches and pains, and Michael obviously can't do it. Would you like Maria to do it?"

"The first year we lived here, you put Santa and nine reindeer up on the roof all by yourself. I guess some things *do* change."

Jim helped with the windows. When he left, he stopped before getting into his car to admire the few Christmas decorations at the front of the house that Dolores had set up only that morning. He glanced up. The roof was bare, save for the new coating of snow.

About a minute later, the lights flickered off and on a few times in rapid succession. Maria gasped in surprise. Michael told her that such flickering used to happen often during snowstorms when he was a kid, and that there was nothing to worry about. Then, just as Bridgett stood up to go to the kitchen to put a pot of hot water on the oven, the lights went off completely. The house fell into darkness. Bridgett stood in place. The snow outside could not be seen because there were neither street lights nor moonlight to illuminate the drifts.

"Wonderful!" Dolores grimaced. "That's just great. How in heaven's name will the four of us be able to get ready tomorrow morning? I knew we shouldn't plan it for December. No one listens to me. We'll have no heat or light tomorrow morning. It will be impossible. Impossible!"

"Calm down, Mom," Michael urged—for his mother's voice was indeed getting higher, tighter, and more desperate. "I heard on the radio that it's gonna be a bright and sunny morning, so you won't have to worry about light. And chances are the power will be back by then anyway. This wasn't a hurricane. It wasn't even much of a snowstorm. You're panicking for nothing."

"It will still be impossible tomorrow morning."

Ken found a book of matches in the end-table draw, but had trouble lighting a match.

"Give it to me, Dad," Michael insisted. "I need the practice."

"What for?"

"Well, Mom doesn't want me to be a cartoonist, but I hear that arsonists make good money. And you can easily light a match sitting in a chair."

"That's an awful thing to say, Michael," Dolores complained. "Awful! What's the matter with you, saying something like that?"

"It's just a joke, Mom."

Just then, they heard a car pull up to the house, then a knock on the door. Jim Crowley walked in.

"I saw the street lights go out down the block as I was driving away, so I came back to see if the house was out, too. I guess it is."

"Maybe the whole neighborhood, for all we know," Ken said. "Maybe the whole Island."

"Is everyone all right?" Jim asked.

"Well, tensions may be running a little high, which I'm afraid is par for the course."

Dolores did not appreciate her husband's sarcasm and let him know that in no uncertain terms.

"You think this is funny, Ken?" she scowled. "Are we really prepared for a blackout? When's the last time you put batteries in the flashlights? Do you even know where the flashlights are? We are completely unprepared, and we have a big day tomorrow, and you're acting like it's nothing but a big joke."

"Everything will be fine," Jim insisted. "When I was getting more spackle in the basement before, I saw a whole bunch of candles on a shelf. Anyone have a match?"

Ken handed him the book of matches. Jim lit one, held it in front of him to navigate the basement, and returned a minute later with five decorative candles, each inside of a thick glass jar. Imprinted on each jar was a gold script logo that spelled out Boston Candle Co. As everyone remained silent, Jim lit all five candles with another match, and then looked around at the tired and impassive faces.

"There. Modern nerves soothed by ancient technology. It's like magic."

Michael particularly enjoyed the phrase and said so. Bridgett and Kim smiled and thanked Jim.

"Welcome to the family," Ken chuckled.

"Nice to be a part of it," Jim responded.

"Thank you," said Dolores to him, in a low, diffident voice. "You're very helpful."

Using one candle, Bridgett and Kim went to the kitchen to make tea on the gas oven. A few minutes later, they brought seven steaming mugs into the living room. Fifteen minutes later, the lights came back on.

•   •   •   •   •

Sunday morning was chilly, but calm. All the roads had been cleared. The limousine driver arrived at nine-forty-five and honked the horn. Dolores and Ken, and Bridgett and Kim, climbed into the roomy back seat at ten o'clock sharp.

Michael and Maria sat in the living room on either side of the Christmas tree and watched through the window as the long, black car pulled away from the house.

"Wow!" Michael said. "The neighbors will either think that Alexis is marrying a Kennedy, or that we found out your mother is really the queen of Puerto Rico."

Maria looked at Michael with a look that mixed amusement with melancholy.

"I have to remember that face and draw it one day," he said. "*That* will win an award." Maria's expression remained. "I have a surprise for you," Michael added. "A special Christmas present. But because of the circumstances, I have to give it to you before Christmas."

"Why?"

"You'll know why after I explain it. Here's the deal. I'm home most of the time, right?—at least for the time being. So I get to watch you and listen to you a lot, and I know beyond a shadow of a doubt that the one person you're curious about more than anyone else in the whole wide world is your mom."

Maria could not guess what Michael was leading to, though her mind was indeed racing.

"One day last month," Michael continued, "when Grandma was out shopping with Donna, and Grandpa was at work, and you were at school, I did a ton of research. Remember I showed you that program from *West Side Story*? Your mom's last name was listed as—"

"Chibas," Maria interjected.

"Right. So I wheeled over to the library, and the librarian helped me look up all kinds of stuff in old phone books, old newspaper articles, microfilm from some government agencies in New York City... It was fascinating, really. I enjoyed it. I even found a review of *West Side Story* in some small Bronx newspaper that said your mother came here from Puerto Rico when she was fifteen. When I got home, I made a ton of phone calls. Guess what."

"You found my mother?"

"Maybe. I think so. I *hope* so. I mean, you have to remember that English isn't the first language of your mother's family. So there might have been a few minor misunderstandings when I was talking to people who I think are your relatives. But anyway, what ended up happening seems real enough."

"What happened?"

"Well, I didn't actually speak to your mother—she may have been out at the time, maybe at work—but I spoke to a girl who translated for everyone else in her house. Her English wasn't great, but it wasn't bad, which was a blessing since my Spanish absolutely sucks. Anyway, I explained as much as I could to her, and this girl confirmed almost everything that I was saying! At least it seemed like she did. I mean, unless there's something really big that I missed, or something that fell through the cracks. The point is, I think I may have found your mother's family, Maria. Which means *your* family. And maybe I even found your mother."

Maria, rarely at a loss for words, was speechless.

"So my Christmas present to you is a round-trip taxi ride to 6876 Woodhull Avenue. That's in a section of the Bronx called Pelham Gardens. Remember my friend Marco from that camping trip I went on last year? Marco Katselis? We've kept in touch. Great guy. He called the other day. Out of the blue. Somehow we started talking about what I found out. About your family. And he came up with this idea. His father drives a gypsy cab, and the Bronx is one of the places he drives to all the time. You know what a gypsy cab is, right? Of course you do. It's like a taxicab that's not really a taxicab. Anyway, he said his father can drive you there, wait for you, and then drive you home, all before Grandma and Grandpa get back home from the anniversary party. I met Marco's father once. He's a great guy, too. His name is Argus. Argus Katselis. Sounds like something from *Star Trek*, doesn't it? So he's either Greek or from another planet. Anyway, he'll be here in about fifteen minutes. The Chibas family is expecting you between eleven-thirty and noon."

Maria was still without words.

"It's okay. You don't have to thank me yet," Michael smirked. "I'm also giving you an old watch of mine, from when I was a kid. Still works. I was gonna throw it out, but I forgot to. Here." He handed the watch to Maria. She put it in her pocket. "Keep an eye on the time. You have to be back home no later than five o'clock, preferably four to be safe, because Grandma and Grandpa will be home from the party at about eight. Maybe even sooner, knowing how your grandma wants this marriage to happen as much as she wants a root canal without Novocain. So even if there's a little traffic back and forth to the Bronx, you'll still get home in plenty of time. That's important."

"You think Grandma would like this idea?" asked Maria.

"You're too smart not to know the answer to that. She'd be—do you know what apoplectic means?"

"Yes. It was in a book I read last week. My teacher explained it to me."

"Good. Because that's what your grandmother would be. She'd hate it, whether it works out the way we hope, or not."

"If she really thought about it, she'd like it."

"Doubtful, sweet pea. As much as she has a hard time admitting to being a grandmother, she has an even deeper seismic fault in her head about... well... about a lot of things. What matters is making sure this plan works, and that we keep it between the two of us... Are you up for this little crazy adventure?"

Maria reached over to hug Michael.

"Yes," she said, and then looked down. "But do you think she wants to find *me*?"

"Your mother? I thought about that, too—about invading her privacy, more or less. About trying to do something she might not be ready for. I've heard stories about that kind of thing."

"Me too."

"So I broached the subject on the phone, as clearly as I could. And I'm pretty sure the answer was yes—that it would be okay. At least that's the impression I got. I mean, there were a lot of pauses and a lot of times I had to repeat myself, but... well... I think it will be okay. I hope so."

"Me too."

"I might be a friggin' nut-job for sending a six-year-old on a taxi ride by herself into the Bronx. I *know* I am. But ever since the first day you arrived, I knew you'd have a few cards stacked against you. Grandma would never even consider trying to help you find your mother. We both know that. But I know how much you want this. I wish I could go with you—and I probably really should—but it would just be too difficult with the cab, their apartment building... But you can do it. I trust you more than anyone else in the world. I mean, you gotta admit, you ain't your average six-year-old."

"This sounds like a story in a book. Maybe my daddy's old friend Daniel Hillman will write it one day."

That gave Michael pause. He looked down.

"That's something else I wanted to discuss with you," he said. "While I was at it, I also did a little bit of research on your dad. But I couldn't find anything. Nothing at all. Wherever he is, he covered his tracks well. And I know you know what *that* phrase means, too. I'm sorry, Maria."

"That's okay. It's not like I'm an orphan. I have a mother and a father somewhere. And I have a whole family right here."

. . . . .

The dark blue Chevrolet arrived on Pearl Drive to pick up Maria an hour and a half later than planned. Argus Katselis said he had stopped to help a stranded motorist on the Meadowbrook Parkway and then ran into traffic after that. Michael was concerned about the delay—but not overly so, since there was still plenty of time to accomplish the plan in full.

Argus tried to make Maria comfortable during the ride to the Bronx by talking to her amiably. That was his way. Maria sat in the back seat bundled in her winter coat. She was nervous, but tried not to show it. This was her first time alone. Argus had a friendly face, and that helped her remain calm. To Maria, he seemed to be close to Grandpa Ken's age, though a bit shorter. That soothed her nerves, as did the man's crisp white shirt, which was similar to what Grandpa Ken wore to work every day.

"Ever drive over a bridge?" Argus asked as he turned the car off the Grand Central Parkway onto the Cross Island Expressway.

"A few months ago I went to Boston, and we went over the Throgs Neck Bridge," Maria said.

"That's the bridge we're going over in about three minutes."

"And last year my Aunt Bridgett took me to see the Christmas show at Radio City Music Hall, but that time we went through a tunnel."

"The Queens-Midtown Tunnel. That's about ten minutes that way," Argus announced, pointing left. "Anything else?"

"Not really. Mostly I stay home."

"Do you mind that?"

"My grandma says I have to," Maria said. "She always says that things happen."

"Do you believe that?" Argus asked. "That things happen?"

"I guess. But that doesn't mean that *bad* things always happen. Good things can happen too."

"Are you a genius or something? 'Cause I'll be honest with you, little girl—you sound like one. What are you—nine years old?"

"Six."

"See what I mean?" Argus had the urge to continue looking at Maria in his rear-view mirror, but as a dependable and dedicated livery driver, he made sure to keep his eye on the road. "You *are* a genius! Right?"

"I don't know," Maria said, with her head down.

"I'm embarrassing you. I'm sorry. Can I tell you a secret?" Maria nodded; Argus saw her do so in his mirror. "I'm a genius, too. I'm not joking. My IQ is one-sixty-five. I graduated from high school at fifteen, college at eighteen. If I told you some of the jobs I've had over the years, you wouldn't believe it. Jobs normal people don't have. But for the last fifteen years, I've been driving a cab. You know why?"

"Why?" asked Maria.

"Because things happen!" He smiled in the mirror. "But guess what? Today I met this adorable little genius in my cab, and you know what she taught me?"

"That good things can happen too?" Maria posited.

"You bet!" Argus said.

·   ·   ·

Argus parked in front of 6876 Woodhull Avenue. It was twelve-thirty-five. The yellow, wooden, multifamily house was tall and skinny, three stories high, with identical tall, skinny houses on either side, nearly touching each other. Each one sorely needed repainting. There was a string of large green and orange Christmas lights draped loosely across the small front porch. The loops of the string were wide and swayed with the breeze.

"Looks like three families live in this house," Argus said. "I see two mailboxes but three doorbells. Crazy, huh?"

Looking for a spot to pull into, Argus drove slowly to the end of the block. He found none, but noticed a driveway with a locked gate in front of it. He parked there.

"Let's see... it's twelve-forty. After I take you inside, I'm gonna go pick up a few local fares and do some errands," he explained to Maria with a familiarity that was reassuring to her. "Then I'll swing back and pick you up in about an hour-and-a-half. About two-fifteen. Your uncle wants you home by four. Look for my car out front. Okay, brainy Janey?"

"Okay."

Argus turned on his hazard flashers, helped Maria out of the car, locked the doors, and walked with her to the house. He looked closely at the doorbells, which were too high for Maria to see. One of them had a little tag underneath that said Carlito Chiba.

"That must be it. That's the name your uncle gave me. I'll wait here with you until I know you're safe inside, like I promised your uncle, then I'll go. Deal?"

"Yes," Maria smiled.

Argus pressed the button. A minute later, the door opened an inch, and a man peered out.

"Sí?" the man said.

"Carlito?"

"Sí."

"This is the girl you're expecting. Maria. Maria Kelleher."

"Ahh — Maria," the man said. "Sí." He opened the door all the way. His white button-down shirt was loosely tucked into baggy black pants. He stood eye to eye with Argus.

"Hey — we could be twins!" Argus said, noticing the color similarity of their attire. "We even look to be about the same age. Except I'm originally from Salonika and I'm assuming you're not."

Carlito understood none of what Argus said, nor why he was smiling so much. Still, he, too, smiled as he gently grabbed Maria's hand and escorted her into the hallway.

"See you later, smarty pants," Argus winked.

"Okay. Thank you," said Maria.

The building smelled like cigarette smoke, and the steps going up the dark, skinny stairway seemed to Maria to be pitched slightly backward. It was disconcerting. She felt she could easily fall off and tumble down the stairs. The man clasped her hand. His complexion and some of his features were not entirely dissimilar to her own, and that was something in which Maria could take some comfort. Carlito led her to the third floor of the house, into a cramped apartment that — as Maria immediately noticed — had small rooms, rusty, old-fashioned radiators, and bare bulbs hanging by cords from the ceiling. Two women waited for them in what appeared to be the living room. One woman was small and slender and looked to be about the same age as Carlito. The other was taller and heavier and seemed much younger.

The younger woman said, "Esta es Rosalita, y yo soy Alexa."

"Alexa?" exclaimed Maria. "I have an aunt named Alexis."

"Alexis?" the woman repeated. "No, soy Alexa."

Maria looked around the small room. On every flat surface were small religious statuettes, dolls, candles, and most intriguingly to her, framed photographs. Without asking permission—for she assumed that asking would fall on clueless ears anyway—she turned around and ambled the perimeter of the room to look more closely at each photograph. She moved from bureau to end table to cabinet to chest, and sometimes returned to one or another, hoping to find a picture of a face that seemed familiar, an older version of her own, perhaps, or maybe a picture of her father, which she could compare in her mind's eye to those she saw at home. As she went from frame to frame, the three family members behind her spoke quietly to each other in Spanish. By their inflections, and the several words she understood, Maria knew they were asking themselves questions and offering possible answers to what they might expect from this unusual visit to their home.

The photos told the story of a close family. She recognized Carlito and Rosalita and Alexa. There were five or six others, some young, some old, and she wondered who they were. They all had genial smiles. In some photos they were laughing, in others they leaned against each other, making silly faces. Some shots appeared to have been taken in New York—two or three bystanders in the background looked on suspiciously—and others, more faded ones, juxtaposed slum-like buildings near muddy farmland. Maria wondered if those had been snapped in Puerto Rico. In those photos, too, the family seemed intent on having a good time.

The happiness evident in the pictures seemed to belie another kind of reality here in the Bronx apartment. Many of the items that crowded the bureaus, end tables, and chests seemed to Maria to have a touch of sorrow attached to them: the pain of a grimacing Jesus, the threadbare shabbiness of an old doll, the angry pencil scrawls, in Spanish, on the covers of booklets from the New York City Office of Puerto Rican Affairs, the melted wax from candles that had long ago dripped onto the countertops... As adventurous as Maria may have felt moments ago, she now felt lost. She had come for a purpose, but was she in the right place to have that purpose served? Why, she wondered, was no one saying anything to her about why she was there?

"Did you speak to Michael?" Maria finally asked, looking at all three of them.

"Michael es tu hermano?" the older woman asked.

"No, my uncle. Tio Michael. He said my mother lives here. Mi madre."

"Tu madre?" asked the younger woman. She looked puzzled, then turned around and called out to someone in the house. "Ana! Ven aqui, por favor." Her voice was loud and explicit.

A girl who seemed to be just a few years older than Maria appeared in the entryway between the living room and the rest of the apartment.

"Ven, ven," Carlito said to the girl urgently, waving his hands. She entered the room uneasily.

"Habla con ella," the man said.

Maria talked first.

"Hi," she said to the girl. "I'm Maria."

"I am Ana," the girl responded softly and cautiously.

"Did you speak to my Uncle Michael on the phone?"

"Sí." Then she reassessed and reconsidered her response. "Yes," she said.

Maria looked at the adults and then back at Ana.

"Is my mother here?" she asked.

"Mother?" Ana spoke slowly, as she still needed to think of each English word before she uttered it.

As the adults stood by listening to words they barely understood, Maria and Ana did whatever they could, given their ages and dissociation, to understand each other implicitly. For Ana, too, was smart and perceptive, and after about three minutes she knew two things for certain: one, Maria was in a deeply emotional search of a mother she never knew, and two, someone—more than one person, most likely—had made a grave mistake.

Through Ana's slow, careful, and methodical recounting, the story emerged. Indeed, her mother's name was Maria. She had been unmarried. She died in Puerto Rico upon giving birth to Ana. That was nine years ago. When Ana was seven, she came to America with her grandparents, Carlito and Rosalita, and her Aunt Alexa. They all lived together in the apartment.

"But my Uncle Michael said that Maria Chibas—"

"Mi abuelo—sorry… my grandfather… he give me the telephone when your uncle call. He say the man on the phone, he is talking about su familia in Puerto Rico. He say Maria Chibas, Maria Chibas. In my head, I think he talks about mi madre—my mother—Maria Chi*ba*, not Chi*bas*. I think he just makes a little…" She looked for a word.

"Mistake?" offered Maria.

"Sí. A mistake. He also say Maria Chibas has a daughter who today would be six. I am nine. I think, another mistake. So in my head, your uncle is a relation. A relation who make many mistakes."

Maria listened with interest—and sadness. Every time Ana mentioned her mother's name, she pictured her own mother Maria, despite not knowing what her own mother looked like.

"We have relations who come to U.S. before I was born. I never met," Ana explained. "I thought maybe your uncle is relation. He wants to visit. This is not smart of me. I did not understand. I feel… what is the word… terra…"

"Terrible?"

"Sí. Terrible."

"It's not your fault," Maria said.

"Sí. Yes. It is my fault," said Ana. "I should have… how do you say it? Understanded."

"Understood," Maria smiled.

"Understood. I *want* relation to visit."

"How come?" Maria asked, sensing Ana's unease.

"Mis abuelos, they worry we will be force to go back to Puerto Rico. I do not know why, but they are worry. Alexa, too. They think if we have more relations in Nueva York, it is a very good thing. I think this is why I tell your uncle okay for you to come. I did not understand. I did not know you were looking for your mother."

Ana paused and glanced down, then looked up at Maria and said, "Lo lanento."

"That's okay."

"But I feel… terrible."

Maria detected tears in Ana's eyes.

Ana turned around and spoke to her family in Spanish. By their faces, Maria could see that they, too, felt bad for her, saddened that there had been such confusion following such hope.

"They saying you look like a nice girl," Ana told Maria when she looked back at her. "They say you can visit any time you want."

"Thank you," Maria said. "Since I can't leave for another hour, do you want to teach me more Spanish? I want to learn as much as I can."

Ana smiled broadly. Her tears disappeared.

$$\bullet \quad \bullet \quad \bullet \quad \bullet \quad \bullet$$

After he dropped Maria off at the Woodhull Avenue house, Argus Katselis drove to the Dyre Avenue subway stop, elsewhere in the Bronx. He pulled in by a fire hydrant for a moment so that he could retrieve his magnetized taxi signs from the trunk and place them on his front doors. He kept the transmission in neutral. Then he reentered the car. Someone rapped on the driver's-side window with his knuckles. Argus saw a man with a blue shirt and black leather vest, upon which was fastened a gold badge on the right lapel. Argus rolled down his window.

"I know this is a fire hydrant, officer, but I haven't parked. I'm pulling out now. Sorry."

"Get out of the car. You're not allowed to park here," said the man, who had a considerable frame, stooped shoulders, curly black hair, and bushy eyebrows.

"If I'm not allowed to park here, why should I get out of the car? As I told you, I haven't parked."

"Out," the man barked.

"Real police officers ask for a license and registration first," said Argus, who suddenly realized that his car was marked for theft and that the burly man was not an actual police officer. His sharp mind considered two simultaneous questions: what would happen if he screamed for a cop, and what would happen when the real cop found out that his car was not a real taxicab? Before Argus could draw any conclusion, the man reached into the open window, pulled up the lock, and grabbed Argus's throat. He squeezed and shook him hard, then let go and opened the door.

"Out!" he snarled.

Argus was so stunned, so pained by the vicious choking, that he sat there without moving. He was aware of the numbness of his throat, but not much else. Two women across the street, in front of their own apartment building, saw the big man drag the smaller one out of the car and slam him onto the sidewalk. They ran inside the building. Argus found a reserve of strength and fought back. He even managed to stand. Swinging his arms and legs with wild recklessness, he kept his stronger assailant from overpowering him. With blind luck, he was able to land some stinging blows to the man's face and stomach. The burly man doubled over in pain, but then threw his full weight on Argus, and both of them fell onto the sidewalk and rolled three or four times into the middle of the street, with blood trailing every inch of the way. A car had to swerve to avoid running them over. More punches were thrown. More blood flowed. Sirens were heard. Two police cruisers came careening down the block and skidded to a stop in front of the struggling rivals. Four uniformed officers rushed out, two from each car, and began separating the men. But the officers needed very little manpower to complete the task, for both Argus and his attacker were unconscious.

Maria took Michael's watch out of her pocket. It was five minutes after two. She and Ana put on their winter coats and went outside to sit on the front steps of the house. They talked about school, about aunts and uncles and grandparents. Maria spoke about Westbrook Hills, which sounded exotic to Ana, and Ana described Caguas, the town in Puerto Rico where she spent her first four years. Maria tried to picture it in her mind, but confused it with images she remembered from a book about Puerto Rico that she had taken out of the library months ago.

Ana saw Maria's watch, and her eyes showed she was taken with its beauty.

"I had a watch one time," she whispered. "But it was stole. Mi abuelo says I cannot get a new one."

"Then I want you to have this one," Maria said. Ana was speechless. Maria handed the watch to her new friend.

"Gracias, Maria. Usted es muy agradable. You know what it means?"

"Thank you, you are very nice... Tu tambien, Ana."

"Gracias."

Ana hugged Maria. Once again, tears fell. Ana apologized for them, and explained that she cried easily, and that so many things happened in the small house that worried her from time to time. She said she had to be stronger. "I have to... how do you say it?... act my age."

"Nueve?" Maria said.

"Sí," Ana responded. "Sometimes it feel like *veinti*nueve."

"Is that twenty-nine?"

"Sí!"

Both of them laughed.

At two-thirty, Rosalita opened the front door and in Spanish told Ana to bring Maria back inside, that it was too cold to stay out on the stoop. Her grandfather, she said, would keep a lookout for the blue car from the upstairs window, which looked out onto Woodhull Avenue. Ana explained all this to Maria to the best of her ability, and the two of them went back into the house. Maria asked if she could use the phone to call her uncle. Ana said that their telephone service had been cut off just that morning because they were unable to pay their phone bill for several months.

· · · · ·

Being wheelchair bound, Michael could not pace, though the urge was strong. His version of it was to spin slowly in half circles, first in one direction, then the other. He did that relentlessly on the living room carpet. It was a few minutes after four o'clock. He had expected Maria home by then—a safe cushion of time before his mother and father were due to return from the engagement party in New London.

Michael ran through his head the conversations he had had with Marco Katselis and his father, Argus. 'No later than five o'clock, no later than five o'clock' was the line he knew he had repeated many times, and so he decided there was no need for panic. It was still early. Marco, his friend, was always very reliable, and there was no reason to believe that his father would be any different. At four-forty, Michael rummaged through the notes and papers on his desk and found the number he had for the family on Woodhull Avenue. He dialed. A mechanical voice came on the line, saying that the number was disconnected. He dialed Marco's number, which he knew by heart, but an answering machine informed him that Marco had stepped out and wouldn't return until the evening.

At five o'clock, Michael called directory assistance and asked for the number of a Bronx precinct of the New York City Police Department. He decided that if five-fifteen came and went and Maria still was not home, he would place that call.

At five minutes after the hour, the front door opened. Dolores and Ken walked in.

Michael was in the middle of the living room floor, the front wheels of his chair at a ninety-degree angle to his seat. Ken noticed it right away.

"Spinning your wheels, son?" he asked from the doorway.

Certainly, Michael was in no mood for levity, and that's what Dolores suspected immediately by his expression.

"What's the matter?" she asked in a low monotone. "What happened?"

Michael stared at his parents. Dolores took another step inside.

"Where's Maria?" she asked in the same manner and tone.

"Michael?" said Ken.

"Why are you home so early?" he asked.

"Your father wasn't feeling well. What is going on? Tell me."

Michael looked down. There was no way out of it. He would have to tell them.

"Maria isn't home — yet."

"Where is she, Michael?" Dolores said, interrogating and convicting him at the same time. Michael could tell by his mother's hastened breaths and twitching eyes that she would soon lose whatever self-control she had. Ken put his hand on her shoulder just as Michael began to divulge the plan. He recounted it with a calm, measured voice, and hoped that by doing so, it would give his mother a reason to be logical about it. For a moment, when he was through telling the tale, it seemed to him as if the idea had worked.

Then Dolores screamed.

"What in God's name is the matter with you? They might have been in an accident, Michael! Or maybe this Greek taxi driver kidnapped her. You don't really know him."

"He's one of the nicest and most reliable guys in the world, Mom."

"Why in the name of Jesus, Mary, and Joseph would you do something so stupid, so reckless?" she howled, ignoring his description of Argus Katselis. "Careless, Michael! Careless and stupid. She's six-years-old, for the love of God! Six, Michael. Why in heaven's name would you ever do something like that?"

"Because *you* never would!" he shouted back. "Never in a million years. And for the life of me I can't figure out why."

He knew there would be repercussions for saying it, but he no longer cared. Why, he wondered, could his mother not see that his intentions were good? Why was she unable to talk to him like an intelligent adult instead of a petulant child?

After Michael's retort, Ken took the opportunity of an awkward silence to put the gears in motion for Maria's return. He did it with a strong, composed voice to prove to Dolores that the gears were most definitely turning. He asked Michael for the address of the Bronx apartment building, then called the New York City Police Department with the number that Michael had previously written down.

"I'm driving out there," Dolores announced when Ken hung up the phone. "By myself, if I have to. Give me the address."

Ken explained to her how the sergeant with whom he spoke strongly recommended that they stay home and wait. He also told Dolores that the sergeant had checked and discovered there had been no road fatalities reported in the last few hours in the Bronx or Nassau County. Either Maria and the driver were stuck in traffic, or Maria was having such a good time that this Argus fellow simply let her stay longer than originally planned. The sergeant assured Ken, who assured Dolores, that everything would be all right.

Dolores was not appeased. She said neither of those scenarios covered the possibility of kidnap or murder. And with that, she went to her bedroom upstairs and slammed the door shut with such force that two framed photos under glass fell off the hallway wall and shattered into dozens of tiny shards on the floor.

"I'd better go clean that up," Ken said.

"Should you be climbing the stairs?" Michael asked. "Mom said you weren't feeling good."

"I coughed once at the party. Once! But Mom doesn't like Jim Crowley's family very much. So that one cough gave her the excuse she needed to come home."

. . . . . .

Without her watch, Maria could not know how much time had passed. She now knew Ana was a sensitive person, which is why she decided not to upset her by constantly asking about the time. That would merely show her own nervousness. Nor did she want to suggest that she and Ana go to another apartment in the building to ask to use someone else's phone to call her Uncle Michael, for that, too, would probably aggravate everyone's nerves. Ana, however, made that suggestion on her own moments later, though when she made the request to Carlito, he refused to let them do that and sounded quite adamant about it. Ana had no explanation for that.

Sensing that Maria was now worried, Ana said that perhaps the man who had dropped her off assumed she was having a good time and that, after consulting with her Uncle Michael on the phone, agreed to let her stay longer. Maria understood Ana's broken English well, but knew that what she suggested was unlikely, since all that Argus had seen was one man who didn't even speak English. He did not know about Ana at all, having never seen her. Still, Maria accepted it as a possibility.

The girls sat on the living room floor looking through a tattered book of yellowed photographs taken in Puerto Rico. It was a quiet, oddly serene way to pass the time. A little later on, a loud knock startled them out of their serenity. Carlito barreled through from another room and opened the door. In the hallway stood a policewoman.

"Sí?" asked a nervous Carlito.

"Is there a Maria here?" asked the officer. She looked past the man and saw the two girls on the living room floor, then stepped around Carlito. "Are you Maria?"

Maria shook her head.

"I'm Officer Parker. I'm going to take you home now."

"Did you talk to my Uncle Michael?" Maria asked.

"My sergeant spoke with your grandfather," Officer Parker said.

"Where's the man who drove me here?"

"We're not sure. We're still looking into that. Say goodbye to your friend, Maria," said Officer Parker.

"Adios, Ana."

"Adios, Maria. Maybe you will come back?" She searched the air for a word. "To visit?"

Maria felt in her heart that returning to the Bronx was an unrealistic prospect, but knew not to say that aloud. So she simply smiled.

"Practicar tu Español," Ana said.

"Lo haré, Ana. Gracias."

"De nada, Maria."

Officer Parker held Maria's hand as they descended the stairway. Maria walked slowly because of the sloped, rickety steps.

"Don't be afraid, Maria," Officer Parker said, mistaking Maria's caution for fear. "I'm your friend. You can call me Rosalie."

·   ·   ·   ·   ·

Dusk had set. The snow from the day before had already been pushed to the side of the roads and highways. When car lights shone on them, they appeared as white mountains, still untouched. Maria buckled herself into the back seat of Officer Rosalie Parker's cruiser.

As soon as they had settled into the car, Officer Parker told Maria that she knew about the plan to find her mother. "Your grandfather told my sergeant," she explained. "But I'm guessing your mother wasn't there. Was she?"

Maria said no, almost under her breath, and then, in calm, well-chosen words, described the entire afternoon to Officer Parker. At that point, Rosalie used her police radio to report to her sergeant that Maria Kelleher was with her, safe and sound, and that the family she had been with was not the one that she or her Uncle Michael had hoped for or expected. The sergeant said he would call the family in Westbrook Hills to relay the information. He asked Officer Parker if she needed directions to the house, but she reported she knew exactly where it was. Then she started the car and drove away.

As they entered the highway, Rosalie began to talk to Maria. She asked about Westbrook Hills, about school, and about her friends. She wanted to know about her aunts and her Uncle Michael, and about her grandmother and grandfather. Maria spoke in short, yet courteous sentences. Though she felt no alarm, she was unsure what to make of the fact that she was now in the back of a police car instead of the gypsy cab in which she had been earlier. Where was that nice man? What had happened to him? Did Michael know he had not returned for her? Would Grandma Dolores be waiting for them on the front stoop when they arrived? And if so, just how mad would she be when they stepped out of the police car?

All these thoughts went through Maria's head as she gave Rosalie Parker simple responses to her questions. She said she liked Westbrook Hills but was only just recently seeing more than her own front and back yards. She liked first grade, she said, but did not feel particularly close to anyone in her class other than her teacher. Her aunts and her uncle were very nice, she reported, and she enjoyed them very much, even more so when she was alone with each of them—especially her Uncle Michael. She said her grandfather was very nice, but worked too hard, and that her grandmother was very smart, busy, and capable, but always seemed to be a little moody.

"Capable? Moody?" asked Rosalie. "Those are pretty big words for a first-grader, aren't they?"

"I see them all the time in books. I read a lot of books," Maria said.

"What book are you reading now?"

"It's called *Little House in the Big Woods*. By Laura Ingalls Wilder. My teacher gave it to me."

"Isn't that for older kids?"

"It's on the fourth-grade shelves in the library at school."

"I see."

They drove for a few moments in silence, and then Rosalie asked Maria if she knew anything about her mother and father. Maria said that she and her mother had the same first name. "Her last name is Chibas. She sings and dances. But I really don't know anything else about her. And I don't know too much about my father, except what my Uncle Michael told me."

"How do you feel about that? I mean about your mother and father not being married to each other, or not living with you."

"My Aunt Caroline says that they probably weren't ready to get married, or even to have a baby. She says it's very complicated."

"I think she's right," Rosalie agreed.

"But I'd like to find them one day," Maria added.

"Your grandfather told my sergeant that your uncle thought he had found your mother. But I guess it was a big misunderstanding. That's too bad. You must have been so excited at first."

"I was," said Maria.

"Maybe you'll still get to meet her one day."

"Maybe my father, too."

"Maybe your father, too," Rosalie said. "What did your uncle tell you about your father?"

Before Maria answered, Rosalie had to swerve and honk her horn to warn a motorist on her left that he was halfway into her lane. Maria gasped and looked anxious.

"You okay?" Rosalie asked, after the offending car had gone back into its proper lane.

"Yes."

"Good." She glared in her rearview mirror at the license plate behind her. "Out-of-towner. Go back to Georgia where you belong, you moron!" she yelled comically for Maria's sake. Maria laughed.

"Do you live here? On Long Island?" Maria asked the officer.

Rosalie explained that she lived on Staten Island, worked in the Bronx, had a boyfriend in Manhattan, volunteered at a homeless shelter in Brooklyn, and often visited her parents in Queens.

"I guess I'm a real New York City girl, huh? I'm in every part of it."

"My Uncle Michael told me all about the five boroughs. Manhattan, Brooklyn, Queens, the Bronx, and Staten Island."

"You're a very smart little girl. That doesn't surprise me at all. Your father was very smart, too."

Rosalie glanced at Maria's face in the rear-view mirror. One eye was half-closed, as if she wanted to ask Officer Parker a question. But she stayed silent. It was only a few seconds later when they arrived at Pearl Drive, which made Maria forget about the question she had wanted to ask. It was almost dark outside. Maria stretched her neck to look at the clock on the car dashboard. It said six-forty-seven.

"Ready to go inside?" Rosalie asked, after she parked the car in front of the house.

"Am I in trouble?"

"Of course not, Maria. Why would you say that?"

The house was brighter than it usually was, whether day or night. Dolores had turned on nearly every light, upstairs and down. She now stood in the vestibule near the living room as Ken opened the front door. With her arms folded and her eyes glaring everywhere except at people's faces, Dolores seemed to teeter on the edge of fury, as she had been for the last hour-and-a-quarter.

Ken hugged Maria.

"Mr. and Mrs. Kelleher?" asked Officer Parker.

"Thank you so much, officer," Ken said with a faint smile on his face.

Maria walked over to Dolores.

"I'm sorry, Grandma," she said, a sullen look on her face. "I really am."

Dolores breathed deeply. She could not look directly into Maria's eyes.

"It's not your fault," she said.

"Don't be mad at Uncle Michael."

"We'll see about that," Dolores said frostily. "Go to your room, Maria."

Rosalie Parker took another step into the house. She stood next to Maria and put her hand on her head.

"Mrs. Kelleher, why don't we all sit down. Perhaps we can—"

"Thank you, officer," Dolores said brusquely. "You can go now. Thank you for your time. We appreciate what you've done."

Ken, embarrassed by his wife's rude behavior, went over to Officer Parker to open the door for her and to say a few words of gratitude.

"Officer," he began—

"You have a son named Doug, don't you, Mr. Kelleher?"

Ken smiled. "Yes," he said. "Doug is Maria's father. Do you know him?"

"I did. And I was actually here once before, in this house."

"Maria," Dolores barked, having realized that her granddaughter was still beside her, "I thought I told you to go to your room!"

"Dolores!" Ken rebuked.

"Don't 'Dolores' me, Ken. Do you know what could have happened to her? It's just luck and chance that we came home when we did? What if we didn't? Then what?"

"Michael would have done something."

"What can he do?" Dolores screeched, her rage finally unleashed. "He's a cripple, for Christ's sake."

From his alcove studio, Michael heard the conversation.

"This cripple was just about to call the police when you walked in," he shouted out indignantly.

When she heard Michael's voice, Maria ran over to him in the art alcove and hugged him.

"I know it wasn't your family," Michael whispered despondently. "I heard."

Maria nodded, though with a tender smile to go along with it.

"But the girl I met is really nice. I'll tell you about her later."

"Did the policewoman say what happened to Mr. Katselis?"

"No. But he was really nice, too. I hope he's okay."

By the front door, Officer Parker searched for a way to calm Dolores down.

"Mrs. Kelleher," she said, "I know this is a family matter, but if I may share a little something with you that I happen to—"

"We really don't have time," Dolores snapped back. "We've had a hard day, a long ride, and now I'll be up all night wondering how to deal with this... this mess." She was nearly barking now, as if to an ill-tempered child. "All night! Goodbye, officer."

Rosalie was too detached from the family to be offended, but still felt the sting and the futility of the situation. She wished her visit could have had a different outcome—but it did not, and since there was nothing she could do about it, she simply returned to her car and drove away.

Maria went upstairs to her room. Though it was only seven o'clock and her bedtime was not until eight, she went to sleep.

•   •   •

Dolores walked into Maria's room early the next morning. The sun had not yet risen. For a moment, Maria took as literal truth her grandmother's pledge to stay up all night, for Dolores looked tired and untidy.

"Maria," Dolores began, standing by the foot of her bed, "I still think it was an absolutely foolish thing to do, and I'm very surprised at both of you—you and Michael. You should have known better because you're a smart girl. And Michael—well, I just don't know what to think. But I tried to put myself in your shoes, and... well... I've decided not to be angry with you. Not too angry, anyway." She let Maria think about it. "All right?"

"I know you already have," Maria said.

The comment baffled Dolores. She had just pivoted to leave the room when Maria said it, but stopped sharply and turned back.

"What do you mean, you know I already have."

"I know you've already put yourself in my shoes. Remember the attic at Nana Mary Ann's house? You wanted to find out more about your parents. I could tell you wanted it a lot. That's why I thought you might understand why Michael did what he did."

Confused, mystified, and speechless, Dolores acknowledged that it was still too early in the morning to start the day. She walked out of the room and closed the door behind her. Maria heard no footsteps after that and had to assume that her grandmother was standing just outside the bedroom door. For just how long she did not know, for she fell back to sleep almost instantly.

6. FISHING FOR COMPLIMENTS

A letter arrived for Michael from *Esquire* magazine. At first he thought it was a joke because it came on April Fools' Day, and two or three of his friends were experts at duplicating logos and recreating letterheads that looked authentic.

After a closer inspection, Michael determined the letter was genuine. It informed him that a cartoon he had entered in a contest sponsored by *Esquire* won second place, and that a ceremony was to be held at the Russian Tea Room in Manhattan on the first Saturday evening in May. The theme of the contest was "Literally Speaking." The cartoon Michael had entered, which duplicated the artistic style of Norman Rockwell, showed a young man sitting lazily at a lake's edge, a long tree branch in his hand, pulling a line out of the water. Dangling on the end of the line are a half-dozen seaweed-covered words, including 'Handsome,' 'Talented,' and 'Intelligent.' The caption read "Fishing for Compliments."

Michael called *Esquire* and spoke to an editorial assistant named Mindy, who confirmed that the letter was real and that they indeed invited him to be honored. He could bring up to five guests. The prize was two-hundred-fifty dollars, publication of the cartoon in the magazine, a plaque, and a mention of his name in all the publicity material prepared and distributed for the contest. "Many past winners have gone on to very good art careers," she told him on the phone. Michael asked about transportation. Mindy said that winners had to arrange their own.

"What if I lived in Lubbock, Texas?" Michael asked.

"But you don't," Mindy said. "You live in Westbrook Hills. I have it right here in front of me. Isn't that on Long Island?"

"Unfortunately, yes."

"Then we'll see you next month."

Michael kept it to himself for several days. He considered hiding the news from his parents and asking the magazine to accept the prize on his behalf. Thanks to Maria, he abandoned that plan.

Maria sometimes did her homework lying on her stomach on the floor of Michael's studio, while he worked at his desk. On the fifth of April, she noticed him reading the same piece of paper three or four times and asked him what it said. "Nothing" was always his response.

"You don't read 'nothing' over and over. Tell me!" she insisted.

"Can you please stop being so goddamned brainy for five minutes and act like a pain-in-ass stupid six-year-old?"

"I will—as soon as you tell me what that letter says."

He wheeled back from his desk and turned his chair to face Maria.

"Fine. Are your grandmother and grandfather around?"

"Grandma's doing something at church and Grandpa just got home and is taking a nap."

Michael told Maria about the "Literally Speaking" contest at *Esquire*, his second prize win, and the ceremony in Manhattan. Maria was happy and excited for him. She hugged him with all her strength.

"Jesus, kid," he said, "I think you just cut off the circulation to my shoulder. Now I might lose an arm to go along with the leg."

Michael made her promise not to say anything to her grandparents; he had to decide when and how to break the news on his own. He knew that his mother would consider the entire affair pointless, convinced as she was that cartooning was not a suitable profession. Neither was she a fan of driving into New York City, and she certainly disliked navigating the wheelchair on city sidewalks and into and out of elevators. All this he explained to Maria, and she stared at him with silence and concern.

"Stop it," Michael said.

"Stop what?" Maria asked.

"When you have only one leg, you develop x-ray eyes. I can see the wheels turning inside your head. So stop it. Because no plan you come up with to get us all to go to the city will work. Trust me. I should know; I'm the king of messed-up plans. Remember the Bronx disaster?

Do you think I'll ever live that down? Chibas, Chiba... How stupid! And poor Mr. Katselis getting hurt on top of it. I just thank God that he'd okay now, and that you got home in one piece. I let the specter of hope make me deaf, dumb, and blind, and I'll regret it for the rest of my life. Wow — that's a great line. I should use it somewhere."

"*I* won't regret it, Uncle Michael. I'll never forget it."

"Thanks, kid. Anyway, Grandma and Grandpa aren't anxious to go to Manhattan to see me get an award for a cartoon. Besides, Grandpa is coughing more than ever now and sleeps whenever he's not working, and Grandma just started a part-time job on Saturdays. So it's a moot point. I won't be going. And since you're Maria, I know you know what moot means."

"I bet you'll go," Maria said. "Let's make a bet."

"You're on, kid."

$$\bullet \quad \bullet \quad \bullet \quad \bullet$$

Ken's coughing concerned Dolores, but it was no great surprise. Over the last few years, Ken had driven longer distances for Aster-Paxton, and also drank, smoked, and ate more than he had in the past. He had put on twenty pounds just since the time of his mother-in-law's funeral in Sherborn. In January, Dolores had compelled him to visit his physician, who told him that if he did not slow down and cut back immediately, his health would worsen quickly.

In February, Ken talked to the senior vice president of sales at Aster-Paxton. Ken, always held in high regard by management, did not fear being honest with the man; the vice president insisted that Ken reduce both his territory and his travel schedule. Other salesmen would pick up the slack, he said. His regular salary would remain the same, but his commissions would decrease.

Dolores was pleased with the doctor's orders, with Ken's acceptance of the changes he had to make, and with the company's support. To compensate for the loss in income, Dolores accepted a part-time job at the local pharmacy, which had recently expanded into new lines of merchandise for home decor. She took on the role of a sales and merchandising consultant every Tuesday, Thursday, and

Saturday morning. The owner of the pharmacy was a client of Ken's, and was pleased because he could promote the fact that his store now had a 'home decor expert' on staff. That brought in many new customers.

Michael resigned to the fact that his mother would avoid the *Esquire* ceremony, and that he, too, would probably have to avoid it. He accepted it and rationalized that the recognition he would get from the magazine was far more important than the dinner at the Russian Tea Room. Fleetingly, he wondered what the ceremony would be like, and just as fleetingly pushed it out of his mind.

The morning after Michael had told her about the ceremony, Maria barged into his studio and startled him out of his private moment of reflection.

"So it will be you and me and Grandma and Grandpa and Bridgett and Kim," she announced.

"You scared the crap out of me, Maria. How'd you know I was thinking about the *Esquire* thing just now?"

"I just knew."

"Like I told you, your grandmother won't want to drive into Manhattan, and after the Bronx fiasco, I don't think she'll let you out of Westbrook Hills ever again."

"This is different. I'll be with five adults."

"Forget it, Maria."

"We'll see," she said.

• • • • • •

Dolores picked Maria up from school the next afternoon. Usually she stood apart from the throng of parents in front of the building, but today attempted to chat with a mother or two. It made her uncomfortable, but she tried. Fortunately for her, Maria was one of the first students to bolt out the door.

"What's the matter, Maria?" Dolores asked. "Is something wrong?"

"No," Maria said. "I just wanted more time to talk to you about something."

Maria said it with such a beguiling mixture of innocence and maturity that Dolores, despite working against it, smiled.

"Okay. What do you want to talk about?"

"I made a bet with someone and I want to see who wins," Maria began.

"What kind of bet?"

"Let's pretend that one of Uncle Michael's cartoons won a prize and that he had to go to New York City to get it."

"Why would Michael waste his time entering comic book contests?" Dolores asked. "In my opinion, if he wants to be a cartoonist, he should try to get a job on a reputable magazine."

"Let's pretend he won the prize from a reputable magazine, not a comic book. Let's pretend it's a magazine that millions of people read. Adults."

With a pitiable smirk, Dolores said, "Okay, fine. Let's pretend. Now what?"

"If a limousine came to the house to take us to New York City so that Michael could get his prize in person—just like the limousine that took you to Alexis's engagement party—"

"Maria, why would a limousine pick us up for something like that? Michael is not famous. He's not a celebrity."

"We're making believe, Grandma."

They turned onto Pearl Drive and approached the house. Dolores saw how much work her garden demanded and quickly tired of the game of make believe. "Maria," she said, "I'm really very busy."

"If a limousine took us to New York City," Maria persisted, "you'd go, wouldn't you?"

"Is that what the bet is about? Who did you make this bet with?"

"I can't say. Well.... would you?"

"I suppose so," she said. "Are you happy now?"

"Yes!" Maria smiled.

Dolores walked up the steps to the front porch. Maria ran toward the backyard.

"Where are you going, Maria? What about your homework?"

"I did it during rest period at school. I want to go to the swings. That's where I do my best planning."

Maria disappeared behind the side of the house. Dolores, lost in thought after that last remark, used the wrong key to try to open the front door.

With part one of her plan settled, Maria needed quality planning time to work on part two.

•　　•　　•　　•　　•

In late March, Caroline broke her contract in Philadelphia and joined a radio station in New York City. She had a program called *Caroline at Night* that was on the air for four hours every Saturday and Sunday evening. In addition to the show, she made guest appearances at various events as a representative of her station two or three times each week. That's why she was so specific when she called her mother to tell her she'd be stopping by next week for a visit.

"Wednesday afternoon. One through five," she said to Dolores on the phone.

"Wednesday afternoon, one through five," Dolores repeated cynically. "I'm glad you can fit us in, Caroline."

"Don't be sarcastic, Mother," Caroline said. "You should be happy that I have my own show in the greatest city on the planet. I mean, it's a new station and it isn't the biggest in the world, but it's doing well. You used to worry that I'd end up running a naked commune up in the hills of California. I don't, you know."

"Yes, Caroline. I'm very happy for you. And I'm happy that you're not at that other vile station anymore. At least I can mention this one to people."

"That's the nicest compliment you've given me in a long time, Mom."

From Michael's studio, where she was doing her homework on the floor, Maria overheard her grandmother's part of the conversation. Since her plan involved chatting with Caroline alone, what Maria heard about her aunt's upcoming visit was good news. The hard part would be to talk to her in private once she was at the house. That wasn't hard at all; Caroline decided on her own to pick Maria up after school on the day of her visit.

Caroline gave her niece a big hug when Maria ran out of the school and into her arms.

"Can you walk with me around the neighborhood and tell me who you used to know?" Maria asked.

"Sure," Caroline consented. "But your grandmother might wonder where we are—so not too long. Okay?"

"Okay."

"See that house over there?" Caroline said, while making a left at the first block after the school. "The second house on the right? That's where Patty Alcott used to live. She was my best friend, for like two years. Until she and another girl decided they didn't like anyone else but themselves, so they formed their own club. They called it a chain gang. You know why?"

"Because they wore paperclip chains around their necks?"

"How did you know?"

"I guessed. I saw a bunch of paperclips on Uncle Michael's desk that looked like a chain."

"You scared me, Maria. Being a big brain is one thing, but being psychic is something else. I don't think any of us could handle you being both."

"I knew you were going to say that."

Caroline laughed so hard that she tripped on the curb and almost fell into the street.

"Just what I need—" she said, "another bruise for Grandma to see. She'll never let me pick you up again."

"Didn't you once say that you had a friend whose father worked on the radio?"

"Yes," Caroline said, as she and Maria turned left onto another block. "Right there. The house on the corner. Jessica Fontana. Very pretty girl. Her father did sports on a station in the city. I spent a lot of time there. Aunt Bridgett used to have to come over to tell me to come home. But we always ended up staying for another hour or so."

"Aunt Bridgett liked to play with Jessica, too?"

"Yes. She liked all the sporting equipment at their house. At least I *think* that's why she used to stick around. Anyway, why'd you ask about Jessica Fontana?"

"I wanted to talk to you about radio stations," Maria said.

"Radio stations? Why? Is that what you want to do when you grow up?"

"I was listening to a station yesterday. Not yours. They were sponsoring a contest to see who could come up with the best idea to get people to stop smoking."

"I wish your grandfather would stop smoking," Caroline murmured, as the two of them turned onto Pearl Drive.

"It was interesting because all these people were calling up, and they even talked about that radio station on television that night."

"Lucky for them. My station could use a shot in the arm like that. It's the smallest station I've ever worked at, even though we're right in the middle of Manhattan."

That was the opening for which Maria had hoped and waited. She told Caroline about the award that Michael would receive from *Esquire* and wondered aloud if Caroline's radio station might consider sponsoring the contest. As part of the sponsorship, Maria suggested, maybe the station could send a limousine to pick up Michael, Dolores, and Ken.

The idea intrigued Caroline, but she knew it was unlikely to happen.

"The thing is," she explained, "*Esquire* is huge. They've got tons of money. They don't need a small station like us to help them promote anything."

"But wouldn't they like it if a radio station talked about them anyway?"

Caroline thought about it.

"Maybe," she said, as she ran various scenarios through her mind. "I know the general manager would love to get an article in *Esquire* about the station. Hmm... Maybe I'll talk to him about it. He's a nice guy, and he likes me a lot. I think he has a crush on me. That's why he moved mountains to get me from Philly."

Caroline liked the idea more with every second that passed.

"Maria," she finally said to her niece, "I'm glad you got dumped on your grandparents' doorstep! Just don't mention any of this to

Grandma before it's all set up. She'll think we're in cahoots. You know what cahoots means, right?"

"Yes."

"When am I gonna learn never to ask you if you know what something means?"

• • • • •

On the evening of Saturday, May 5, 1985, *Caroline at Night* devoted all four hours to *Esquire*'s "Literally Speaking" cartoon contest. The event was broadcast live from the Russian Tea Room. *Esquire* planned to run a feature article in an upcoming issue about the fledgling radio station. All the contest winners, as well as three editors from the magazine, gave exclusive interviews to Caroline during the broadcast. A wheelchair-accessible limousine, hired by the station, had picked up Michael and Maria, and Bridgett and Kim. Dolores and Ken, who had originally planned to attend, had to cancel at the last minute because Ken was rushed to the hospital the night before for what the emergency room doctor called a 'cardiac episode.' Everyone knew that was just a slightly nicer way of saying he had a heart attack. According to the doctor, it was not at all life-threatening. From his hospital bed, Ken insisted that Michael still go to the ceremony and that Maria, with Bridgett and Kim as chaperones, go as well.

On the drive into the city, as the limousine exited the Queens-Midtown Tunnel, a rumpled young man rushed over to the car from the side of the road and washed the windshield with Windex and rags. The driver turned on the wipers to discourage him. The whipping wipers slapped the rumpled man's hands, and he barked out an angry "Fuck you, you son of a bitch" before moving on to the car behind them.

Maria seemed frightened by the man's anger. Kim, who was sitting next to her in the plush rear seat, hugged her close.

"Sometimes I can understand why Mom refuses to drive into the city," Bridgett murmured quietly.

"Oh, it's not so bad," Michael said. "I mean, that guy was a jerk, but most of them are just trying to earn a buck. Our society really isn't set up to give everyone the opportunities they deserve."

"Why don't you run for office, Michael?" asked Bridgett. "I'm totally serious."

"I can't," Michael said.

"Why not?"

Maria was eager to beat Michael to the punch-line.

"Because he can't run," she said.

The four of them broke into laughter. The limo driver, a dapper, silver-haired man in a tuxedo, looked in the rear-view mirror to see what all the fuss was about.

"In fact," Michael added, "if Mom and Dad finally throw me out of the house one day — which is my goal, by the way — I may become a street entrepreneur myself, just like that windshield washer guy."

"A street entrepreneur?" asked Kim. "What does that mean? What would you do?"

"I'd set up an easel on the sidewalk, put a bucket beside it, draw cartoons, and hope that people throw money into the bucket."

"If Mom heard you talking like that," Bridgett said, "she'd —"

"Cut off my other leg?"

"God, no. For some reason she feels guilty enough as it is. She doesn't need embarrassment on top of it, and what you said, Michael, is embarrassing."

"Well," added Kim, attempting to lighten the mood, "maybe when she listens to the radio tonight, she won't feel guilty or embarrassed."

"We can only hope," Michael sighed.

· · · · ·

In his private room at Nassau Hospital, Ken told Dolores that he was very comfortable and that she should stop worrying. She looked at him dubiously; the new lines on his face, the permanent furrow in his brow, and the oxygen tubes in his nostrils seemed to contradict his assertion.

Dolores sat in a blue plastic chair to the right of his bedside. She had taken with her from home the radio from the kitchen counter and turned the dial in search of Caroline's station.

"It's one hundred point nine," Ken said.

"Your temperature or the radio station?"

"Don't make me laugh. All these wires on my chest will pop out. My temperature is probably thirty below. I'm freezing."

"Do you want me to call the nurse?"

"No."

"I'll bring your warm pajamas from home."

"They won't let you, Dolores. This is a hospital."

"What law says you can't look nice and feel good in a hospital?"

"The same law says that if you want to look nice and feel good, don't go to the hospital."

Dolores had actually planned her own outfit carefully, despite the short amount of time she had to prepare. Once Ken was in stable condition, she drove home to change and pack a small suitcase to bring back with her to the hospital. She knew that in a way—as in so many ways before at various events and locations—she had to represent the entire Kelleher family (past and present, as she mumbled to herself occasionally), and as such, needed to look presentable. While in the emergency waiting room, Dolores saw several things that, to her pleasant surprise, made her appreciate her matriarchal role more than she might have otherwise. She saw three candy stripers walk through lackadaisically, offering lollipops to people waiting for loved ones. When Alexis was a teenager, she, too, had been a candy striper at Nassau Hospital and had become a favorite among the patients because of the enthusiasm she brought to the role—much more so than these three candy stripers. Then she noticed two teenaged ball players with broken limbs who were complaining bitterly about the pain. Bridgett, she recalled, had been a star athlete in junior high and high school, and she, too, had broken a few bones. Never, though, did she whine the way these two athletes were whining. Following that, she saw an open copy of the *New York Daily News*, with an article on page three about members of a high school 'security team,' as it was called, who beat up a group of innocent classmates. Caroline belonged to a dozen clubs in school and had been featured in many newspaper stories—stories that were far more interesting and admirable than this one in the *Daily News*. Finally, she saw an angry husband curse and throw things at a grainy television set mounted on the wall. Ken, for whatever faults he had, would never do anything as crass. He was a well-liked professional respected by dozens of businessmen and businesswomen across Long Island.

These various, seemingly random glimpses in the waiting room, and the memories that went along with each one, made Dolores realize that in their own special way, the Kelleher family was not at all inconsequential on this part of the Island. Through the years, she had complained to Donna about this, that, or the other thing; was it all justified? While perhaps not quite royalty, weren't the Kellehers a prominent family? And now, Michael was receiving an award from *Esquire* magazine, which made Dolores wonder if it would get infinitely easier for her to be more sympathetic to his passion and vocation than she had been before.

Why, then, did she still sense an ache in her heart about the way things had turned out? This is what she thought about while Ken was being examined, but was unable to come up with a satisfactory answer.

In his private room, Ken closed his eyes to rest while Dolores found Caroline's station on the radio. She kept the volume low while she searched. In those few moments of near-silence, she considered the current situation. Silently, she wondered if she should have demanded that all the children stay nearby until the doctors assured them that everything would be fine. Should she have allowed them go to New York City? Yet, was it not Ken himself who had insisted that Bridgett, Kim, and Maria accompany Michael to the ceremony? Ken, she decided, was right. She knew he was. They must not underestimate the validation Michael would embrace. One could not help but feel pride when all the siblings and Maria engaged in activities together. One of Ken's favorite self-styled proverbs was that when all his progeny were together, laughing and joking, the world was at peace. Dolores recalled hearing him say it many times.

"You don't mind that the children aren't here, do you?" she asked quietly.

"Mind? I *wanted* them to go to that ceremony. Did you find the radio station?"

"Yes."

"I think it's time. Turn it up."

She did, and they listened.

Dolores and Ken heard Caroline's cheerful voice. With his eyes still closed, Ken instinctively smiled; Dolores had trained herself to hold judgment until she knew no judgment was necessary. Caroline interviewed an *Esquire* editor about the contest, and while her quips were silly, her tone was respectful.

"That's our daughter," Ken said.

"Yes it is," Dolores responded.

They listened in silence while Caroline and the editor discussed *Esquire's* history with cartoons. Almost as if on cue, a nurse entered the room during a commercial break to record Ken's vital signs and ask if there was anything he needed.

"I'm fine," Ken said. "We're listening to our son get an award," he told the nurse proudly.

"Oh, how nice," the nurse said. "I was wondering why you brought in that radio. Most patients just watch TV."

"I guess our son has a face only for radio."

The nurse chuckled.

"Stop it, Ken," Dolores said, embarrassed by her husband's attempt at humor. "We're both very proud," she assured the nurse.

"I know," the nurse responded warmly, as she prepared to leave. "I live in Westbrook Hills. I remember *all* your children, Mrs. Kelleher."

The nurse departed as the program resumed.

"Yes, ladies and gentleman, he has the same last name as mine," Caroline announced, "and that's because he's my baby brother. All of you conspiracy theorists, all you miserable menaces to society, and all you bottom-feeding lawyers out there whose antennas just popped up like big ol' sausages, be assured that *Esquire* independently selected all the winners, without any involvement whatsoever of WNYG. We are pleased to share with you Michael Kelleher's second-place cartoon..."

Dolores and Ken heard both laughter and applause coming from the little radio as Caroline continued her narration.

"It's such an odd coincidence," Dolores remarked.

"What is?" asked Ken.

"Caroline's station cosponsoring a contest that Michael entered and won. What are the odds?"

"You really think it was a coincidence, Dolores?" Ken said. "Have you forgotten about that little girl who lives in our house? The one named Maria?"

"Maria?" The notion surprised Dolores—but only for a moment. She realized she should not have been suprised at all. "You think she somehow put this all together? By herself? How do you know that?"

"Oh, little bits and pieces over the last few weeks. I know she really wanted Michael to go, and I'm pretty sure she engineered the whole thing. But they don't know I know." Ken wanted to laugh, to shake his head in wonderment and amusement—but because of all the medical trappings, all he could manage was a delicate smile. "She's something else, that kid. Isn't she?"

"She's a challenge, Ken. You know that. Let's listen to the show."

Ken stared at her.

"Don't turn off your radios," Caroline announced toward the end of the segment, "or I'll come to your houses and unplug your heart-lung machines. There's one more segment."

"That wasn't very nice," Dolores chided, as if she had been speaking directly to Caroline through the radio. "Why does she have to say things like that?"

"Caroline's Caroline," Ken whispered. "And you're you."

Dolores turned to him.

"What does that mean?" she asked.

Ken was silent for a few moments.

"That radio is the one your mother bought a few years ago, isn't it? The one that was in her kitchen."

"Yes," Dolores said. "Is that an issue? What does that have to do with anything?"

"You never really wanted to leave Massachusetts, did you? Sherborn. Boston. I always wondered why you did."

Dolores rose slowly from the chair, stood stiffly beside her husband's bed, and leaned in ever so slightly.

"I left because I wanted to be married to you, and you insisted that we move to Long Island. Is there anything terrible or mysterious about that?"

"You were pretty convinced that you'd get me to move back there one day. Am I right?"

"That's ridiculous, Ken," Dolores said, her voice steady and firm. "What's gotten into you? You say you're cold, but frankly it sounds like you have a fever."

"It's not ridiculous, Dolores. You lost that battle. But if you think about it, it's really the only battle you ever lost."

On the radio, a commercial played in the background and, despite its jumpy tune and overeager announcer, neither Ken nor Dolores heard it.

"Do you remember," Ken said, "how I really wasn't all that interested in getting married so quickly?"

"Do you regret it?"

"Not at all. But that's not the point I'm getting at. Do you remember how I resisted? How I came up with excuse after excuse? How I wanted to wait a little longer? And yet, somehow, you managed to get me to do it. We got married when you wanted to, and where you wanted to, and how you wanted to."

"Ken..."

"Lower that," he said, nodding to the radio. Dolores turned the volume knob. "Remember when we moved into the house, how I wanted to turn the basement into a poolroom, and paint black and white squares on the garage door like a checkered racing flag—"

Dolores closed her eyes and shook her head.

"Stop it, Ken."

"Let me make my point! Somehow, Dolores, it ended up being a Sherborn house through and through, a Farrell house, just the way you pictured it."

"And you hate the house?"

"No, I don't hate the house. But again, there's a point here that I'm trying to make that you're not letting me make. Sherman Oaks. Remember? Who was it that wanted to try something new in California? Was it Douglas, or was it you?"

"You were as willing as Douglas and I, Kenneth!"

"But you were the one who pushed for it and made it happen."

"Because if I don't make things happen, they don't happen!"

A doctor poked his head into the room to see if everything was all right. Dolores assured him that everything was fine. The doctor continued on his way.

"Why don't you just say what you want to say, Ken? Enough with this beating around the bush."

"Heredity," he said. It was almost a whisper.

"Heredity? What in God's name are you talking about?"

"Maria. She's cunning. Bright. Shrewd. Determined... The contest, the limo... Now I know where she gets it from, Dolores. She's your granddaughter, all right."

Ken closed his eyes once again. The discussion had tired him to the point of exhaustion. Dolores turned around and sat on the chair. It was only when a nurse walked in to record Ken's vitals once more that she realized another half-hour had passed.

7. NO EUPHEMISMS

"Mine's bigger than yours," Michael said to Father Thomas Woodward at Saint Matthew's Church. Father Woodward laughed the moment he realized Michael was referring to their wheelchairs.

"With a sense of humor like that, it's a miracle your mother lets you stay in her house," the elderly priest joked.

It was the second Sunday in June, a half-hour before the scheduled ceremony that would unite Alexis Kelleher and Jim Crowley in marriage. Father Woodward struggled with his wheelchair in the church lobby. He had started to use it just that week after begrudgingly accepting the fact that he could no longer get around on his own.

"If you need any help figuring things out," Michael offered, "just ask. I'm a pro. If you don't mind my saying so, I think you need a different model. That one looks a little snug."

"Thank you, Michael. I tend to agree. I'll mention it to my orthopedic guy at my next appointment. But before *that* holy hell, there's holy matrimony to contend with."

Michael smiled.

"With a sense of humor like *that*," he said, "it's a miracle my mother still comes to this church."

"She's been one of my most loyal parishioners since your family moved to Westbrook Hills. And one of the most challenging, I might add."

Ken, several steps away, had overheard the entire exchange between Michael and Father Woodward, and was pleased that Dolores was not nearby. She was tense enough.

Over the past few months, Ken noticed how his wife had been making an effort to feel more relaxed with each family member and to enjoy them more. She hadn't been entirely successful, but he was proud of her. Despite the earnest steps that Dolores took forward, the wedding of Alexis and Jim seemed primed to force her back a step or two. There were at least three reasons for that. First, her brothers and sisters would be at the wedding, and whenever they boasted about their own children—her nieces and nephews, all of whom had that decisive Farrell look that her own brood, other than Michael, seemed to lack—Dolores could not submerge a tinge of melancholy. Among her six nieces and nephews were three attorneys, two physicians, one vice-chairman of the English department at Harvard University, and one head of investments at the Bank of New England in Boston.

There was also the fact that whenever Alexis, Bridgett, and Caroline were together, they formed a tight, chattering circle in which Dolores was rarely invited. As far as Ken could tell, there was nothing malicious about it. Dolores got along relatively well with her three daughters; the chattering circle was simply a consequence of many years of shared family experiences. And since the three of them would be at the wedding, with Kim a fourth musketeer, it was likely that Dolores's pensive feelings would return when she saw all the younger women together.

The last reason was that for all of Dolores's contributions to the landscaping of Saint Matthew's, of which she had been very proud, a newly hired business manager had recently removed three of her four gardens to install a playground and a basketball court. Ken feared that at the church, Dolores would feel an unwelcome sense of personal injustice.

"Are you okay, Dolores?" Ken asked as they walked into the sanctuary.

"Yes," she said. "Why?"

"No reason."

The ceremony was simple yet elegant, and Dolores took solace in the fact that several guests commented on the one garden that remained.

The reception took place at a catering hall in Syosset, a few towns away from Westbrook Hills. Jim had paid for everything and spared no expense. It was a lovely affair. For all of Ken's worries, Dolores seemed to have a pleasant time. Her smiles were not expansive, but she did smile, and often. Her graciousness to guests, while subdued, was sincere. She spoke at length with her sisters Katherine and Patricia, and to her brothers Timothy and Randall, as well as to their spouses and children. She chatted for a few moments with Ken's brother, Joe, and was cordial to Caroline's boyfriend, Larry Katzenberg. As Dolores told Alexis when they found themselves alone in the bathroom, Caroline merely loved the company of men and was almost never without a boyfriend, so it was folly to think that she would ever be serious with anyone in particular. Alexis pointed out, however, that Caroline and Larry appeared to be quite fond of one another, and that Caroline seemed to treat this man more reverently than any of her previous beaus.

"That's just wishful thinking on your part, Alexis," Dolores said. "Perhaps it's simply that you don't want to be the only married sister."

Alexis seemed poised to respond, but held her tongue—for a few moments, at least. "Are you having a good time?" she finally asked her mother.

"Of course," Dolores said. "Why wouldn't I?"

"Well, families are funny... And I noticed that Donna isn't here. I know how much you two like each other and always talk..."

"Darren had to go to Cape Kennedy. Something about the space shuttle. Donna was told she could stay with him for a week. All expenses paid. How could she refuse?"

"Are you upset?"

"Why should I be upset?"

Ken sat for most of the reception to avoid exacerbating his near-constant state of exhaustion. He, too, was cordial, and even danced once with Dolores to a ballad from the nineteen-forties.

There were no children Maria's age at the wedding, but Maria had a fine time eating and chatting and dancing. Michael danced with her by letting her stand on the footrests of his wheelchair. The sight unnerved Dolores, but Ken assured her it was all right.

"No birthday party this year?" Michael said to Maria, as the two of them made slow circles on the dance floor. Guests parted the way whenever the wheelchair came near and always smiled brightly at the unusual yet affectionate picture. "Are you sad about not having a fiesta de séptimo cumpleaños this year?"

"It was my idea," Maria said. "Grandma asked me about it."

"What did you say?"

"I said that one gigantic event each summer is enough. And this is it."

"Well, you could have had a tiny party instead."

"What would be the point of *that*?"

Michael laughed so raucously that he bumped into his Uncle Timmy, who promptly joked that he'd sue him for every penny he had. Michael assured Timmy that every penny he had amounted to a paltry sum hardly worth suing over.

Maria was pleased by the attention she received from her Massachusetts relatives. At one point, aware of how disappointed her grandmother was that Donna was unable to attend, Maria whispered to Timothy's handsome twenty-seven-year-old son Richard that he should ask his Aunt Dolores to dance. Richard did as suggested. No one could tell by her expression whether Dolores felt delight or dismay.

·   ·   ·   ·   ·

A week after the wedding, on a Tuesday afternoon, Maria handed Dolores a letter when she went to pick her up at school. According to Maria, Miss Besher, her first-grade teacher, called it a very important note that her grandparents should read right away.

The handwritten note informed Dolores and Ken Kelleher that they had to decide whether to allow Maria to bypass a year of class and begin third grade in September. All that Dolores and Ken needed to do was to send back a signed note of approval.

"You knew about this, didn't you?" Dolores said offhandedly to Maria after she read the note on the walk home.

"Sort of," Maria smiled. "What are you going to write back?"

"I'll talk to your grandfather about it tonight."

Michael was not yet home. He was at the YMCA for a day-long meeting of handicapped counselors scheduled to work at the Y that summer. The meeting was scheduled to end at eleven at night.

As midnight approached, Dolores realized she had forgotten to speak with Ken about the note. He was not in the living room. She glanced toward his bedroom; the door was open.

"Ken, I need to discuss something with you," she said as she took a step closer to the room. That's when she noticed Ken, sitting in his desk chair, was leaning precariously to one side.

"Ken?"

Dolores walked in and saw that his left eye was closed, that the eyeball in his right eye was hidden, and that his tongue was hanging out of his mouth. Drool dripped onto the arm of the chair. When he sensed her presence, he mumbled unintelligibly.

"Ken!" she shouted. "Kenneth! What's the matter? What's happening? Ken!"

She cupped his face in her hands and shook it gently, but that merely made him look even more frightened and caused him to lean even further to the side. Slowly, he slid to the floor.

"Ken! Ken!"

Dolores assumed Maria had heard her shouting and was awake by now.

"Maria," she called out, hoping her granddaughter was at the top of the stairs, 'it's Grandpa. Something's happened. Maybe a stroke. Or another heart attack. I don't know. Call someone. I don't know who. Just call someone."

Maria went to the phone in the kitchen and dialed Alexis and Jim Crowley's number, which she knew by heart. The two of them had returned just that morning from a short honeymoon in Cape May, New Jersey, and were living in a small house three miles from Westbrook Hills that Jim had purchased after the engagement party. Jim answered and instantly knew that something was amiss; it was already past midnight. Maria told him what her grandmother had said and asked him what to do. Jim told her to dial nine-one-one; he instinctively knew that Maria could relate the problem and provide the nine-one-one operator with whatever additional information was needed. Jim said that he and Alexis would rush over to the house.

While they waited for the ambulance, Dolores did everything she could to make Ken as comfortable as possible on the floor. She straightened his head and put pillows underneath, gave him a glass of water, put a cool washcloth on his forehead, and covered him with a blanket. He remained eerily quiet. Three vehicles arrived at nearly the same moment. One was the ambulance, the second was Jim and Alexis, and the third was the handicap van from the YMCA. On the front lawn, in the darkness, Alexis explained the situation to Michael, who wheeled himself to the ramp at the back of the house to go inside. Alexis went through the front door and hugged Maria. Jim followed and moved some furniture aside to make it easier for the paramedics to wheel the gurney in and out of the living room.

"I'll get my pocketbook," Dolores said in a shaky whisper. "I don't know where it is. Maybe I should go to the bathroom first. I feel a little ill... And cold. I mean hot. Oh God..."

"Stay here, Mom," Jim said sternly. "You're in no shape to go right now." The two paramedics wheeled the gurney, with Ken upon it, through the living room. "Do you have some kind of sedative you can take?"

"I think so," Dolores said. "A little blue pill that the doctor gave me last time, when... well... when..."

"Take it. Just one. Now listen, Mom. Alexis and I will follow the ambulance, find out what we can, and then we'll come back in a little while." Jim was not asking her — he was *telling* his mother-in-law what the plan was. "Then I'll drive you to the hospital — you shouldn't drive yourself — and Alexis will stay here with Michael and Maria. Maria, will you be all right staying with Grandma and Uncle Michael for about an hour or so?"

"Yes," she said.

"Good girl."

Jim and Alexis went to Jim's car. The paramedics put the gurney in the back of the ambulance, then drove away swiftly with the siren off. Dolores looked out the living room window and was glad the siren was off; that way, few if any neighbors would know that something serious had happened. "I can't go through all those questions again," she said to no one in particular. "All the explanations..."

"Mom," said Michael, who had wheeled himself into the living room, "can I get you anything?"

"No." She looked at him. "You're home so late. It's past midnight."

"I told you I'd be home late. The meeting lasted until eleven-thirty."

"What meeting?"

"At the Y," Michael reminded her. "For the camp I helped set up. Remember?"

"What about Maria..."

"What *about* Maria?"

"Camp. This summer. She should go."

Maria listened and knew that her grandmother's mind was a jumble of nerves and colliding thoughts.

"Grandma," she said, "should I find the little blue pill for you?"

"How do you know about that?"

"Maria," said Michael, "it's probably upstairs in her bathroom. But I don't know if you're tall enough to find it in the medicine cabinet."

"I'm good at reaching tall things," Maria smiled at Michael. "Remember?"

"No ladders!" Dolores barked erratically.

"No. I'll use a chair," Maria assured her. "I'll be careful."

Maria found a little bottle of blue pills and took it downstairs to show to Michael. He confirmed that they were the right ones. He gave one to his mother with a glass of water. Dolores sat on the couch and within minutes fell asleep. Michael, as alert as if it were midday, wheeled himself over to his studio. He told Maria to follow him.

"Are you okay?" he asked once they were both in the alcove.

"I guess. It's a little scary," Maria said.

"I know. It is. But we'll get through it. So don't be scared, and don't be sad, because your grandfather is a tough guy, and your grandmother is a tough lady, and Aunt Alexis and Uncle Jim are really good people. Everything will be okay. Okay?"

"Okay."

Jim called an hour later. Michael wheeled into the kitchen to answer the phone. Ken had had a mild stroke and another cardiac episode, Jim explained. The doctors said his prognosis was fair. He'd never be the same, but was in no risk of dying.

"Cardiac episode?" Michael said. "If you're gonna stay in this family, Jim, you have to know that I despise euphemisms."

"Sorry, Michael. A heart attack."

"Listen, Jim. I know you said you'd come back and drive her to the hospital, but she took one of those pills and is out like a light. Why don't we tell her first thing in the morning?"

"She won't get mad about that?" Jim asked.

"Oh, she will! But I don't think even an atom bomb would wake her up right now. She looks more peaceful at this moment than I've ever seen her. I don't think that's a bad thing."

Jim agreed with the plan. Michael would tell her the moment she awoke, then Jim would stop by to take her to the hospital.

Michael hung up the phone and looked at Maria. "Was that mean of me to say?" he asked. "About Grandma?"

"A little," Maria said. "But as long as everything will be okay, you can be forgiven."

"Thank you."

8. A NEW GARDEN

Donna returned from her brief vacation on the Space Coast of Florida. Darren had to remain longer for the late June liftoff of Space Shuttle Discovery. When she heard the news that Maria qualified to skip second grade, Donna called Darren in his Cocoa Beach hotel room. He said he had planned to leave for the airport in an hour. Donna asked him to please stop by the Cape Kennedy visitors' center first and buy a school lunchbox she had seen there during her stay. Darren arrived home after dinner and gave the lunchbox to Donna. She put it in a bag and rushed next door.

"I have a present for you, Maria."

She had come in through the kitchen door unannounced. Maria was putting away silverware from the dishwasher. Michael was in his studio.

"A present?" Maria asked.

"For third grade!" Donna took the lunchbox out of the bag and handed it to Maria. "It's the Discovery. The Space Shuttle. See all the stars and the moon, and there's Earth in the distance."

Maria found the lunchbox captivating.

Donna said, "I'm sure that most second-graders will have 'Rainbow Brite' lunchboxes and 'Inspector Gadget' lunchboxes, and things like that. But a special *third*-grader like you should have something different. Do you like it?"

"I love it. Thank you, Donna."

"You're welcome, honey."

Dolores had been in Ken's room giving him his last dose of medicine for the day. When she came to the kitchen, she and Donna chatted a while. When Donna left the house to return home to her husband, Dolores asked Maria to sit with her.

"I had been planning on asking you this for a while, Maria, but something always came up. Do you think you might like to go to camp this summer?"

Dolores had seen an article in *Newsday* about a camp fair to be held on Saturday on the football field behind John F. Kennedy High School in Bellmore. That was a fifteen-minute drive from Westbrook Hills. There would be representatives from day camps all over Long Island. Dolores read the article twice and noted that some of the camps had book clubs while others had music lessons, theatrical productions, and art workshops. They all had sports programs. She mentioned all this to Maria and showed her the article from the newspaper. Maria seemed both receptive and uncertain at the same time.

"But Michael said he's going to teach art at the YMCA and coach a basketball team," she said.

"So? What has that got to do with anything?"

"Well, that means Michael won't be home a lot this summer. And Grandpa is sick and is in his room a lot, and... well... you'll be all alone if I'm at camp all day. I just thought..."

"You're seven years old, Maria. There aren't many children on the block your age. Your friend Debbie goes away for most of the summer. Don't worry about me and Grandpa. Just because I let so many people down doesn't mean I have to let you down, too. I think you should go to camp."

Michael, who overheard the conversation from his studio, wheeled into the kitchen.

"You haven't let anyone down, Mom," he said. "Why do you say things like that?"

"I didn't mean anything by it, Michael. Forget I said it. It's late. I'm tired. I don't know what I'm saying. Goodnight, you two."

And with that, Dolores left the kitchen and retired to her bedroom.

"Cool lunchbox," Michael said to Maria, once he knew that his mother had climbed the stairs. "I wish I could go to outer space sometimes. It's far away from Westbrook Hills, and you don't have to use your legs to get around! Wanna come?"

"No thanks," she said. "Grandma needs me." Then she, too, retired to her bedroom, leaving Michael alone in the kitchen, perhaps more perplexed than he had been in quite a while. Still, he smiled.

●　　　●　　　●　　　●　　　●

Several hundred adults and children crowded the football field at John F. Kennedy High School. The weather was delightful, which no doubt encouraged attendance. Ice cream and popcorn were free for all attendees. As part of the festivities, a woman painted faces with watercolors, a man created animals out of balloons, and a clown rode a tall unicycle while juggling plastic bowling pins. Dolores and Maria went from one booth to another and listened to representatives from each camp talk about activities and counselors, and snacks and buses.

"I don't know if it's easier or harder to have so many good choices," Dolores said to no one in particular as she and Maria walked away from one booth. A woman several feet away overheard her and laughed.

"That's so true," the woman said. "So many good ones." When she and Dolores looked at each other, a flash of recognition registered between them.

"Dolores? Dolores Kelleher?"

Dolores could not put a name to the face.

"It's Michelle Shepherd," the woman said. "Jodi's mom. Bridgett's friend from high school."

"Oh, of course. How are you, Michelle?"

"We must be the only two grandmothers here. I'm here with my son-in-law Ryan, and my grandson, Billy. This is your granddaughter, Maria, isn't it? We've heard all about her."

"Say hello, Maria," Dolores instructed.

"Hi," Maria said. "You knew my Aunt Bridgett?"

"I did! Always playing sports, as I remember. I heard she became a gym teacher, which isn't a surprise, I suppose. Is she married?"

Despite how affable Michelle appeared to be, Dolores wanted to move along. Maria gave her just such an opportunity by wandering a few feet toward another booth.

"Maria!" Dolores shouted, feigning panic.

"Oh, she's fine," Michelle said. "From what I heard, that girl can probably go across the country by herself if she wanted to."

"Well, I'm not sure about that. She's still only seven years old."

"Douglas's girl, is that right?"

Dolores wished for a second invisible tug in another direction.

"I'm sorry, Michelle. She has a habit of wandering off. So nice to see you." Dolores ambled away. "Say hello to Jodi. And to your husband."

"I will. Bye."

After another twenty minutes of walking around, Dolores and Maria settled on Rolling Hills Day Camp, in the town of Albertson, a few miles northwest of Westbrook Hills. She gave the representative a check. Dolores said she liked the diversity of its programs. Maria said she was happy it was close to home.

• • • • • •

It was not a premonition but a certainty: With no doubt that Maria would receive an exemplary final report card, Dolores arranged a family get-together on the evening of her last day of school. On that day, Maria did indeed bring home a report card filled with E's, for Excellence. In the teacher comment section, Miss Besher wrote: "Maria has been a pleasure to have in class. Her progress is always surprising but never unexpected. Second grade will miss her, but as we all know, she will not miss second grade. I am certain she will thrive in third! "

To Dolores's pleasant surprise, everyone had accepted her invitation. No one had a conflict. Bridgett and Kim arrived first, just after four-thirty, followed by Alexis and Jim at five. Caroline and Larry ran into some tunnel traffic on their way out of Manhattan and showed up at the house just as dinner was being served at six o'clock. Donna and Darren Kelsey also were invited and walked over to the Kelleher house just as Caroline and her beau were parking by the curb. Donna held a Tupperware carrier, inside of which was a cake she had baked for the party.

"Hi. I'm Darren Kelsey. I don't think we've met before," Darren said to Larry on the front stoop of the Kelleher house. "We live next door. My wife Donna and Caroline's mother have been friends for years."

"Hi. I'm Larry Katzenberg. Caroline's fiancé."

When she heard what Larry had said to her husband, Donna's eyes opened wide with surprise. Then, as the two women hugged, Caroline whispered into Donna's ear.

"You sure you want to stay?" she said. "We're telling my mother later tonight. There could be fireworks. And not the good kind."

"I'll take my chances," Donna said.

The party got underway with Ken sitting in his pajamas and bathrobe in the living room, chatting quietly with Michael, Jim, and Darren. The women listened to Maria's funny descriptions of her former first-grade classmates. Caroline told stories of her own first-grade memories. Then Dolores served the chicken dinner she had prepared, and following that, Donna handed out pieces of her chocolate cake. The time passed quickly. After dessert, the party took several unexpected turns that made Dolores anxious. Thanks to the prevailing mood, and a few glasses of wine, none of the turns brought the party to a screeching halt.

First, Alexis revealed she was pregnant and had given notice at The Birch Tree Cafe. There were congratulations all around. Jim said that it was he who insisted that Alexis quit her job immediately. "I want her to concentrate on being the least-stressed pregnant woman on Long Island," he said proudly.

Then, Bridgett and Kim announced that in September, a foster child from Vermont would come to live with them, and that adoption was a possibility. The two of them took turns describing some benefits and challenges both of foster-parenting and adopting, and proved expert at calmly and quietly diverting whatever concerns Dolores threw their way.

After that brief discussion, Larry lifted Caroline's right hand in the air to signify for all that the two of them were engaged, and that the wedding would be in Manhattan in October.

"We've discussed everything," Larry said with a gleam in his eye, "and there's only one thing, out of the millions of things we discussed, that we can't agree on."

"Which one of you should get pregnant?" Michael jested.

"No," Larry chuckled. "She can't decide if she wants to be Mrs. Caroline Katzenberg or if I should be Mr. Larry Kelleher. I'm opting for the former, of course."

There were giggles and hardy congratulations from all, other than Dolores, who instead managed a pleasant smile and the wish for good fortune to follow her daughter and future son-in-law.

Darren lifted his glass high.

"Well, as if all that isn't enough... I have some news of my own," he announced. "Bittersweet, I'm afraid."

"*You're* pregnant too?" Michael said.

"No. Donna and I are moving to California. Near Burbank. I accepted a job with Lockheed. Senior director of propulsion research," he said proudly.

Donna looked at Dolores, who remained silent with a surprised expression on her face.

"I'm sorry, Dolores," Donna said. But Dolores shook her head to signify to her friend and neighbor that being sorry was an absurd notion, given the reason for the move.

"That's wonderful, Darren," Dolores said. "I know that's the kind of job you've been hoping for. You deserve it."

The final surprise of the evening was Michael's announcement that *Playboy* had purchased three of his cartoons for four-thousand dollars, but that modesty prevented him from sharing the single-panel adult-oriented drawings with anyone in the family. "Sorry, Mom," he said curtly. His sisters, though, would not hear of it, and crowded into his tiny studio to see the cartoons. They tried to curb their laughter, but that merely made them laugh even more.

While her aunts and uncle were in the studio, Maria asked her grandmother if she could help bring the dinner dishes from the dining room to the kitchen. Dolores consented. Donna helped too. Ken and Darren, and Jim and Larry, remained in the living room to chat mostly about the Yankees and the Mets.

By ten-o'clock, Maria's eyes were closing. Kim took her upstairs. As they ascended the stairs, Maria thanked everyone for coming. She was happy with the party in her honor.

Ken had fallen asleep in the living room easy chair. Dolores asked Jim and Larry to help him into his bedroom. They took off Ken's bathrobe, switched the lounger to a bed, put him comfortably on top, and pulled a blanket over him. It wasn't long afterward that the house was completely silent. All the guests had left. Dolores sat on the couch, somewhat dazed, thinking arbitrary thoughts on random topics for perhaps a half hour, oblivious to any sights or sounds around her. Then she willed herself to stand so that she could finally straighten up the living room before going to bed. As she rose off the couch, she looked around and noticed that the living room was already in perfect order. Michael was in his wheelchair by his studio.

"Did you do this?" Dolores asked.

"It was a nice thing you did for Maria. And the chicken was really good," Michael said. "I wasn't tired, and I'm a hell of a good cleaner-upper. So..."

"Thank you, Michael."

"Don't get too used to it. I may move out one day."

Dolores walked over to the stairway.

"I wouldn't mind if you stayed," she yawned softly.

•   •   •

"No matter what the weather, sometimes it seems like the sun is shining, and sometimes it seems like there are nothing but dark, gray rain clouds up there," Dolores said. She was at Saint Matthew's on a Wednesday morning..

Father Woodward looked through the small latticed opening of the confessional. His side of the confessional was now wheelchair-accessible, allowing him to see his confessors simply by turning his head.

"Are you quoting a poem to me, Dolores?" he asked.

"No. It's like when Alexis used to try to lose weight when she was a teenager. A month of trying, two months of giving up, another month of—"

"Dolores, my dear," the elderly priest interrupted with an exasperated sigh, "unfortunately my mind sometimes realizes that it's as old as my body. Frankly, I don't know what the heck you're trying to say."

"I'm sorry, Father." She closed her eyes and embraced the dark and the quiet of the confessional in an attempt to focus on what she wanted to articulate. "I don't know if you remember my last confession."

"Your last confession? I don't remember what the heck I had for breakfast," Father Woodward said. Dolores looked bewildered. "Forgive me, Dolores. For over thirty years, I've tried to get through your stubborn head with a little sarcasm and a little humor. Maybe I shouldn't have. I don't ever want you to think that I don't take—"

"No, it's fine, Father," Dolores interjected. "I know you mean well. I always have. In fact, I appreciate it, even though I may not have shown it all the time. It always made me take a step back and see where I could try to improve."

"That's nice of you to say, dear. You see—your kind words are helping me get through another day. Quite frankly, the days are getting a little harder to get through because that darn Father Time never wants to slow down. So if you want me to help *you* get through this day, please do it without crazy analogies or metaphors, if you don't mind. Father Time has taken away my patience for all those gosh-darned things."

"I understand. What I'm trying to say, Father, is that something always happens to make me want to change the way I am, to become a better person, and then something *else* happens to stop me in my tracks. I don't think I have the strength, or the willpower, to change. That's such an unholy feeling. It makes me think that life isn't always righteous. It scares me. "

Father Woodward clasped his wrinkled hands in front of his chin, and through the lattice, Dolores could see that they shook considerably. That made her think momentarily about the phrase he

217

had just used — Father Time — and she grimaced while wondering when she herself would be too old to get on her knees for confession. What then? she asked herself; can it be that by then I won't need confession? Or even want to seek it?

"Dolores," Father Woodward said, "what's better — boring or interesting?"

"Interesting, I suppose," Dolores answered.

"Good. What's better — fairly normal or strangely deviant?"

"Fairly normal, of course."

"Fine. Knowing you, Dolores, I have a feeling that the things that happened that stopped you in your tracks, as you say, despite what you may think, are interesting and fairly normal things. You don't *need* extra strength. You don't *need* extra willpower. You need to just be yourself, and to let all your loved ones be themselves. One day you'll believe what I've been telling you for years — that each one of them is a blessing."

After he pronounced her simple penance for having evil thoughts about the holiness of her life, Father Woodward instructed her to return home. "Go," he said. "I'm sorry, Dolores. I've gotten cranky in my old age."

Despite having promised herself not to, Dolores drove home in a foul mood. Father Woodward had assumed that she was thinking only of her children when, in fact, she was also thinking of Donna, who was moving far away, and of Larry Katzenberg, who seemed to be a brash young man. She was also thinking of Toni Moore, the Aster-Paxton saleswoman who had mailed Ken no less than three affectionate get-well postcards. Why, Dolores asked herself, does Father Woodward make such assumptions that everything is a blessing? Why does he refuse to ask more questions, to delve more deeply? Does he now have as much patience for me as he has for analogies and metaphors?

It was on the ride home that Dolores decided to make another effort to build some sort of career for herself, not unlike her previous attempts, but this time with more resolve. She thought that might ease her distressed mind. Her job at the pharmacy was not nearly enough; it was only nine hours a week and rather tedious. Maybe an interesting and important avocation would allow her to more easily accept things, accept change, accept people, regardless of what they did or how they behaved.

So instead of going home, Dolores drove to the Westbrook Hills Public Library. She asked the reference librarian where she could find information on all the major nonprofit and charitable service organizations on Long Island. The librarian took her to the periodicals section and handed her a copy of the *Northeast Nonprofit Times*. "This is the current issue, and it happens to be their annual rundown of all the nonprofits in the northeast."

"Thank you," Dolores said. The reference librarian went back to her section, and Dolores took the periodical to the check-out desk.

"Oh, I'm sorry," said the college-aged volunteer behind the desk, "this is the current issue, and current issues of magazines, newspapers, and periodicals don't circulate."

"What does that mean?"

"You can't check it out."

"My granddaughter takes out a few children's magazines every time she comes here."

"Yes, previous issues. You can read this one here at the library," the young woman said, "or you can take out an older issue."

"But I have to go home now."

"You can take out an older issue," the volunteer repeated.

"I don't think older issues will have this information. The librarian said something about this one being an annual rundown."

"I'm sorry."

Dolores returned to the reference librarian's desk and asked for the same periodical, the annual rundown, from twelve months earlier. The librarian had to go into the basement to retrieve it. Dolores took that issue to the check-out desk, only to be asked for a library card, which she did not possess.

"But my son and my granddaughter have cards. They're both here all the time. Can't I use theirs?"

"No. I'm sorry."

"Everyone's sorry," Dolores said—and when she heard her own words, she was instantly mortified that she had uttered them in such a tone to the blameless teenager. Powerless to turn back time, and clueless how to make it right, she attempted a smile, placed the periodical on the desk, and left the library in a hurry. She sat in her car for over twenty minutes before starting the engine.

When Dolores arrived home, Maria was on the floor of Michael's studio reading Laura Wilder's *On the Banks of Plum Creek*, and Michael was by his drawing table with a crumbled piece of paper in his hand. Dolores peeked into the studio on her way to Ken's room.

"That's terrible for your posture, Maria," she said. "And you look like you haven't washed in days, Michael."

"I thought you said you'd be home by eleven," Michael said to her. "It's almost twelve."

"I had things to do."

"But the YMCA van was here to pick me up at eleven-fifteen. I couldn't leave Maria here alone with Dad because he's not feeling too good. The van had to leave without me."

"You don't have to go to the Y all the time, Michael," Dolores grumbled.

"Yes I do!" Michael shouted. "I'm a counselor. Remember? It's a job, Mom. A real job."

"Camp doesn't start until next Monday anyway."

"No!" he shouted again. "Maria's camp starts next Monday. Mine started yesterday. You're not thinking straight. What are you so stressed out about?"

"Are you kidding me, Michael?" she bellowed as she marched upstairs. She forgot to check on Ken.

Maria looked sad.

"Don't worry," Michael said to her when he was sure that his mother was in her bedroom. "She'll get over it."

At that moment, Maria was thinking more of her uncle than her grandmother. She knew Michael loved working at the Y camp. He was a bit of a celebrity there, due both to his basketball prowess and to the four or five newspaper articles recently published about his cartoon work. Michael very much enjoyed working with the handicapped children, and Maria knew that to have missed the second day of camp must have been emotionally jarring for him.

"Can the van come back for you? " she asked hopefully.

"No," Michael said. "I'll just have to wait for tomorrow. Don't some people say that tomorrow is always a better day anyway?"

"I hope so. I hope it's better for Grandma, too. What do you think is wrong?"

"I don't know. Maybe Father Woodward told her to get the hell out of his confessional. That could be a good thing. Maybe she'll start accepting reality, instead of making excuses for her shattered dreams."

"I know that Grandpa yelled at her about something this morning, and he *never* yells."

"Really? Well, that can't be good. Although, with everyone on her case, maybe she'll start to see the light. You never know, right?" Michael's face took on a pensive look. "Hey," he declared. "That's it!"

"What?" Maria asked.

"I've been wracking my brain for an idea for a weekly newspaper cartoon. You know—like 'Calvin and Hobbes' or 'The Family Circus.' I met a guy at the *Esquire* awards who works for a syndication company, and he told me if I ever have anything to pitch..."

"Do you?" Maria asked.

"How about this: a cartoon called 'Hey, You Never Know.' It could feature a different character every day. Each one of them is miserable or depressed about something at first, but then they figure out a way — a funny way or a silly way or a really sweet way — to turn misery and depression into optimism. At least *cautious* optimism." He looked at Maria. "What do you think, kid?"

Maria pursed her lips.

"Hey, you never know!" she said.

• • • • • •

The next day turned out to be one of the most consequential for Dolores. However, as she went through the morning and then the afternoon, the episodes she experienced, one after the other, made it feel like one long, wretched day. Those events included Michael getting injured, a problem at the bank, and an unholy mess in the Kelleher living room.

The YMCA van had picked Michael up at eleven-fifteen. By two o'clock, he was back home with a dislocated shoulder, which had occurred during a basketball game. The YMCA had its own infirmary, where Michael's wound was dressed. He was given a sedative and told to spend the rest of the day at home. The van made a special trip.

Michael was wheeled into the house by a YMCA volunteer, and Dolores immediately saw that her son had a large bandage on his elbow and that his right arm was in a cloth sling looped around his neck. She stayed quiet, unable to decide on whom to place the blame. Despite Michael's strength, coordination, and skill, why, she wondered, was he foolish enough to make basketball coaching one of the focal points of his camp activities? Why did the camp leaders allow it? Was Ken to blame? After all, time and time again, Ken had told Michael that he could do whatever he set out to do. Or should she simply blame herself for seeing it all unfold in front of her and doing absolutely nothing to stop it?

Moments later, Dolores received a phone call from Rolling Hills Day Camp. The check she had handed in at the camp fair had bounced. She said to the woman on the phone that her husband usually handled all the banking and bill-paying, but that he was ill and that she had been doing it instead, and may have made a simple mistake. How she wished she could yell into the phone all the reasons her head was full of tension, all the reasons a silly financial error could so easily have been made. But to shout all this to a clueless, innocent camp lady who was merely doing her duty was, of course, out of the question. All Dolores could do was apologize and promise to rectify the situation as quickly as possible.

After she consulted briefly with Ken, Dolores decided that a visit to the bank was the quickest and most decisive way to clear up any inconsistencies with the family bank account. So, with Michael home to watch Maria, she jumped in the car and drove to the Emigrant Savings Bank. After ten minutes of tense discussion, the bank discovered that Dolores had been making all of her and Ken's recent deposits into their savings account instead of the checking account. She now worried about how many other checks would soon bounce. Shaken by the experience, she drove home in a state of distress. Her inattention to the road caused the car to hit the curb on Hempstead Turnpike with such force that the front right tire was punctured and instantly flattened. It was Ken who had always handled car problems in the past, but now, of course, he could not do so, and Dolores had inadvertently let their emergency roadside service membership lapse. She waited in the car for fifteen minutes before a police cruiser pulled up beside her and offered to use his car radio to call a mechanic.

While Dolores was still out of the house, Maria had gone into Michael's studio to sit on the floor. She asked him if his elbow and shoulder hurt.

"It hurt like hell when it happened," he explained. "I think I literally saw stars. But I don't feel anything now. I'm just mad at myself."

"Why?"

"Because it was avoidable. I reached out for something and tipped my chair over. Careless. Speaking of being mad," he added, "remember how mad you got when the library didn't have that book you really wanted, 'Greenish Anne of Gobbledygook' or something like that?"

"It's *Anne of Green Gables*, silly," Maria said, knowing full well that Michael had mixed up the title on purpose just for fun. "What about it?"

"I found it for you."

"Where?"

"It was in the library at the Y. I put it on the bookshelf in the living room."

"Thank you, Uncle Michael." She kissed him on the cheek.

From that moment on, Maria wondered if Michael's announcement was actually part of a practical joke. Maybe he *did* find the book for her—but did he really put it on the bookshelf in the living room? Why wouldn't he have simply handed it to her?

Maria went into the living room to check. She found what on the outside appeared to be L. M. Montgomery's *Anne of Green Gables*, but discovered upon opening it that the dust jacket actually covered Pearl S. Buck's *Portrait of a Marriage*. She put that book on the floor and returned to the shelves to look for the Pearl Buck dust jacket. When she found it, she realized it covered *The Bostonians* by Henry James. By this point, Maria knew without question that it *was* part of a practical joke. Michael had played the same joke once before, but on a smaller scale. One after the other, Maria took books off the bookshelves and removed the dust jackets until she finally found *Anne of Green Gables*. By then, nineteen books, and nineteen detached dust jackets, covered the living room floor.

A minute later, Dolores walked into the house, drained and trembling from her experience at the bank and her adventure with the flat tire. Maria wasn't there. What Dolores saw on the living room floor enraged her even more. To her mind, it seemed as if there were not nineteen, but fifty or seventy-five books strewn across the floor, their dust jackets removed and scattered about. The sight so incensed Dolores that her pocketbook, which she had been holding in her left hand, dropped to the floor as her right hand covered her mouth. She wondered for a moment if the house had been robbed, or if there had been an earthquake, or if Ken had tried to look for a book on a bookshelf and suffered another seizure.

Maria walked into the living room from the hallway and startled her grandmother out of her frozen position.

"I'm sorry, Grandma," she said. "I was just about to clean it up, but I had to go to the bathroom first."

Dolores did not ask for an explanation, though Maria was prepared to tell the story of how the hardcover muddle came to be. Michael wheeled out of his studio and stopped beside Maria. Both of them stared at Dolores, whose hand still covered her mouth. A tear rolled down her cheek. She seemed unable to move or even to speak.

"Mom?"

Dolores remained eerily quiet and still. More tears fell.

"Grandma?"

"I can't do it," Dolores said in a desperate, listless whisper.

"Do what?" Michael asked. "Maria and I will clean up the books."

"I can't do it," she repeated.

"Do what, Mom?"

"Everything. The banking. The car. Looking after the two of you. The house... This wasn't supposed to happen to your father. This wasn't supposed to happen. I can't do it alone."

"Sit down, Mom—"

"Things happen," Dolores cried. "You can plan and pray and try, and still things happen. And then you lose control over everything. Everything! The house, the family... Everything. This isn't my house. This isn't my life..."

"Sit down on the couch," Michael repeated, this time with a more adamant tone.

Dolores sat.

"It *is* your house, Grandma," Maria said. "If you're mad about the books, it was just a silly practical joke—like your father used to do in Sherborn when you were little."

Dolores threw a sharp look at her granddaughter.

"Aunt Trish told me. Uncle Randy, too."

"This isn't Sherborn," Dolores said. She lowered her head and closed her eyes.

"I'm glad it isn't Sherborn," Maria continued as she took a step closer to her grandmother. Michael lifted an arm to stop her, but then held off as he perceived her determination. "I'm glad it's Westbrook Hills. I love this house. It's where I read all my books. It's where Aunt Caroline practiced talking into hairbrushes. It's where Uncle Michael became a cartoonist."

Dolores raised her head and looked at Maria quizzically, trying to accept the fact, once again, as she had done so many times before, that these mature thoughts and words came from the mind of someone so young.

The words sunk in.

"Hairbrushes..." Dolores said despondently. "Cartoonist.... If I had been a better mother..."

"It's what I *want* to be, Mom," Michael said demonstrably. He wheeled over to be side-by-side with Maria. "Don't you know how happy I am? Can't you see it? Can't you feel it? Sure, I'm sarcastic, and I'm twenty-eight and still living at home. But I know who I am, and I *like* who I am. I enjoy my life. I'm doing what I want to do. Can't you take any goddamned credit for it? I *want* you to, for Christ's sake."

"You never had a chance, Michael!" Dolores yelled. "How could you know?"

Her words bounced back at her and stung. She was shocked that she had spoken them so loudly and crudely; her dismay showed in her expression, at once mortified and embarrassed. Yet they came from somewhere real, regardless of how painful that reality. And that recognition made her cry uncontrollably.

"What are you talking about, Mom?" Michael asked. "What do you mean?"

"No one ever had a chance." Dolores put her face in her hands. "I never let your father have the house he wanted. I always tried to make the girls into something they weren't. Maria... inside with books all day long... never allowed to go to a friend's house... I never even took you to Jones Beach, Maria. What kind of grandmother am I? It's all my fault."

"Grandma," Maria said sturdily, "you didn't do anything wrong!"

"Of course I did!" Dolores wailed. "I've caused nothing but pain in this house. Nothing but pain. I hate this house. I hate it."

"Well, I love this house. There's no other house like it on the block, Grandma," Maria continued. "Our rooms.... the things you built... the things you fix... even the garage—"

"The garage! No!" Dolores wept. "No!"

"Grandma—"

"No! That's my fault, too. It is... It is..."

Dolores stood up brusquely and walked through the living room, then into the kitchen. Michael and Maria looked at each other. They heard the backyard door open and so they, too, went into the kitchen. Maria ran down the backdoor ramp ahead of Michael's wheelchair. Dolores had entered the garage through the green door at the back. The garage interior was as clean and neatly ordered as it always was. But it was very dark, because the lightbulb ten feet above the cement floor, controlled by a switch to the left of the green door, had burnt out weeks earlier. Dolores went to the side of the garage, where there was a glass-jar candle and a book of matches on an aluminum shelf, and hastily lit the wick. Then she walked to the center of the garage and stopped, facing the closed automatic door at the front. Maria walked around to look at her face and saw in her grandmother's pained expression all the unspoken blame she had assigned to herself, and in the silent moment that followed, Maria tried to understand it all.

"It wasn't your fault, Grandma," Maria whispered.

Dolores lowered her head.

"I thought I could fix it myself," she said in a low, tight, broken whisper.

"What did you think you could fix by yourself?" Michael asked.

"The door. The automatic garage door. When the button was pushed, it opened only halfway, and then always got stuck."

Michael and Maria took a step closer to her. They held hands. There were tears in Dolores's eyes. She stared at Michael.

"Your father wanted to call the company that installed it, but we were trying so hard to save money. Every time, it went only halfway up, and then the motor made a horrible noise when it was in the stuck position. Clack clack clack clack clack... Like that. It always woke you up, Michael, when Dad had to open the garage door in the morning to go to work."

Dolores stopped to take a tissue out of her pocket, and with it she wiped her nose and dabbed her eyes.

"The chain was getting stuck on something. I knew I could fix it. So I put up the ladder and disconnected the door from the chain."

With her weeping still untapped, Dolores felt compelled to stop speaking. She took a breath and held it for an extended moment. When she finally spoke again, she strung her words together into short, unstable sentences.

"I took out the screws," Dolores said. "One by one. And then... then the door... the door came slamming down to the ground. I didn't know you were there, Michael. You were only two. You wanted to show me some dandelions that you had picked. I didn't know..."

Her voice became higher, shriller, more choked with tears and grief. She lowered herself gently onto the cement floor, and there she stayed on her knees, crying.

"It came down with such force... it sounded like it weighed a thousand pounds... Like a freight train was coming through the garage. Like a bomb had exploded. It took just a second, maybe two, that's all. And you... your leg.... Oh Michael... Oh God... Michael..."

Dolores sobbed uncontrollably.

"I'm so sorry. I'm so sorry, Michael. Oh God. Please forgive me. You'll never be able to forgive me... Please..."

Michael wheeled over to her and put his hand on her shoulder.

"I don't have to forgive you, Mom," he said softly. "It was an accident. But everything you've done since then, to turn me into who I am—that's been on purpose. And for that I'm grateful."

"Grateful?" Dolores said incredulously. "Grateful?"

"Yes. And Alexis, Bridgett, and Caroline? I've never seen them all so happy. It's almost disgusting. You must have done something to get them that way. Whether on purpose or not, I don't know. But does that matter? And Maria? You've never had to do anything on purpose for her. She's always done everything on purpose for herself. You just helped it along—by doing whatever you did! By letting her become her."

Dolores looked up, a touch of good-natured cynicism in her gaze.

"Sometimes I wonder if I had anything at all to do with it," she said. "I mean, well... I haven't exactly been the best grandmother. That's the truth."

"I think you have," Maria said. "Besides, it's not like you had much of a chance to prepare."

Dolores shook her head slowly, deliberately, as her lips formed into a simple smile. She felt lightheaded, yet was still able to run all that she had just now heard through her mind—the compassionate words of Michael and the discerning ones from Maria. She continued to stare at the two of them as the words echoed in her memory.

"Maria," she said. "Michael."

Finally, she stood up.

"Goodness gracious... Come... Let's all go inside. Please, both of you, hold my hands..."

So, holding hands, with Dolores in the middle, the three of them went back into the house.

• • • • •

The Rolling Hills bus was scheduled to arrive at eight-ten in the morning on Maria's first day of camp, Monday, July Sixteenth. By seven-thirty, she had already showered and was outside covered with dirt. She was on her knees, carving out a new garden at the side of the garage, where previously there had been only crabgrass and weeds. She had a small shovel in her hand, a hoe by her side, and a bucket by her feet. It was a clear and beautiful summer morning.

"Maria?" Dolores called out from the front stoop. "Maria?"

"I'm on the side, Grandma," Maria called back.

Dolores joined her there, saw what she was doing, and folded her arms.

"You heard me talking to Aunt Kat on the phone the other day, didn't you?" she asked. "About planting more gardens around the house?" Maria asked.

"Yes," Maria acknowledged. "And something about a horticulture club. Are you starting one?"

"Just thinking about it," Dolores said.

She helped Maria stand up.

"Goodness, Maria, you can't go to your first day of camp looking like that — as if you just crawled out of a cave. Thank goodness you're not wearing your new camp tee-shirt."

"I still have time to wash up and change. But first tell me about the horticulture club."

"Why?"

"Because Aunt Kat has a loud voice and I heard her through the phone say that you were nuts! I want to hear why you're nuts, Grandma."

Dolores laughed.

"She *does* have a loud voice, doesn't she? And she's right. I *am* nuts. I'm thinking of creating gardens all over the backyard. Some on the ground, some in raised beds. Some all the way back there just in front of that little patch of woods. With walking paths all around, made of beautiful slate and stones and... oh, I have all kinds of ideas, Maria."

"That doesn't sound nuts, Grandma," Maria said as she brushed dirt off her knees.

"I told Kat that I was planning on having plants and flowers that everyone knows about, and just as many plants and flowers that most people don't even know exist. There are quite a few of those, you know. I thought I'd invite horticulture clubs from high schools and colleges to come visit. I'd put out the word that scientists and botanists and horticulturists from all the big colleges on Long Island could come by to examine things. Maybe I'd even rent out the yard to wedding photographers. Oh, there are so many ideas. Maybe it's just a pipedream. I don't know. Maybe it isn't. Who knows? You don't think it's nuts, Maria?"

"No," she said. "And your mother and father wouldn't, either."

Dolores looked at her.

"You're right. They wouldn't!" she acknowledged. "Now go inside and make yourself presentable. It's your first day. You look like Scout in *To Kill a Mockingbird*, for crying out loud. But please tell me you don't know what I'm talking about. That would be too much for me to take. I can't handle any more surprises."

"Don't worry. I didn't read the book," Maria said as she ran toward the front of the house. "But Michael and I watched the movie, and I'm gonna read the book next month."

•   •   •   •

A half-hour later, Dolores sat on the front stoop to wait for Maria. It was a few minutes after eight. She noticed at least a dozen large black garbage bags on the curb in front of the house across the street and recalled that Beverly and Murray Hillman were getting ready to leave for Florida. She wondered if their grown children, Lori and Daniel, were staying over there to help them prepare for the move.

Behind her, only the screen door of her own house separated her from whatever was going on inside. Sure enough, she heard Maria's energetic footsteps skipping through the foyer. When she came out, Maria's knees were clean, her shorts spotless, and she was wearing her new, bright-white Rolling Hills tee-shirt.

"That's better," Dolores smiled. "Are Grandpa and Michael up?"

"No," Maria answered. "I think they're both still sleeping. Michael's bus doesn't come until nine-thirty. He'll stay asleep until nine-twenty."

Maria sat down next to her grandmother.

"I still think he should give it a few more days, with his elbow and shoulder bandaged up like that. It's only been three days. But he insists, and he knows best, of course. What about you, Maria—do you wish you can sleep longer, too? I mean, with school over and all, I guess it might be nice to—"

"No. I *want* to go to camp, Grandma. Thank you for sending me."

"Well, I still want you to be a child, even though you might be in college before I can build these damned gardens I'm yapping about."

"Can I help you build them?"

"You'd better! Maybe Michael will help, too. There's so much he can do. If he doesn't move away, that is. Although I hope he does. Just not too far."

"I'm glad Alexis and Jim live so close," Maria said. "And Bridgett and Kim. You know what? I heard Larry whisper to Caroline that he wants to come over as much as possible because he always has such a good time here."

"Really?" Dolores was pleasantly surprised.

"Yup. And I bet with everyone around all the time, Grandpa Ken is gonna get better really quickly. Just like Dorothy got all better when she realized that everyone she loved was all around her after the nightmare."

"Dorothy?"

"In *The Wonderful Wizard of Oz*. I just finished it."

"And Grandpa is Dorothy?"

"Just this once," Maria smiled.

Dolores laughed so loudly that Michael heard her in his bedroom.

"Hey," he shouted from inside, "there's a handicapped man in here with a sore shoulder trying to get some shut-eye!"

"Sorry. Go back to sleep," Dolores called back. She leaned in close to Maria. "Crazy family, huh?"

Maria smiled.

"Let's keep it that way," Dolores added.

"And when 'Dee's Gardens' become famous," Maria said, "more people will know how crazy we are!"

Dolores grinned.

"Dee's Gardens, huh?"

Maria leaned her head against Dolores's arm, which prompted Dolores to reposition that arm so that it wrapped around Maria's shoulders. They sat in silence for a while.

" I love you, Grandma," Maria said softly.

"Maria.... Maria," Dolores whispered longingly. She held back a tear. "I love you too."

They sat like that until the bus arrived.

EPILOGUE: DOUG'S REPLY TO DANIEL

Daniel Hillman had to kick ten magazines off the couch with his foot in order to sit down, for in one hand he held a cup of coffee and in the other a stack of mail.

A bit earlier that afternoon, he and Emily had been having 'a picnic,' as Emily called it, on the floor of his living room. Emily was a young woman that Daniel had met the week before on a flight back to New York from Los Angeles. She had put a blanket, some couch pillows, and two small scented candles on the floor in front of the coffee table. As she explained, she had once played the part of Jill in *Butterflies Are Free* in Chicago, and in the play the two main characters, Jill and Don, have an impromptu midweek picnic on the living room floor of Don's Greenwich Village apartment. Emily wanted to duplicate the scene in a real-life Greenwich Village apartment with her new real-life boyfriend. She had lit the candles while Daniel was pouring the wine. Then the two of them relaxed on the floor to kiss, talk, drink, and get to know each other better.

Emily inadvertently knocked a few magazines off the bottom shelf of the coffee table with her feet when the kissing became a bit more impassioned. She apologized. Daniel told her not to worry — that they were just some old magazines for which he had written articles he didn't think were among his best. It impressed her anyway, and she inquired further. Daniel was more interested in kissing than boasting, but Emily insisted on learning a little more.

Much to Daniel's relief, the interlude lasted just a few minutes. He showed Emily each magazine, turning quickly to the pages on which his articles appeared. She asked a few questions. Daniel kept his responses brief. The slightly tipsy Emily took each magazine after he had flipped through and tossed it onto the couch. Soon, all ten were there, haphazardly spread over both large cushions..

Then they made love and fell asleep on their picnic blanket.

Daniel awoke three hours later. It was mid-afternoon. He realized he had not retrieved the mail from his tenant slot in the lobby for the last few days. He let Emily sleep while he put up a pot of coffee to diminish the wine-induced buzz; after all, he had promised to drive her home by nightfall because she had an audition early in the morning at the Papermill Playhouse in New Jersey and needed time to prepare.

With the coffee machine brewing, Daniel threw on pants and a shirt and took the stairway to the lobby three floors below. The mailbox, as always, was full. He returned to the apartment and poured a cup of coffee. With the mug in one hand and his mail in the other, Daniel walked over to the couch, cleared off the magazines with his foot, and sat down.

There were half a dozen fliers from local restaurants, a check from *Gentleman's Quarterly*, the new issue of *Vanity Fair*, a bill from Con Edison, a subscription renewal notice for the *Paris Review*, a "Hello from Boca Raton" postcard from his parents, and a small, battered envelope with a return address that said Socorro, New Mexico. It was from Doug Kelleher.

Daniel had nearly forgotten that he had sent the three-part manuscript to his old friend Doug. There had been a whirlwind of activity since the time he had mailed it several months earlier. He had been on two assignments for two magazines, one that took seven weeks and the other three. He spent five days in Washington State at a writers' conference, and then stayed in Los Angeles for three days to attend meetings with a television producer who was interested in a feature article he had written for *New York* magazine. Also, there were two weddings he attended, one on Long Island and one in New Jersey. With all those activities, the three-part Farrell/Kelleher project had simply slipped his mind.

As he tore open the envelope, he felt himself becoming eager, perhaps even a little nervous. Emily groaned and repositioned herself on the blanket. She probably smelled the coffee, but was not yet ready to commit to a cup of her own. Daniel was happy about that, for he wanted as much time as possible to read and absorb the seven-page handwritten letter from Doug in its entirety. He took a deep breath and began to read:

> *May 14, 1989*
> *Dear Daniel:*
> *How's it going? I received your package a few months ago. I read all three stories as soon as they came, but didn't get around to writing you back til now. Sorry.*
>
> *My first thought was, How the hell did you find out where I live? My second thought was, Well, you've always liked writing, and you even said you were a writer in your letter, so I guess research is probably one of the things you're really really good at. Believe it or not, right after I finished reading your stuff (all during one long day with a few beers), I started to look through Playboy and saw an article you wrote about George Harrison, and you were listed as (at least I <u>think</u> this is what it said) a New York-based journalist who writes frequently on the arts, entertainment, and international culture. Or something like that. So now it's all perfectly clear to me. Well, sort of.*
>
> *Remember when we used to make believe we were in that old Superman TV show? I always made you be Inspector Henderson and I always had to be Clark Kent and Superman. Sorry about that. I feel bad. I guess I was pretty arrogant back then. <u>You</u> should have been Clark, because I didn't know the first thing about making believe how to be a reporter. And <u>I</u> should have been Inspector Henderson since (as I know you know because you wrote about it in "Officer Doug Kelleher") I was actually a cop for a little while in New York.*
>
> *Seems like a million years ago.*
>
> *Besides, I've never been much of a superman. I'm pretty much of a <u>stupid</u>man, if you ask me, only because of some of the stupid things I've done. Though I do have some super*

stories about my life over the last few years. But to be honest, I hope you don't decide to try to turn any of my super stories into Part Four of your project! I don't think anything needs to follow "Dolores and Maria." I don't think I'd like that very much. Even just "Dolores and Maria" by itself was incredibly difficult for me. Who needs more? Right?

Which brings me to the letter you sent along with the three manuscripts, or whatever the hell they're called. You wrote that you aren't sure what you're going to do with them. You mentioned maybe you'd make a book out of one or two, or all three, or maybe try to have a movie made out of them. I think you also mentioned a series of articles for a big magazine or something. I don't really remember exactly what you said. (I can't even find the letter anymore! It's somewhere in this hellhole.) I do remember, though, that you said you might change the names. Have you decided yet? Frankly, I hope you do change the names and some other stuff, because the whole thing with Maria, and then little Maria — well, it's still kind of delicate in my head, if you know what I mean. It's personal, painful, and plenty embarrassing. (That's an alliteration, right?)

You also said that you might need a release form from me. I'm not a hundred percent sure what that is, so maybe you could write back and explain it to me. I mean, this kind of stuff isn't like anything I deal with on a daily basis here in lovely New Mexico. You didn't say whether or not my mom and dad and my sisters and Michael are going to give their permission to use their real names. I guess you're not required to tell me. I was just wondering.

Which brings me to my last question. About Maria Chibas (little Maria's mother) and her parents and her sisters. I'm guessing they're not even in New York anymore. If they're not, would you even need their permission to use their real names? Just curious.

For a long time after the Maria episode in my life, I used to find myself looking in the mirror, or laying in bed, or driving my car, just saying "Maria, Maria" over and over and over again. It was almost like asking God for a clue to how to make things right, or how to get happy, or how to find something meaningful in life. I don't know if I'm making any sense, Daniel, but I know what I felt. Again, please don't get any ideas. I don't want a story written about any of the stuff I'm telling you in this letter. Like I said, what you wrote is enough, in my opinion. Maybe too much.

I know I said that was my last question, but I guess I lied. I didn't know I lied when I said it. Now I know. Because I have to ask about little Maria, too. She's gotta be what now, almost 11? In fifth or sixth grade? Or eleventh, if you know what I mean! College, maybe? I'm still trying to wrap my head around the whole thing.

Another thing you didn't ask me is whether or not I ever plan on visiting Long Island. I doubt it. It would be a really dramatic thing for me to do — dramatic for me, for my mom and dad, my sisters, Michael, and of course little Maria. I mean, imagine if I just showed up there one day. I don't think the world needs that much drama, do you? Plus, I just don't have the balls. I'll be honest — I have thought about it. From time to time I still mull it over in my head. But if you have any visions of looking out of a window one day and seeing me sitting on the front stoop hugging someone, I think you should just forget about it. Besides, you have no reason to drive all the way out to Westbrook Hills anymore. Right? According to one of the stories, your parents moved away. (Which should also prove to you that I did actually read the whole damn thing!)

If I had time I'd write more, but I'm working a second job now because I need more money to pay for this tiny little crumbling mansion of mine. Gotta run out in a few minutes. My landlord just threatened me for the third time for back rent. On top of that, I'm involved in some kind of stupid lawsuit having to do with a lady racecar driver who claims that the pit crew I'm on sexually harassed her. We didn't. It's bullshit. But we have to go to court anyway. Life's nuts.

Speaking of life being nuts, someone left a Sunday newspaper in the diner the other day when I was pigging out on pancakes and bacon, and I saw a cartoon called "Hey, You Never Know" that was signed emkay. Could that be my brother Michael? I know you wrote about him becoming a cartoonist and all, and I think you even said that he signs his stuff emkay. But that would be just too weird. I mean, way out here in New Mexico? Anyway, it was a strange cartoon. It shows this guy who I guess is homeless, because he's wearing a barrel instead of a shirt and pants. There's a white line painted on the front of the barrel, in the shape of an upside down U, which looks like a frown. He says to his little dog, "You wonder if things will ever get better?" In the next picture, the dog sort of cocks his head, as if he has an idea that he'd like to share with the homeless guy. Then, in the last picture, the guy apparently had taken off the barrel and put it back on, but with the bottom now at the top, so that the white line looks like a smile. So he says to the dog, "Hey, you never know!"

Like I said, it was strange. But it was also kind of nice, in a way. It sort of made me think that things can always get better. But it also made me realize that we actually have to do something about it, if we want things to get better. You know what I mean?

Anyway, it sounds like things worked out fine for Michael. More than fine, actually. God bless him for the way he's been with little Maria. Right? Seems like my sisters are doing pretty damn good, too. I'm happy for that. I hope my dad will be okay. He was always a good guy. A good father. I'm sure my mom is doing whatever she can for him. Because she's actually a very capable woman. She's tough, right? She sure as hell can be a challenge, as you know. But I think being tough and capable is more important than that. Don't you?

So I'll wait to hear from you again. I'm assuming I'll still be here in New Mexico. In this cave I call home. Then again, I thought I'd be in Tacoma for years, where I worked for a fence company. But I left. (I guess you can say I felt fenced in! Ha ha.) And before that, I thought I'd stay in Daytona for at least 8 or 9 years, but I left there too. I actually owned a traveling bratwurst truck there for a while. (Don't ask me why bratwurst. World's weirdest story.) I even spent some time in Alaska, where I worked on a crab boat in the Bering Sea and almost got killed about five times! But chances are I'll still be in Socorro if you write back, at least in the next couple of months.

Hey, you never know!

I guess I'm a little bit like the crew of the Starship Enterprise: an explorer. Always exploring new things. I watched reruns of that show every night for three weeks straight after I had my third accident at the track and was laid up with a broken leg and a broken arm. All I could do was watch TV. If we ever get together again, we can play "Star Trek" and you can be whoever you want. Captain Kirk. Spock. McCoy. Whoever. Your choice. I promise.

That's it for now, Daniel.

Take care.

Your old friend, Doug

Daniel folded the letter and put it back in the envelope. As unsure as he had been concerning what to do with the stories he had written, he was even less sure now.

Emily rolled over onto her back and yawned. She looked up at him on the couch.

"Daniel?" she said. "Is everything all right? Are you okay? You look kind of... confused? Or bewildered. Is that a good word to use? You're the writer, not me."

Daniel sighed. His answer came several moments later.

"I'm fine," he said. "I'll get you a cup coffee."

END

ABOUT THE AUTHOR

Joel's career began in 1974 when he worked as a stringer for his hometown newspaper on Long Island at age 17. He has since written for many newspapers and magazines, and is the author of five nonfiction books, including *Grandpa Had a Long One*, about his comedy-musician grandfather, and *Some Kind of Lonely Clown*, about Karen Carpenter. That book sprung from a report he wrote and narrated about the late singer for NPR's *All Things Considered*. His 2019 novel, *Blowin' in the Wind*, is about the boy who lives across the street from the Kellehers in *Almost Like Praying*. Joel and his wife Bonnie have three grown children, five grandchildren, a tabby, and two Maine Coons who are expected to grow as large as his first car, a 1972 Chevrolet Impala.

Amazon page: https://www.amazon.com/-/e/B000APLCG6
Literary blog: http://hey-you-never-know.blogspot.com
Almost Like Praying blog: https://almost-like-praying-new-novel.blogspot.com

NOTE FROM THE AUTHOR

If you enjoyed *Almost Like Praying*, please consider leaving a review online—either on Amazon or other book-related sites. In today's digital world, word-of-mouth promotion via the internet is one of the most powerful tools for marketing. That's what my fellow authors and I need in order to validate what we enjoy doing for the reading public. Your online comments allow others to more easily find our work—and your help would be much appreciated.

Thanks.
Joel Samberg

We hope you enjoyed reading this title from:

BLACK ROSE
writing™

www.blackrosewriting.com

Subscribe to our mailing list – *The Rosevine* – and receive **FREE** books, daily deals, and stay current with news about upcoming releases and our hottest authors.
Scan the QR code below to sign up.

Already a subscriber? Please accept a sincere thank you for being a fan of Black Rose Writing authors.